CHRISTMAS
— IN THE —
LONE STAR
STATE

CHRISTMAS
— IN THE •—
LONE STAR
STATE

JASON MANNING

St. Martin's Paperbacks

CHRISTMAS IN THE LONE STAR STATE

Copyright © 2016 by Jason Manning.

All rights reserved.

For information address St. Martin's Press, 175 Fifth Avenue, New York, NY 10010.

ISBN: 978-1-250-09116-1

Our books may be purchased in bulk for promotional, educational, or business use. Please contact your local bookseller or the Macmillan Corporate and Premium Sales Department at 1-800-221-7945, ext. 5442, or by e-mail at MacmillanSpecialMarkets@macmillan.com.

Printed in the United States of America

St. Martin's Paperbacks edition / November 2016

St. Martin's Paperbacks are published by St. Martin's Press, 175 Fifth Avenue, New York, NY 10010.

10 9 8 7 6 5 4 3 2 1

For Texas Rangers past and present,
who risk all to keep us safe.

Day One

CHAPTER ONE

The winter of 1876 was the hardest Bill Sayles could remember in all his years in Texas. He had come from Tennessee with his father and older brother at the age of fifteen, just in time to ride scout for Sam Houston in the fight for independence from Santa Anna's Mexico. That had been forty-five years ago, but Sayles was willing to concede that this particular winter might just *seem* the most severe because he was getting long in the tooth. There was something about being on the wrong side of three-score years that forced him to accept that he was not quite the man he used to be. Even so, this *was* a winter to remember.

Several blue northers had come sweeping down from Canada, freezing rivers clean down to the bottom and causing trees to shatter. When in Waco, where his Ranger company was headquartered, Sayles often visited the White Elephant Saloon to enjoy a bottle of Old Overholt, Abe Lincoln's whiskey of choice. Prior to his departure for the state prison at Huntsville, he had been in the saloon when a cowboy down from Kansas swore he had been an eyewitness to a whole herd of cattle frozen dead in their tracks along the banks of the Smoky Hill River.

Sayles didn't doubt that a cow could freeze to death. He had seen the same thing happen to a few men in his time. But why the cattle the cowboy had seen would not lie down to die intrigued him for days.

Sayles didn't mind the forest at all—except in one respect. He had grown accustomed to the more open plains and prairies west of the Brazos, where a man could see trouble coming even if trouble was trying to sneak up on him, assuming he was experienced in reading the signs. The same could not be said for these piney woods. A whole band of cutthroats could conceal themselves in the gloom and the undergrowth not a pistol-shot away. "Be just my luck," he murmured, "that after surviving Santa Anna, Cortina, and that damned Comanche shaman Isatai, I'd be put down by some down-on-his-luck highwayman." He was addressing the coyote dun under his saddle, as he was wont to do, since the horse would sometimes snort and nod when it heard its owner's voice. It was like they were having a conversation. The dun didn't acknowledge him this time, though.

As he rode down the narrow snow-packed road winding through the forest, a bay horse trailing on a long lead, Sayles mused that there were plenty of men down on their luck these days, ever since the Panic of 1873. Being one who had been content to live off the modest wages of a Texas Ranger his entire adult life, Sayles knew little about things like a gold standard, or how cheap silver could result in devalued government greenbacks, leading to the failure of numerous business enterprises, such as railroads, which could not pay their creditors with the same nearly worthless paper money they paid their employees—before laying off those employees. Thousands of men had come to Texas after the war to work on the iron roads sprouting up all over the place, only to be stranded stone-broke by the financial crisis. More than a few of these men had turned to crime. The deep and in places almost impenetrable forests of East Texas sheltered a good many such desperadoes.

Sayles had wondered if the man he was riding to the state prison to fetch had turned to outlawry on account of what had befallen the economy. All his Captain had told him was that Jake Eddings had been sentenced to fifteen years by a judge in Cameron for his part in a stagecoach holdup in which the driver of the coach had been shot and killed. It was said that the killer had been Eddings's partner, who had chosen to end his life in a hail of bullets courtesy of a posse that had run the two men down rather than face the hangman's noose. Hearing this, Sayles was a little surprised that Eddings had escaped hanging too, since details like which member of an outlaw gang had committed murder were usually ignored by a frontier judge and jury. The Captain was of the opinion that Eddings had the silver tongue of his lawyer, a Temple Hanley by name, to thank for him still being above snakes.

It was Hanley, surmised The Captain, who was responsible for the order from Governor Coke that Eddings be delivered to Cameron so that he could be present when his young son was buried. "Never heard tell of such," The Captain had said, when he handed the job over to Sayles in his cluttered Waco office, with its walls papered over with maps and a pall of gray smoke hanging over the battered kneehole desk. The smoke was produced by the lighted Mexican cheroot Sayles was chewing on. "There was that Tonkawa, Yellow Wolf, the one who murdered a farmer and his wife over at Brown's Mill, then defiled and killed their two daughters. As I recall, the Bureau of Indian Affairs asked the governor to let Yellow Wolf visit his family before the Tonkawas were relocated to Indian Territory.

But that time the governor said hell no." The Captain shrugged. He wasn't angry or upset by this peculiar turn of events, just surprised.

Sayles stood there in front of the desk, arms folded, listening and not saying a word, feeling sick to his stomach and trying not to show it. Hearing that Eddings had lost his son made his blood run cold. But it was The Captain's recounting of the murders committed by Yellow Wolf that affected him the most. He couldn't be sure if The Captain even knew or had forgotten about the fate of his own family or just assumed that a Ranger like Bill Sayles had too much hard bark on him to be troubled by hearing tales of loved ones lost. He was resentful, but his creased, leathery features betrayed nothing. He didn't much care for The Captain. Having served under legends like Jack Hays and Ben McCulloch, Sayles held other Rangers he worked with these days to very high standards and usually found them wanting.

In the two and a half days it took him to make the ride to Huntsville, Sayles had plenty of time to get over his resentment, and even managed to stow in the back of his mind the painful memories woken by his talk with The Captain. Mostly he kept himself occupied by ruminating on the changing times. The Waco Indians, the Tonkawa, even the peaceful Caddo bands had been moved north in the Indian Territory. The Quahada Comanche chief Quanah Parker had surrendered and been relocated to Fort Sill in Oklahoma following the Second Battle of Adobe Walls and the Red River War. The buffalo of the southern plains were nearly wiped out and that, coupled with cholera and smallpox epidemics, had played a major factor in the collapse of the once great tribe that had been the chief antagonists of the Texas Rangers for the past thirty years. Not since the Second Cortina War in 1861 had the Mexicans posed much of a threat, apart from occasional horse-stealing raids. The Civil War hadn't brought much fighting to Texas soil. So the Comanches had been the greatest foe Texas had ever had to face. And now they too had been herded onto reservations north of the Red River.

It made a man wonder if soon there would even be a need for the Rangers. From that day over fifty years ago when impresario Stephen F. Austin had formed a small group of mounted militia charged with defending the Anglo colonies from Indian raids, the Texas Rangers had fought to defend the frontier. These days, though, as far as Sayles was concerned, he and his compadres were just glorified lawmen dealing with common outlaws. This job The Captain had given him was a case in point. Escorting an inmate to a funeral and back to prison again was a far cry from being in hot pursuit of Comanche raiders. Sayles figured he ought to be glad that the threat to the settlers on the Texas frontier posed by the Comanche had been dealt with. But the truth was he knew he was going to miss the passion of the hunt. Things were never going to be the same.

The road he took through the tall gloom of the forest was a narrow one, covered with ice-encrusted snow. Throughout the day he saw no sign of human passage save for the track left by several wagons pulled by mule teams coming out of the woods to turn east in the direction of Huntsville. Taking into account the scattering of wood debris on the road, he surmised they belonged to woodcutters, probably hauling firewood, and that made him think he was nearly to his destination, since Huntsville woodcutting crews would have no reason to venture very far into the forest. Soon the road rose into rolling clay hills. The timber thinned out and small homesteads began to appear. In the distance he could see a pall of chimney smoke marking the location of the town.

The seat of Walker County, Huntsville was on its way to recovering from the economic disruptions that had followed the War Between the States thanks in large part to cotton and lumber and the arrival of the International and Great Southern Railroad. Even so, the broad streets between rows of tightly packed false-front buildings were nearly empty; anybody who didn't need to be outside was behind closed doors and curtained windows striving to stay warm. The smell of wood smoke was strong, carried by the blustery, bone-chilling wind channeled down the streets. This at least diminished the pungent effluvium produced by so many people living together in one place. He had a sense of smell that was more sensitive than most. He had heard Bigfoot Wallace claim that living a life of danger day in and day out would heighten all of a man's senses, and while the legendary Bigfoot was renowned for his hyperbole, Sayles had felt there was something to what Wallace said. Sayles understood why folks congregated like this—for the sake of commerce and work, companionship and safety—but he hadn't needed to rely on a town for any of that, at least for any length of time.

Pausing at an intersection to take a long look around before heading south for the state prison, Sayles stood in the stirrups a bit just to ease aching bones as memories assailed him. "Real shame about Callie Owen," he murmured, talking to the coyote dun. "She was quite a gal." Ears turning, the horse whickered in response. A pensive smile touched the corners of the Ranger's mouth. Callie had been a lady of ill repute when he had first met her, back in the Republic years, a wild and wanton woman-child who wore her "shame" like a badge of honor. Sayles had visited her fairly often back then, in the years after he had served as scout and courier during the fight for Texas independence, and before his company had been mustered into service to the United States Army as guides and guerrilla fighters in the Mexican War. He had gladly paid a dollar a poke and sometimes added another dollar, in the hope of making her remember him. Two dollars was no small thing when you earned thirty dollars a month and had to pay for your own room and board and your mount's too, but Callie Owen was worth it.

He had been a brash and lively young man in his twenties back in those days and Callie made him feel like he hung the moon, to such an extent that one day, emboldened by a strong dose of liquid bravemaker, he proposed to her. She turned him down, of course. Spurned and heartbroken, he could never bring himself to show his face again, though often he longed for her touch. Only when he was older did he realize that women like Callie made every man they did business with feel special. The yellow fever epidemic of '67 had taken her. She died a respectable woman, happily married to a storekeeper.

Sayles hadn't learned of Callie Owen's passing until four years later, when he had come to Huntsville after a personal friend, Leander McNelly, captain of the newly formed state police, was shot and wounded when local sympathizers smuggled weapons into the local jail to arm three men who had been convicted of the murder of a freedman. The killers escaped and even though a militia unit was dispatched to Walker County, and a state of martial law existed for two months, justice was never served. The state police were disbanded soon after. McNelly and thirty-five other men who had served in that short-lived unit were enlisted into the Texas Rangers. Due to professional rivalry, Sayles hadn't been sorry to see the state police go. But now he *was* sorry, figuring that this job he had been given was one better suited to the glorified lawmen of McNelly's old bunch than it was to a Texas Ranger.

Stopping at the telegraph office in the small railroad depot—telegraph lines generally followed the iron roads where possible—he had a message sent to the Cameron lawyer, Temple Hanley. HAVE EDDINGS. BE THERE THIRD DAY. RANGER SAYLES. He added the "Ranger" since he wasn't sure The Captain would bother wiring Hanley to let him know who was bringing his former client to Cameron. Then he rode south about a mile to the prison. He had last seen it two decades ago, when it had been but a few years old. It looked much different than he remembered. Outside the prison walls near the West Gate was a massive three-story red-brick building with WARD, DEWEY & CO. painted on a front window. Sayles moved on to the gate. A prison guard in forage cap and overcoat who was leaning on the gate straightened up and approached him, unsmiling and steely-eyed. "State your business, mister."

Sayles winced as he stiffly swung down out of the saddle. It was a courtesy to the guard, as he was of the opinion that remaining mounted when talking to a person on foot was discourteous. "Sayles. Texas Ranger," he said, matter-of-factly. "I'm here to see Goree."

CHAPTER TWO

⁂

The guard's expression changed immediately from bumptious to respectful. At first he had seen a short, gaunt old man with a deeply lined and leathery face who was far from nimble when stepping down off his horse. But once Sayles identified himself, the guard noticed the piercing, hooded eyes as cold as gray ice below the brim of a battered campaign hat, eyes that the old man's smile never reached. The visitor displayed none of the deference that older folks adopted out of necessity when they knew they could not stand up for themselves. "Yes, sir, Mr. Sayles, if you'll wait right here." The man pounded a gloved fist on a door set into one of the stout wooden gates buttressed with iron. There was the rattle of chains, a bolt pulled back, and the creak of weather-beaten hinges as the door opened and the guard vanished inside.

Sayles didn't have long to wait. He knew it wasn't his reputation that had wrought the drastic change in the guard's manner, but the reputation of the unit he worked for. As far as he knew, he didn't have a reputation at all, except within the brotherhood of hard men he rode with, who knew him as one who could be relied on. He wasn't famous, like the fearless John Coffee Hays, who not only led the Rangers during the Republic but trained the men under his command to load, aim, and fire their pistols and long guns while on horseback, giving them an advantage over their enemies. Or like Rip Ford, who had led his company of Rangers against the Comanches in retribution for Indian raids all along the frontier, and battled the guerrilla forces of Juan Cortina along the Texas-Mexico border, to boot.

A few minutes later that side of the gate opened and Sayles walked his horses through. Before him was the prison yard, covered with a blanket of white snow crisscrossed with muddy tracks. Directly across from the gate was a large building with a plume of white smoke rising from a massive brick chimney. Immediately to the right was a long two story building forming part of the prison's west wall. The guard led him there. Sayles tied the dun to a post, left the bay on its lead rope, which was secured to his saddlehorn, and pulled his Winchester Model 1873 carbine from its saddle boot. A Ranger he had known, Boone Dooley by name, had gotten into a dustup with drunken hidehunters at a trading post out at the headwaters of the Lampasas River. After some lead-slinging inside, the last skinner left standing had stumbled, wounded, from the post and grabbed the first firearm he saw—Dooley's saddle gun. Dooley went out after him and was shot dead with his own carbine. Ever since, Sayles had made sure never to leave a loaded gun on his horse when going inside.

Shaking a mantle of snow off his sheepskin coat before crossing the threshold, spurs jingling, and entering a small unheated room, Sayles waited while the guard knocked on the door to an adjacent room, opened it when bade to enter, and said, "Ranger here, sir. For Eddings."

Then he turned to Sayles. "The superintendent will see you now." He stepped aside.

T. J. Goree rose from the chair behind his desk, and as they shook hands Sayles gave the office a quick but thorough survey. There was a pine sapling in a bucket full of rocks in a corner, with decorations made of tin and wax. It seemed out of place in a prison. He doubted there was much Christmas cheer within the walls. A tree like that evoked memories of happy times, and made sad and lonely men sadder and lonelier. He turned his attention back to the superintendent, identified himself, and produced a letter signed by the governor. "I'm to show you this."

Goree nodded, sparing the letter a mere glance. "Authorizing me to release a prisoner into your custody." He gestured at a potbelly stove standing between two windows that provided a good view of the prison yard. "Reasonably fresh coffee on the stove, Mr. Sayles." He indicated the chairs facing his desk. "Then please, have a seat, as you must be tired after your journey. There is a room upstairs where you can sleep tonight."

Sayles leaned the carbine against the wall, took an enameled cup from a wooden shelf, and filled it with coffee. It was hot and strong and had good flavor; Arbuckle's, he guessed. He sipped and then settled his stiff form into one of the chairs and felt like he was beginning to thaw out in the warmth of the robust fire crackling in the stove. He could tell he smelled strongly of horse and wet leather. "I'll be heading out today." He checked a clock on the wall and fished his Elgin keywinder out of the pocket of a vest he wore under his coat. Consulting this, he commented, "You're about eight minutes slow."

Goree was a lean, dark-haired man in a fashionable

high-buttoned sack coat of brown wool with waistcoat and four-in-hand. Sayles didn't know much about him, except that he had been on the state prison board of commissioners before taking over as superintendent. But in a glance he pegged the superintendent as an ambitious man who pushed himself and others hard. "It's only a few hours until dark," Goree observed, glancing out the window. "Perhaps it would be better to get an early start in the morning. You look like you could use a hot meal and a long rest."

Sayles's bushy brows furrowed. "I feel better than I look," he muttered. "Enough daylight to get six, maybe seven miles behind me. There's a dead boy lying in a wood box for nigh on a week now and I reckon his people would like to see him buried. Seems they don't want to do that until his father gets there."

Goree rose from behind his desk to open the face of the wall clock and move the minute hand ahead eight minutes. "Bring Eddings here," he told the guard, who was standing at the door. Then the superintendent sat on the edge of the desk, arms folded, looking mildly perplexed. "I didn't think the governor was a sentimental man. I can only conclude that this has something to do with the clamor raised by some newspapermen regarding the treatment of prisoners here. Or maybe Coke is heading for the United States Senate and wishes to polish his image, since some called him inhumane for refusing to fund the state asylum."

He began to pace, hands shoved into the pockets of his wool trousers. "You see, we've made some changes here. Changes for the better. The prisoners are no longer a burden on society. They work for their keep. A few years ago the prison commission struck a deal with Ward, Dewey and Company out of Galveston. The state was no longer able to afford the prison's operating costs. Ward-Dewey paid three hundred and thirty-five thousand dollars for a fifteen-year lease on the labor of the inmates. We make wool and cotton clothing, as well as furniture and wagons, shoes and boots. Work crews are hired out to lay track for railroads or to cut timber. Ward-Dewey profits from all of that, and in return has paid for improvements to the prison itself. New fireproof brick buildings, forty new cells, an infirmary."

Goree returned to his chair and sighed. "The problem is . . . human nature. A man will work if he thinks he profits from it, or if it's something he's born to do. We have had to persuade many of the inmates that work makes it easier for them to do their time. That it keeps them healthy in body, mind, and spirit. Slackers must be strictly dealt with. Examples must be made. Some people disapprove. They don't understand. The newspapers only sensationalize what is done here to boost their sales." He studied Sayles a moment, a slow smile curling the corners of his mouth. "But you aren't interested in all of this, are you?"

"Not really," admitted Sayles and drank the rest of his coffee. He didn't think much about prisons except to believe that the people in them deserved what they got whether it was working till they dropped or languishing in a six-by-eight cell. He himself had been in jail a few times, but usually just to sleep off a drunk, to be cut loose the morning after and sometimes pay a fine. He had never stolen anything—a matter of self-respect—nor killed anyone that hadn't been trying to kill him first—a matter of pride.

"Single-minded in purpose," said Goree. "A much-admired trait of the Texas Rangers. I read somewhere that a Ranger rides like a Mexican, tracks like a Comanche, shoots like a Tennessean, and fights like the devil.

You may know I served as an aide to General James Longstreet and saw many Texas units serve with valor in Northern Virginia. Did you serve in the War?"

"Not the last war. I did some shooting down in Mexico in the one before." Sayles was uncomfortable talking about himself. He rose, grimacing as his stiff and saddle-sore body complained, and moved to the potbelly stove, relishing the heat that emanated from it. He was warm for the first time in three days. "During the last war, what with so many Texicans back east fighting, the Indians were kicking up some dust, so I had plenty to do right here."

Goree began elaborating on his wartime experiences, but Sayles tuned him out. Looking through the window, he saw two men crossing the yard. One was the guard Goree had sent to fetch Jake Eddings, so he assumed the second man was Eddings himself. The prisoner was a gaunt man of medium height. He wore a shapeless brown woolen coat over faded black-and-white-striped prison is-sue. His arms were crossed, hands shoved into armpits, hugging himself against the blustery wind that whipped at his baggy clothes, He walked with the shuffling gait of a man who'd had to learn how to walk in shackles, even though his ankles weren't chained now.

A moment later Sayles was getting a better look at Ed-dings as the guard ushered him into Goree's office and stood him in front of the desk. There was an unhealthy grayish pallor to the man's skin. His hair had been clipped short to the scalp, which made lice easier to deal with. His eyes were deep in their sockets, and it looked to Sayles like there wasn't much life left in them.

Sitting behind his desk, Goree said, "Eddings, this is Bill Sayles, Texas Ranger. He will be taking you to

Cameron so you can bury your son. He will then bring you back to me so that you may serve out the remainder of your sentence. Make no mistake. If you try to run, he will shoot you down."

Eddings had been looking at the floor, and when Goree stopped talking he looked not at the superintendent but at Sayles. "I just want to see my son one last time. And . . . and my wife."

He said it so earnestly that Sayles didn't doubt him. He could tell Eddings was struggling to maintain his composure. The words, though, cut like a knife in his gut. "I don't reckon he and I will have a problem," he told Goree.

The superintendent was studying the inmate's face. He knew what prison could do to a person. A few individuals managed to adapt to incarceration. Many more, though, were embittered by the experience and became a danger to others as they felt they had nothing to lose. And then there were those who had the life sucked right out of them by the experience of life behind bars. He decided that Eddings belonged in the latter category. "I'm not so sure," he murmured, then rifled through the papers on his desk and produced a document, which he held up. "If you would sign this, Mr. Sayles. Shows we released the inmate into your care."

Sayles turned to the desk, took the metal-nib pen Goree provided, dipped it in the inkwell, and scratched out his name. "I'll have him back in six days, a week at the most," he informed the superintendent.

"Splendid," said Goree, studying the Ranger's indecipherable scribbling on the release form. "Then we will have him back in time for our famous Christmas dinner."

Sayles, who was studying Eddings and wondering if the man would even make the three-day trip in the dead of winter in the condition he was in, glanced at the superintendent because he couldn't tell if Goree was being serious or not. Then the prison guard standing by the door snickered at his boss's comment.

A moment later Sayles was outside, with Eddings and the guard. After the stint in Goree's warm office he was particularly susceptible to the bitter, breathtaking cold of the winter wind that whipped around in capricious zephyrs out in the wide-open space of the prison yard. He clenched his teeth to keep them from chattering as he snugged the Winchester carbine into its scabbard, brushed snow and ice off the worn hull on the bay horse, and told Eddings to mount up. Once the prisoner was aboard, he brandished some wrist irons from the saddlebags on the dun and put these on him, with the hands behind his back.

"How am I supposed to ride like this?" asked Eddings.

Sayles didn't waste breath replying, since the answer would be evident soon enough. He made a noose knot in one end of a rope, then took several turns of the rope around Eddings's ankle, over the muddy, down-at-the-heels half boots the inmate wore. Threading the rope through the knot, he tossed it under the bay's barrel, walked around to the offside of the horse, and lashed Eddings's other foot. He checked underneath to make sure the rope, now taut, rested on the cinch strap; he didn't want it chafing the bay's underside. There wasn't much extra length to the rope; he had used it before, binding a prisoner's feet tight to the mount's barrel so the former couldn't kick the latter into motion or a faster gait. Besides that, it would help Eddings stay in the saddle since he couldn't grab the pommel or have hold of the reins.

While Sayles hauled himself up into his own rig, the guard made for the nearby West Gate, getting one side open in time for the Ranger to exit the prison, leading the bay with Eddings on board. He gave the guard a nod, rode about thirty feet, and, when he heard the gate close, reined in the dun. The bay, no stranger to following in the dun's wake, stopped immediately. Sayles twisted his upper body, gloved hand on the cantle of his saddle. Eddings was half turned as well, looking back at the gate,

"Reckon I know what you're thinking," drawled Sayles. "What just about every man would think once he come out of there. That you're not going back in no matter what."

Eddings looked at him sullenly. "You going to threaten me now, is that it?"

Sayles shook his head. "Nah. Just saying, you *will* be back here. I'm not going to have to shoot you because you're not going to have a chance to run. You got no good options, son, but the best one is doing your time and getting out a free man." He glanced up at the thick gray clouds that stretched from horizon to horizon. There was still not a piece of blue sky to be seen. He shook his head, tugged the collar of his coat up under his chin, pulled the brim of his battered campaign hat down over his already frozen face, and nudged the coyote dun into motion.

CHAPTER THREE

❦

Sayles put six miles between himself and Huntsville before stopping with just enough light left in the western sky to turn off the road, venturing about a hundred yards into the forest and finding a site that looked suitable for a night camp. An big uprooted oak tree had toppled over, leaving a depression in the ground on a slope rising slowly to the north. The oak had fallen within the year, and Sayles found plenty of wood debris dry enough to burn underneath the massive trunk, sheltered somewhat from the constant drift of snow filtering through the forest canopy. He got his prisoner down off the bay and started a fire in the depression. Eddings hadn't said a thing since they left the prison, and Sayles hadn't tried to engage him in small chat. That silence was broken only after the fire was well started.

"Can't feel my hands, Ranger," said Eddings, through teeth clenched to keep them from chattering. "Cut me loose. Let me thaw them out over the fire."

The rope that had bound the prisoner's legs together under the barrel of the bay was still tied to one ankle, and Sayles used that to secure Eddings's feet before unlocking the shackles from his wrists. Though thinned by two

years in prison, Eddings was a rawboned man with thick
wrists, and Sayles could see how the shackles had been
tight enough to cut off the circulation. He circled around
to his side of the crackling fire before dropping the irons
and, sitting on his heels, fed the voracious flames a few
more sticks of deadwood. That done, he stripped saddle
and blanket off his dun and put them on the ground near
the fire. Taking the Winchester with him, he fetched
the bay's rig next, along with an extra bedroll consisting,
like his own, of two woolen Cherokee blankets. This he
dropped near Eddings.

That chore done, Sayles sat down and pulled a .45
Smith & Wesson Schofield from the holster under his
coat, broke it open, and used a small cloth he carried in a
coat pocket, which was blackened from years of blood and
grime, to dry the pistol. When he was done he put both
the cloth and the pistol into his coat pocket.

Holding his hands close to the flames, Eddings was
starting to feel his fingers. He watched the Ranger but
didn't speak again until Sayles had put the pistol away.
"You don't have to worry about me," he said. "I told you,
I'm not going to try anything."

Sayles smiled a crooked smile. "As desperadoes go,
you ain't too worrisome. I just don't want to have to shoot
you, should you decide of a sudden to do some damned
fool thing. Might be another owlhoot or three right around
here, you know. Ain't likely they will see our fire, but on
a night such as this a gunshot'll be heard a far piece. Gunshots make desperadoes nervous, and to see if there's a
reason for being nervous they would take a look around
if they were smart. Other reason is if I have my druthers
I'll deliver you alive to Cameron. I reckon your wife would
not care for buryin' you alongside your son."

Eddings grimaced, his eyes glimmering as he stared

into the dancing flames. Seeing the profound grief etched into the prisoner's face, Sayles quickly busied himself making supper. He scooped some untrammeled snow into a small cooking pot and placed the pot near the fire. The snow melted quickly. The fire was burning hot and fast, and he set up his rig, a long stout length of bamboo driven at an angle into the frozen earth to one-third of its length, set in a forked stick firmly pushed into the ground upright, the upper end of the bamboo directly over the flames. He added some frijoles to the water and hung the pot from a notch in the high end of the bamboo. Melting more snow in a second pot, he pushed this into the bed of glowing embers and poured two handfuls of ground coffee into it. Quite satisfied with the setup, he told Eddings, sounding almost cheerful, "Did you know this here bamboo won't burn? Don't matter what you try, it can't catch fire. Damnedest thing."

"Her name is Purdy." Eddings looked up, his eyes glancing off the Ranger's steel-gray gaze. "Been married . . . eleven years next March. I was born on a farm outside Cameron. Her pa was a steamboat captain. Back before the war steamboats could sometimes get up the Little River to town. Times were good for everybody. For a while. Then the war came, and the river trade moved to Nashville and Port Sullivan. Purdy and me, we never knew our mothers. Mine died in childbirth. Hers . . . well, no one is quite sure what happened to her, though one rumor is that she ran off with another man after Purdy was born. Whatever the truth, Purdy never knew her. Purdy's pa died of the consumption in '67, mine the second day of the next year. He just . . . went to sleep one night and didn't wake up next morning. Neither of us had anybody else and she just . . . took up with me. I was nineteen, she was some younger. Billy was born the day before Christmas of '68. Until then the best day of my life had been the day Purdy became my bride." He choked on the words and tried to clear his throat.

Sayles dug into his possibles bag and produced a large wooden spoon. He grunted as he stood up, stiff and sore from the cold and all the riding. He stirred the beans cooking in the now boiling water of the cooking pot that was suspended from the makeshift bamboo crane, then got back down on his heels to shake the pot containing the coffee. His nostrils flared as he caught the java's aroma while he produced two hard biscuits from a smaller sack, meticulously checking each one in the fire's light for any bugs. He tried to focus on his cooking and ignore his own memories, stirred to life, this time, by the prisoner's words. But he didn't entirely succeed in that endeavor, and this perturbed him. "Won't do you no good thinkin' on such things," he said, his tone gruffer than usual.

"What else am I supposed to think about in prison?" asked Eddings, resentfully. "That I've got nearly five thousand more days before I'm a free man?"

Sayles looked off into the darkness. "Man's got to live with the choices he makes."

Eddings lapsed into silence, for which Sayles was grateful. He pulled two tin plates out of his possibles bag and, after scooping out the foam that floated on top of the water in the cooking pot, piled some beans on each plate, adding a pinch of salt and placing a single hard biscuit on each plate as well. He filled two tin cups with steaming black coffee and walked one plate, one cup, and a spoon around the fire to set them on the ground next to the prisoner. "Hurry up and eat. It'll get cold quick."

Watching Eddings wolf down the food, Sayles ate his beans then broke the biscuit in two, soaking each half in his coffee to soften it. He had lost about half his teeth in one way or another, and softening up the biscuit made it a lot easier to chew. When done, he collected his prisoner's plate and cleaned it and his own with snow. Because he was a man who wasted nothing, there were no beans left in the cooking pot, so he cleaned that in the same manner, working at it diligently, and after a while the pot was as clean as it would have been had someone taken soap and water to it. Pouring the rest of the coffee into Eddings's cup, he commenced to unrolling the extra bedroll, anchoring the end of one blanket with the bay's rig and laying the top blanket over the first. He was shackling the prisoner's hands behind his back when Eddings spoke up.

"You don't *always* have choices," he said defensively. "First few years we did just fine. Then in '71 there was the drought. The next year the big floods came and we lost the whole crop. The pigs got sick and died that same year. Someone ran off with our milk cow. The storekeeper in Cameron said I had to pay my bill before I could add anything else to it. I didn't blame him. He wasn't running a charity and he had given me a lot of rope over the years. Times were hard for everybody. My pa had taken out a loan on the homestead during bad times, a couple years before he died. I'd paid a lot of it off but there was some still owed and the bank wouldn't lend me anything more to tide us over. There wasn't no work to be found what with the railroads going belly-up. Couldn't push cows north since I didn't have a single pony, much less a string."

He paused and studied Sayles as the Ranger circled back around the fire, hoping to see at least a glimmer of sympathy. But Sayles gave no sign he was even listening as he fixed his own bedding. "Game was scarce," continued Eddings, perturbed. He was arguing whether a person always had a choice and in the process hope to make the case that he wasn't a bad man, just an unlucky one—but the man he was trying to convince wasn't even paying attention. There hadn't been a living soul in prison who had cared one bit about his story or his plight, and now that he was on the outside the man he was going to be spending his time with couldn't care less either. "My wife and son were hungry, you know. That's when I met Underhill."

With a weary sigh, Sayles settled cross-legged on his blankets, digging under his coat and coming up with a half-smoked Mexican cheroot, which he lit with the flickering flame on the end of a half-burned stick plucked from the dying fire. He looked up at Eddings, puffing to get the cheroot burning evenly. "Never heard of him."

"I hadn't either. He said it was because he had never been identified, much less caught. He was proud of his . . ." Eddings couldn't think of the word. "Being unknown. He enjoyed coming into Cameron, where everyone knew about his stage robberies but no one had any notion that he was the bandit. I was angry, desperate. I told him everything. He bought me a meal and then we rode out to a shack a mile or so from town and we got drunk on Forty Rod. He said he didn't 'talk business' in town and that was when he told me he was the road agent. He was talking bad about all the 'money people'—the banks, the railroads, the merchants, the politicians. How they got rich off the poor. How they wouldn't lend a hand to people in need. He said that was why he held up mail coaches. To strike back at the money people. To take from them the only thing they cared about—their money. He had his eye on the Sawyer coaches coming into Cameron from Tyler. Said he didn't need a partner but he would take me along just the same." He looked sullenly at Sayles. "You still say I had a choice?"

He didn't expect an answer so he didn't wait for it. "There were no passengers on the mail coach the morning we stopped it. Just the driver and the guard. We had sacks over our head, holes cut out so we could see. We got the drop on them. The guard threw away his coach gun. I got the strongbox while Underhill cut the horses out of the traces. Then the driver pulled a hideout and took a shot at me. I don't know why he did it—or how he missed. Underhill put a bullet in his gut. He wasn't dead when we rode off but I guess I knew he would be. Funny thing is, Underhill cut the horses loose so the guard would have to walk the rest of the way to Crockett, giving us plenty of time to get away, but the horses ran straight to town. I reckon they were so used to the route that for them it was like going home.

"The posse caught up with us the next morning. Must have been a damned good tracker among them. We were breaking camp. Didn't hear or see them until they came out of the brush. Underhill turned to me, said he was sorry. I'll never forget the look on his face. The look of a man who knows he is a heartbeat away from eternity. Then someone put a bullet in the back of his head. I was standing right in front of him and his blood got in my eyes. Blinded me. Underhill pitched forward and knocked me down. When I tried to get up someone knocked me down again with a rifle butt. I thought for sure they were going to kill me too. But they didn't. The guard was in the posse, and told them it was Underhill who had done in the driver. I think killing Underhill like that took the bloodlust out of them. It was cold-blooded murder. Kind of funny if you think about it. They were after us for shooting the driver in self-defense, and they committed cold-blooded murder."

Sayles waited a moment, but Eddings was done, so he

said, "Still, you had a choice. You could've sold the farm to pay what was left of your debt, and what you owned the storekeeper. Should've had enough left over to take you and yourn to San Antone, or Galveston, someplace where more work could be found."

"My father carved that farm out of the forest. I told him I would work it, pass it on to my . . ." Eddings suddenly looked like he had been poleaxed.

Sayles didn't see the prisoner's expression, being busy using a stick to poke at the fire, herding the still-burning pieces together. "The dead are dead," he said brusquely. "He wouldn't have held it against you. He wouldn't have known. The dead don't know anything. Don't even know they're dead."

He heard Eddings make a choking sound and looked up. The prisoner hung his head. He was shaking, but not from the cold. He was trying to stifle the sobs that racked his body, that came welling up from his grief-and guilt-stricken soul. Sayles knew what the prisoner was going through. *Damn you, you old fool*, he chided himself. Eddings raised his head as though it took great effort. He was breathing raggedly, looking like he wanted to say something, but couldn't manage. Instead he lay down on the ground blanket, managing, with hands shackled behind him, to partially cover himself with the other. He rolled over to put his back to Sayles.

Finishing the cheroot, Sayles flicked it into the fire. The cold crept into his bones. It made his muscles spasm. It burned his nostrils. He pulled his bandanna up over his nose and lay down, propped up against his saddle. His right hand was in the coat pocket where his pistol resided. He could reach up with his left hand and grab the Winchester, which he had put back in its scabbard. But he didn't think anyone would be moving around tonight unless they had to. He was about to drift off to sleep when Eddings spoke, and he was speaking from the depths of his tortured soul.

"I should have been there. To hold him. To tell him I loved him. To . . . say good-bye."

Day Two

CHAPTER FOUR

Every morning for a week Temple Hanley visited the Cameron telegraph office, in the hope of hearing something from someone regarding Jake Eddings. A very punctual man, he woke at seven, had his breakfast at home at seven thirty, and was in his office on Cameron's main street by eight. He found comfort in routine. It gave one the sense that one exercised control over one's life. It was order in the midst of the chaos that was a frontier town. And while he was relieved to get Ranger Sayles's telegram from Huntsville, he was also ill at ease. It meant he would have to put a notice on his office door informing whoever might be looking for him that he would be away for much of the day. Then he would have to hire the buggy at Cornell's Livery and ride out to give the news to Purdy Eddings that her husband was on his way. And it made his full stomach feel unsettled just thinking about that poor woman. It was difficult to face someone who had lost everything—even, it seemed, the will to live. Purdy challenged his most cherished belief—that a person was the master of his or her own fate.

He was making for his office, the telegraph grasped excitedly between pudgy fingers, when Emmett Placer approached him in an ungainly run across the street, a hand on top of his straw boater to keep it from blowing off, as the north wind was gusting down the town's wide muddy thoroughfares. His hat's security was further threatened because he kept looking up at Hanley then down to try to differentiate between slush and mud and horse and mule excrement. Getting mud-caked shoes was bad enough without sinking to the ankles in shit.

"Lawyer Hanley! Lawyer Hanley, a moment, sir!"

Hanley sighed, hastily folding the telegram several times so he could conceal it in the palm of a clenched hand, as it was too much trouble to secrete it in a pocket of his low-cut vest, which was beneath his buttoned tailored frock coat, which in turn was under his buttoned buffalo coat. He would have to nearly undress to do so, and it was much too cold for that. He pushed his bowler hat down more firmly on his head, then combed his thick but well-groomed rust-red beard at the chin with thumb and forefinger, a nervous habit, as he was very self-conscious about his appearance. He felt it was his duty to set an example of civility and good taste in dress, speech, hygiene, and behavior in this rough-and-tumble frontier community. Never mind that technically the Texas frontier was at least a hundred miles farther west—and with the removal of the Comanches to the Indian Territory, it would likely move still farther west at a much quicker pace in years to come.

Hanley assembled a polite smile on his lips, turning up one corner of his mouth and then the other, and remembering to unfurl his brows as he waited for the newspaperman's arrival. "Good morning, Mr. Placer, you're out and about early, aren't you?"

"Morning, Lawyer Hanley," said Placer affably. "I've noticed of late you've been going to the telegraph office first thing each day." He glanced at Hanley's apparently empty hands. "And correct me if I'm wrong, but I could've sworn you left there with a telegram just a moment ago."

With a sigh, Hanley said. "You are very perceptive, Mr. Placer."

"I cannot help but think the telegram has something to do with Jake Eddings. Will he arrive soon? At long last can his poor wife give a decent Christian burial to the mortal remains of her young son, so tragically wrenched from her loving arms at such a tender age?"

Placer often spoke to others employing the purple prose with which he wrote articles for the local newspaper, and Hanley was of the opinion that he was writing the story in his head and giving voice to snippets here and there to let his ears—and those of others—luxuriate in their worthiness. Hanley normally found this habit of Placer's mildly amusing, but this morning it put him in a bad temper. He straightened his spine so as to tower imposingly over the slightly built newspaperman, and puffed out his barrel chest. At six feet six inches he towered over most, just as did Sam Houston, who was of the same height. His girth was quite a bit greater than Houston's, though.

"Sir, where is your sense of decency?" he boomed, in the voice he normally reserved for cross-examining a witness or admonishing a jury to remember that a defendant was innocent until proven guilty. "Where is your compassion? You cannot seriously consider profiting from the great misfortune that has befallen that family!"

Put on the defensive, Placer bristled. He wasn't easily intimidated, and it helped that he knew Temple Hanley, as impressive as he was in size and voice, did not pose a physical threat to anyone. "I have a duty to the people of this community to keep them informed of important matters. And you must admit, Lawyer Hanley, that Jake

Eddings being allowed to attend the funeral of his son at the order of the *governor*, no less, is newsworthy. You had something to do with it, too, did you not? You wrote Governor Coke, that much I know. What possessed you to do that, Lawyer Hanley? Why did you set in motion a chain of events that will result in a desperate man being set loose among us? A man with blood on his hands!"

"It's called compassion," replied Hanley, wrapping himself in the impenetrable and somewhat haughty calm he summoned when he felt himself becoming the target of verbal slings and arrows. "And Mr. Eddings will not be 'set loose.' He will be in the custody of a Texas Ranger."

Placer's eyes widened. "A Texas Ranger! Indeed! Well well, this is news, indeed! A Texas Ranger coming to Cameron. Who is this man? What's his name?"

Sometimes, a commitment to being unerringly truthful was a burden, but Hanley wouldn't lie, even though he had a sinking feeling that the forthcoming revelation would guarantee that poor Purdy Eddings would have to suffer the torment that no mother should have to suffer while in the public eye. "His name is Sayles."

Cupping chin in hand, Placer looked off into his memory a moment, then shook his head. "Never heard of him. No matter. A Ranger coming to Cameron is certainly newsworthy!" He touched the brim of his boater with a crooked grin that infuriated Hanley. "Thank you, sir, thank you!" And off he went, returning to his lair, again trying to distinguish mud from excrement en route.

A disgruntled Hanley walked to his office and from there to the livery, stopping first at the general store to put together a box of foodstuffs, informing the storekeeper he would come back by to pick it up. At the livery he paid for the buggy and stood outside the barn while waiting for a sturdy piebald mare to be hooked in its traces. He was quite warm in his buffalo coat, though his cheeks were numb and rosier than usual. He glumly studied the depressing gray overcast while reflecting on God and the vicissitudes the Almighty often visited upon individuals to gauge their worthiness to enter the Kingdom of Heaven. In his opinion, the worst was the loss of a child, and while it was not always so, today he was glad that marriage and family were not in the cards for him. He had seen first-hand the terrible effect the loss of her boy had wrought upon Purdy Eddings, and one's first impulse was to believe no one deserved that. But his religion informed him that it wasn't about what a person deserved in this life but what he—or she—deserved in the next.

With these thoughts he was trying, without fully realizing it, to buttress himself for the unpleasant duty that took him to the Eddings homestead out by the Little River. By then it was midmorning, but it was impossible to distinguish midmorning from any other part of the day with this dreary sky. Hanley fervently wished for a little sunshine, as so many consecutive gray and lifeless days were depressing. Not as depressing, however, as the sight that he beheld when he rolled up to the plain but sturdy Eddings farmhouse—a sight that would remain etched in his memory to his dying day.

On one side of the porch, resting on sawhorses, was a plain pine casket. Hanley knew it contained the body of eight-year-old Joshua Aden Eddings. On the other side, Purdy Eddings sat in a rocking chair. She was barefoot, clad in a plain brown walking skirt and gray blouse buttoned at the neck. The only hint of color was in the crocheted green-and-brown shawl around her shoulders, and also her auburn hair, which he remembered to have been quite full and lustrous at one time but which now lay in unwashed and tangled strands around her shoulders. Her complexion was ashen and her violet-blue eyes were sunk deep in their sockets. It profoundly saddened him to see how tragedy had sapped the life right out of her. Once upon a time she had been such a lovely, vivacious young woman.

As Hanley drew closer his heart lurched, because she didn't move, didn't look his way, just sat there, quite still, in the rocking chair. A shotgun lay across her lap, and for one frightening instant he wondered if she was alive. He was so focused on her in that moment that he didn't see the big yellow field dog at first. The beast lay half under the porch, but as Hanley brought the buggy to a stop in front of the house the beast came charging out with a deep and menacing series of barks that scared him. The sound animated Purdy. The chair began to rock and she shushed the dog, which responded at once, clambering up onto the porch to sit beside the chair, tail swishing across the snow-swept and weather-warped planking, panting with its big pink tongue lolling. But its gaze never left Hanley.

"Good morning, Mrs. Eddings!" said Hanley, managing to sound cheerful. It wasn't easy. In fact, the scene before him nearly broke his heart. A lawyer had to be part stage actor. Knowledge of the law and of human nature was not all that was required for an effective summation or cross-examination. One had to be able to portray confidence, conviction, skepticism, compassion, indignation, whether one felt anything or not. He was vastly relieved to see that Purdy was, indeed, still among the living— and that the dog, which had to weigh a hundred pounds and appeared to be all bone and muscle and gristle, was at bay.

Purdy looked at him then. "Mr. Hanley," she said, her voice as drawn and melancholy as was her expression.

Hanley descended from the buggy and walked around

it to approach the porch, keeping a wary eye on the dog. He noted that Purdy had spared him a mere glance and was now focused on the coffin to her left, staring at it as though she expected something to happen over there. He tried to distract her with the box of foodstuffs purchased at the general store, placing it on the porch beside the rocking chair. The yellow dog watched every move he made with his strange eyes—one was a bright blue, the other a golden brown—and now that he had come closer to Buck's owner, his tail had stopped wagging.

"I've brought you a few things, Mrs. Eddings. Let's see what we have here. Flour, sugar, baking soda, oatmeal, molasses, dried beans, crackers, coffee, some airtights—peaches and tomatoes—as well as . . ." He pulled each item out of the box as he named them, then stopped, noting that she wasn't paying any attention. It was as though she hadn't heard a word he said. He rose and touched her cheek with the back of his hand—briefly, since a menacing rumble rose up from down deep inside the yellow dog. His name was Buck, but Hanley preferred to think of him as the Hound from Hell. "You're freezing cold," he told her, alarmed. Moving circumspectly, he took off his buffalo coat and draped it over her like a blanket. The dog was grimly watching his every move while sniffing the coat suspiciously.

"Thank you," said Purdy, flatly. "I'm not really cold." But she didn't remove the buffalo coat.

Hanley sighed and was about to place a comforting hand on her shoulder when the dog's head came up and he thought better of it. Instead he turned up the collar of his frock coat and held it closed at the throat. Without the buffalo coat the bitter cold wasted no time in chilling him to the bone. He looked down at Purdy, alarmed by how much Joshua's death had changed her. He remembered her as such a pretty young woman-child, one of the prettiest in the country, with such a sunny disposition, such a breathtaking smile, so full of life. Every man in Cameron and the surrounding area had desired her. Of this he was sure. Even he, in a moment of bittersweet whimsy, day-dreamed about what it would be like to live his life with such an angel. And an angel she was. Her father, a steamboat captain, had turned to drink after Purdy's mother ran off with a gambler. His health rapidly deteriorated as he grew old, and Purdy had taken care of him, doted over him, working menial jobs in Cameron to keep a roof over their heads and a little food on the table. Though at times it was a real trial for her, she was always ready with a kind word and that breathtaking smile of hers.

But now there was a palpable sadness in her, so intense that he found himself thinking she would surely never smile again. Never laugh again. This was why every time he laid eyes on her, it felt like his heart was going to break.

He glanced out across the snow-carpeted fields that stretched from the house to the line of bare-limbed cotton-woods and willows that marked the course of the Little River. Though he knew nothing about farming, he could sense the allure of this river bottom land even under the harsh veil of winter. In a perfect world a family could grow this land and prosper from it, and he knew that the start Jake and Purdy Eddings had made here had been a promising one. But the weather had wreaked havoc. Hanley sometimes hated the weather in Texas. It was brutal, extreme, unpredictable. In a broader sense this was true, he mused, about much of the West. Why would anyone endure such conditions, such uncertainty? Because there was land for the taking, for farming or mining or raising livestock, and land not only nurtured dreams but sometimes made them come true. There was land enough for everyone out West, but not everyone had the grit—or the luck—to succeed in an environment that was routinely hostile.

Hanley knew something about real estate, though he had never aspired to own a farm, or "spread" as they called it in these parts, being quite content with his house in Cameron. This farm should have provided the family who lived on it with a comfortable life—if one could remove the vagaries of the weather from the equation. Which led him to speculate about Purdy's future. He did not see her holding on to this land for the next thirteen years, until her husband got out of prison. Her father dead and her mother vanished, she had no other family as far as he knew. Had she and Jake owned the land outright, she could have sold it for a handsome sum. But Jake's father had put the farm up for collateral to secure a loan from the Cameron bank, money he had spent to weather a stretch of hard times a decade ago. Paying on that loan was what had driven Jake to the commission of a crime, and now Purdy carried that financial burden alone. Hanley doubted that she could. But until her boy was buried he could not bring himself to broach the subject of the farm and the possibility of giving it up. After all, the farm was all she had left of what had been a happy life with bright prospects.

Purdy rose from the chair with a suddenness that startled him. The buffalo coat slipped off her body and onto the porch as she lurched, swaying on unsteady legs toward the casket. She gripped the shotgun by the end of its two barrels, dragging the stock. She was shaking, and Hanley bent to retrieve the coat, but the yellow dog was on all four feet again and bared its fangs at him. Hanley left the coat where it lay and went after Purdy, gently taking the shotgun from her. She didn't resist, didn't even seem to notice. He quickly lay the shotgun on the porch, as he had a powerful aversion to guns.

Hanley realized then that the top of the casket was propped up against the wall of the house, and he caught a glimpse of the dead boy's face, as white as the snow that lay on the ground. A primal chill ran right through him, and it had nothing to do with the winter wind that occasionally whipped the woolen trousers he wore against his stocky legs. He tried to interpose himself between Purdy and the casket, thinking it would be better if she did not see her son's corpse before he began to consider why the casket was open and who had opened it.

"I need to see him," Purdy explained, trying to go around him. "I *need* to see my son," she said, louder, frowning at him as he continued to be an obstruction. "I have to make sure he's still there!" she shrieked, when he gently took her by the arm. Now very agitated, she wrenched her arm free and pushed away from him.

"Of course he is still there, Mrs. Eddings," Hanley replied, employing his most soothing tone. "He is resting peacefully . . ."

"Resting peacefully?" She began to back up, staring at him indignantly. "*Resting?* He's DEAD! My beautiful boy is dead! He's not *resting*!" And then she turned away from him, covering her face with her hands, her body racked with anguished sobs that managed to bring tears to Temple Hanley's eyes.

At a loss what to do, he stood there a moment, feeling quite helpless and demoralized as he watched her suffer so horribly. Hanley's self-worth was vested in his belief that with all his gifts, he could set things right for others. That he could employ his agile mind, his gift with words, his kind and compassionate nature, and sometimes his talent in a courtroom to that end. He had tried to do this by representing Jake Eddings pro bono because he believed Jake was a good man and feared he might face a hangman's noose. But confronted by Purdy's inconsolable, soul-wrenching grief, he concluded he couldn't do anything to help apart from trying to see to her physical well-being. He was not a brave man, but Purdy was in such need he risked antagonizing the yellow dog. His nape hairs rose as the beast snarled at him when he picked up the buffalo coat to wrap it around Purdy again, buttoning it at the collar.

"I certainly did not mean to upset you, dear Mrs. Eddings," he said, getting her back in the rocking chair and tucking the voluminous coat around her.

She wiped the tears from her cheeks and then looked around in dismay. "The shotgun. Where is the shotgun!" She looked at him, her eyes pleading for help. "I must have it, or the coyotes will come steal my boy away. I stayed out here all night to keep them away."

"My God," murmured Hanley, fetching the shotgun and laying it across her lap. Standing there, hugging himself against the numbing cold, he considered his options. He would have to subdue and tie her up to take her back to Cameron, of that he was certain. And then what about Joshua's corpse? He could not transport it in the buggy. Was there someone he could cajole—or even pay—to look out for her? Perhaps his own housekeeper, Miss Bishop, would be a Good Samaritan, and if not he was willing at this point to pay her to do it.

But right now, this instant. he had to do *something* for the unfortunate Purdy Eddings. He remembered the box of foodstuffs and picked it up. "You must be starving. When was the last time you had anything to eat?"

She looked at him blankly. "Thank you, but I'm not hungry." She seemed more composed now.

"You must keep your strength up. I'll make something

and perhaps you will find your appetite. I'm quite a good cook, you know. I don't have a housekeeper because I need someone to cook for me. I just hate cleaning up the dishes." He chuckled, trying to convey that it was meant as humor. He had elicited laughter from others using that same line, but it was lost on Purdy. She didn't seem to hear him or even know he was there, anymore. She was gazing off across the fields, now barren of life, not to mention hope and dreams, though Hanley didn't get the sense she was even seeing them.

With a sigh, he carried the box inside, put it on a table, and looked around. The house was a two-room affair and the main room, the one in which he stood, had a neglected look. It was dusty and unkempt. He built a fire in the stone hearth. On one knee, he warmed himself for a while, glancing several times at the table. He saw with the mind's eye a tableau that had Purdy and her husband and son around that table. It was suppertime, in a cabin that was warm with color, filled with life and laughter and loving smiles. He couldn't get it out of his head.

CHAPTER FIVE

✵

After a quick breakfast of coffee and a biscuit at the break of dawn, Sayles was on the move again. Eddings didn't eat. He didn't say a word. He hardly acknowledged Sayles at all. He seemed lost in his own private hell and Sayles let him be, relieved that there would be no more talk about lost loved ones, at least not for a while and hopefully never again. They rode accompanied by the creak of saddle leather, the soft plodding of iron-shod hooves on the blanket of snow covering the road, an occasional whicker from the bay or coyote dun, and the whisper of the wind that moved the upper branches of the thick forest closing in on both sides, without a word passing between them for hours.

The day promised to be a replica of the one before, and the one before that, and so on—a heavily overcast sky, cold north winds, desultory patches of light snowfall. Sayles figured it had been a week at least since he had seen so much as a patch of blue sky. Although he had prided himself on being virtually impervious to the harsh Texas weather—or at least appearing so—Sayles caught himself thinking fondly of his room in Mrs. Doubrett's boardinghouse in Waco. At first he had been skeptical about living under the same roof with a woman, but the widow was a quiet and unobtrusive sort and it was better than a room in one of Waco's two hotels, since Mrs. Doubrett didn't allow whores or whiskey in her house and was very effective at enforcing the embargo.

It wasn't that Sayles had anything against whores and whiskey, but he did enjoy peace and quiet and there was nothing about a soiled dove or bottle of who-hit-john that was conducive to that. He calculated he would make it back to Waco the day after Christmas, which suited him just fine, since Mrs. Doubrett liked to cook a special Christmas dinner and had finished decorating her house days before Sayles had embarked on his journey to Huntsville. She relished making it seem that she and her three boarders were one big happy family. Sayles preferred to forget about Christmas because it stirred painful memories. He could endure physical pain that would bring most men to their knees, but no one could become inured to the effect of emotional wounds. So, while relieved that he would miss his landlady's Christmas dinner, he looked forward to treating himself to a full bottle of Old Overholt and one of the soiled doves at the Paradise brothel to ring in the new year with as much relish as he could muster for anything these days. That was another good thing about whores and whiskey—they helped you forget.

An hour down the road Sayles started to get a funny feeling at the base of his spine. He checked the road behind them a time or two, and squinted into the verdant gloom of the forest to left and right, but he didn't see anything. This didn't make him feel any easier, as he had spent most of his adult life fighting Indians, and you often didn't see an Indian even when you were right on top of him. He had learned to trust his instincts, at least when it came to being watched, because time and again during his service patrolling the frontier the same feeling he was having now prefaced a hair-raising pursuit or a bloody fight.

Sayles mulled over the possibilities. Odds were good that whoever was out there wasn't an Indian, as all the tribes had been relocated—unless it was a renegade. There was no good reason for a farmer or a hunter or a woodcutter to be shadowing him. Most likely it was one of those outlaws who used the forest to elude justice, and if so then bushwhacking was a possibility. He considered veering off into the brush, which was quite thick in places, but discarded the notion almost as soon as he thought of it. His preference was fighting out in the open where he had a better chance of seeing what he was up against.

He untied the bay's lead rope from his saddlehorn and looked around at Eddings. The prisoner was bound as before, ankles lashed snugly under the bay's barrel, hands shackled behind his back. He rode slump-shouldered, looking down at the ground.

"Grab the cantle and hold on," drawled Sayles. "We're going to run our god-dogs and warm 'em up a bit."

Eddings looked up, puzzled. "God-dogs?"

Sayles was already kicking the coyote dun into a canter, gripping the lead rope in his gloved left hand. "What the Comanch' call that animal under you."

Eddings grabbed the cantle with his bound hands and clenched his legs against the bay's barrel to keep his seat in the saddle. He had never been much of a horseman, and he was sore from the seven-mile ride out of Huntsville the day before, a soreness exacerbated by being cold clean through, that kind of cold that made one's bones and joints hurt. He hoped this horse-warming bit would be short-lived. He tried to keep his teeth from chattering. He had never been this cold for this long before, and the faster the horse under him moved the colder it felt. It made him almost nostalgic for his prison cell. At least those thick stone walls kept the wind at bay.

The coyote dun liked to run, and Sayles had to keep it in check. In his experience, a bushwhacker usually had a yellow streak and preferred a sure thing when it came to doing violence upon another. By putting the horses into a faster gait, Sayles had made himself a harder target for anyone who wasn't a sharpshooter, and hoped that by doing so he had lessened the chance of someone putting a hole in him. Giving the coyote dun its head and taking off in an all-out gallop might have swung the odds even more in his favor, but it also would have increased the chance that Eddings would lose his seat, and if that happened there was no telling how the bay might react. Sayles doubted that whoever was out there would shoot the dun out from under him. Good horses were a commodity. They had value. A dead horse meant less return for a highwayman, unless he was starving.

The first man he saw came out of the woods behind them. He rode up the road at the same gait, not trying to close the distance, and a moment later Sayles knew why. Two more men appeared, emerging from the forest on either side of the road a hundred feet up ahead.

Sayles checked the coyote dun. The bay carrying Eddings stopped too, behind and to the right of the Ranger's horse. The two men in front rode closer, checking their mounts about twenty feet away. One of them was an older man with an unkempt salt-and-pepper beard and a lazy eye. He sported a ragged butternut-gray overcoat and a bowler-style hat, and he carried a 10-gauge coach gun. It wasn't pointed at Sayles, but rested on the man's right leg. With him was a burly black man wearing a blanket serape belted at the waist and a battered sombrero that looked like someone had bitten off chunks of the brim. An old Walker Colt was secured under the belt. Sayles took a look over his shoulder to see that the third man had come to a stop about thirty feet back. He was a young, lanky, tow-headed kid wearing a lot of clothes under his yellow duster to keep warm, and was throwing back the tails of the duster to reveal a brace of pistols in cross-draw holsters. He flashed a cocky grin at Sayles, who wondered just how fast the kid was with those two smoke-wagons.

Eddings was the next to get a glance from Sayles, who thought the prisoner looked nervous. That was understandable. With hands bound behind him he was helpless, unable to defend himself, and being roped to the bay he made a good target—and there wasn't a thing he could do to change that.

"Well well," drawled the older man, flashing yellow, crooked teeth in an untrustworthy smile. "Howdy, boys. Where y'all headed?"

Sayles wasn't going to waste time on an answer that nobody really cared about. "Reckon you men better throw those guns away. I'm going to have to haul all three of you to the nearest jail." There was no bravado evident in his reply, no emotion at all. He was just stating his opinion.

The older man chuckled, a raspy sound. "So you're a lawman, then." His one good eye left Sayles and focused on the ropes around Eddings's ankles.

"Not a lawman," said Sayles, flatly. "A Ranger."

The sombrero-wearing black man had been scowling belligerently at Sayles during this exchange, but now he grunted skeptically and mumbled. "Old man don't look like no Texas Ranger to me." His hand rested on the Colt Walker stuck in his belt. His dark sullen gaze swung toward Eddings. "What you do?"

"I broke the law," replied Eddings, nervously.

"Maybe you ride with us."

Eddings looked at him, the lazy-eye man, the kid who was grinning like a coyote, and finally at Sayles.

"I doubt it," he said.

The man with the bad eye and the ragged Confederate coat wasn't smiling anymore as he looked into Sayles's squinty, gunmetal-gray eyes. That one good eye flickered over Sayles's buttoned-up coat, and to the Winchester rifle still in its scabbard, and finally to Sayles's gloved hands, both of which were empty since he had dropped the bay's lead rope, unnoticed by anyone. He had ridden with the ex-slave for a year now, and the towheaded kid about half that long, and he knew that the former was capable of killing and the latter had been bragging about being capable for so long now he was aching for an opportunity to prove it.

As for the old codger on the coyote dun, he didn't look like much. If he was sporting a holstered sidegun it would take him a moment to get it out from under his coat— probably a fatal moment. Everything about Sayles might have encouraged him to stand his ground—but for one thing. He kept coming back to those hooded eyes in Sayles's gaunt, beard-stubbled face. The old man's gaze was intense and unafraid. Those steel-cast eyes seemed to bore right through you. They were the eyes of a killer. Maybe he was too old and slow to kill now but he had in the past, and often. You could tell because he looked at you like you were a target, not a human being. It was the ambivalence in those eyes that worried him the most.

The man with the bad eye took a deep breath and, realizing he had just lost his nerve, said, "Maybe we'll just ride on by, boys."

The black man looked at him incredulously. "You scared of this codger, Ben?"

Sayles figured the shotgunner had calculated the odds—balancing the likelihood of getting shot against the possibility of collecting horses, saddles, weapons and whatever else that could be used or sold—and decided they weren't good enough. "Don't matter if he is," he drawled. "Not letting you ride away. Start slinging some lead or throw down those guns."

Eddings was staring at Sayles in much the same way the black man was staring at Ben. Somehow the Ranger had buffaloed the leader of this gang of cutthroats, but instead of letting them turn tail he was pushing them into a corner, thus pretty much guaranteeing that there would be some shooting. It didn't make much sense to Eddings, but then again it didn't come as a surprise based on his first impression of the Ranger.

"Damn it," muttered Ben, and now he looked scared. His voice had a hollow, despairing ring to it. "Damn it all."

Sayles saw the barrel of Ben's coach gun begin to lift up off his leg. Without hesitation the Ranger raked the coyote dun with his spurs. The horse was already nervous and fiddle-footing, sensing the tension in the air. It leaped into a gallop that took Sayles between Ben and the black man in a heartbeat. His right hand dove into the deep pocket of his coat and closed around the Schofield revolver he had put there the night before. He passed to the left of Ben, and the latter had to bring the coach gun up and over the neck of his mount, so Sayles shot the black man first, firing two rounds through the coat pocket since pulling the pistol all the way out would have wasted valuable time. Both bullets struck the target where he had intended—in the chest—shattering ribs and tearing through lung tissue. The black man slid off the saddle to his left but couldn't seem to let go of the reins, and when he went to the ground he turned his horse's head so sharply to the right that it brought the animal down to roll on top of him.

The coach gun boomed. Sayles could tell by the sound that only one barrel had been fired. Sensing he didn't have time to slow and turn the dun, he twisted in the saddle and just let his horse run for the time it took him to bring his right arm across his body, lifting the Schofield to shoulder level. He was surprised to see Ben's horse going down.

Ben was focused on surviving the fall and wasn't even looking behind him at the Ranger, who put two bullets in his back. Ben's arms flew up and the coach gun cartwheeled through the air.

Sayles didn't watch the road agent go down, turning his attention to the third man, the lanky yellow-haired one who had come up the road behind him and Eddings. This one wasn't in the fight, though. He had spun his pony around and was kicking it into a headlong gallop back down the road.

Shoving the Schofield back in the coat pocket, Sayles yanked hard on the reins. The dun locked its front legs and nearly sat down in the road as its rider swung a left leg over the pommel and came down on both feet, whipping the Winchester out of its saddle boot before the horse could even stand up. "Ho-shuh," he said. "Ho-shuh." He turned the dun to stand crossways in the road. It was Indian horse-talk meant to calm the animal, and Sayles knew for a fact it worked on the dun. There was already a round in the Winchester's chamber so he laid the long gun across the saddle and draped his left hand over the barrel, reins threaded through the fingers. He curled the forefinger of his right hand against the trigger. It took him two heartbeats to gauge distance, elevation, wind, and trajectory, and he fired with the fleeing highwayman about three hundred feet away. Then he stepped back into the saddle, levering another round into the chamber, prepared to give chase and, if necessary, get a shot off from horseback. But the yellow-haired kid slid sideways off his saddle and lay still while his horse galloped right on out of sight around a curve in the road.

Shoving the Winchester back into its scabbard, Sayles looked around for his prisoner. Trying to make himself the smallest target possible, Eddings sat hunched over on the bay, which had wandered off to the edge of the woods to get away from the gunfire. But that was as far as it would get away from the dun. Sayles stuck thumb and forefinger into the corners of his mouth and whistled. The bay looked around, then turned and plodded back up to the road. It was then that Sayles realized his hands were shaking. He had always had the ability to focus exclusively on how to deal with a threat to life and limb, and only after the threat was dealt with did he entertain thoughts of what *might* have been. That was when the shakes took hold of him. The best way to deal with them was to keep busy.

Dismounting, he ground-hitched the dun and turned his attention to Ben. The right side of the cutthroat's horse was a bloody mess. It was an easy mystery to solve. Ben had been nervous and in too big a hurry and instead of bringing the coach gun up and over had banged the weapon against the animal's neck and triggered one barrel; the buckshot had taken off the side of the animal's face. The old scofflaw was dead, as Sayles had known he would be even before he had put two bullets in his back.

The black man's horse had rolled on him, and was back up, standing with haunches aquiver and a little wild-eyed. Sayles Indian-talked the animal long enough to grab the reins. The blanket serape the black man wore was soaked with blood in front, and he was coughing up more blood, his eyes wide and wild with the abject fear of a person desperately clinging to life for just a few seconds more. Sayles reached into his coat pocket and had the Schofield halfway out, intent on putting the man out of his misery, when the man gave up the ghost, drowned in his own blood.

"What the hell were you *thinking*?" shouted Eddings, angrily. His voice was high and his tone edgy with fear "They backed down! They were going to ride away! But you kept pushing!" He pointed back down the road, at the corpse of the towheaded robber. "He was running away, for God's sake!"

Sayles nodded as he sat on his heels next to Ben and began going through the dead man's pockets. "That he was. But I warn't going to let 'em go so they could rob and most likely kill some other folk riding down this here road." All he found were three buckshot shells for the coach gun and half a plug of chewing tobacco. He tossed the plug, pocketed the shells, picked up the coach gun to inspect it, and nodded. "Might keep this," he murmured, thinking aloud. "Be good for killin' snakes and other var- mints." He spotted a possibles bag tied to the dead horse's saddle and took it, opened it, made a face, and dumped some yellowish-green sowbelly and worm-infested hard- tack into the snow. He shook the burlap bag once more for good measure then folded it up and stuck it under his belt.

Eddings watched, incredulous, as Sayles stood up and went over to the black man and began searching him. He couldn't believe a Texas Ranger was looting dead bodies. That just didn't seem right.

Sayles found a wadded-up handful of greenbacks, which he threw away. "Ain't worth the paper they're printed on," he said, again talking to himself. Then he found the Sheffield bowie knife in a buckskin sheath shoved under the belt at the dead man's back. He pulled knife from sheath and admired the twelve-inch blade with soft brass along its spine and a brass quillon. He knew something about such knives, though he had never carried one himself. A man by the name of James Black, who had made the first such knife to the specifications of James Bowie in 1830, continued to produce the weapon for more than thirty years after Bowie—and his knife—went down in history at the Alamo. The knives were so popular that factories in Sheffield, England, produced them by the hundreds for export to America even before the War Between the States. The knives were so devastatingly effective in a fight that some eastern states had outlawed carrying them concealed. Sayles didn't figure that would ever happen in Texas.

Shoving the sheathed knife into his right boot, Sayles grimaced as he straightened up. He didn't know anything about adrenaline but he knew that after a dustup he felt stiff and even older than usual. He secured the reins of the sorrel mare the black man had been riding to the pommel of the saddle Eddings was sitting on, then hauled himself back up into his own rig, where he checked his Elgin keywinder and frowned. This delay had cost him about fifteen minutes.

"Christ," muttered Eddings. He was still shaking. "You just killed three men with five shots in about half a minute. Don't you feel anything?"

Sayles looked up at the prisoner, then at the two nearby corpses, and nodded. "Yep. I'm relieved they're dead and we ain't."

Eddings sat there atop the bay, shivering uncontrollably from the cold and overwrought nerves, bitterly contemplating the irony that this Texas Ranger had just gunned down three men in cold blood, one of whom had been trying to flee, while he was going to spend the best part of his life in prison because of the death of a man he hadn't even fired a shot at. "You're not even going to bury them?"

"Nope. Critters are hungry this time of year."

"You don't mind killing them but you're dead set on getting me back to Huntsville alive."

Sayles nodded. "True words. You heard the superintendent. It's what's expected of me."

"And you always do what's expected of you, don't you?"

Sayles leaned over to retrieve the bay's lead rope. "One time I didn't," he said bleakly.

He urged the coyote dun into motion and headed back down the road toward the body of the towheaded youngster, whose brace of pistols and cross-draw rig he intended to sell or barter in the next town, along with the sorrel mare. By the time they were headed west again they would be half an hour behind schedule, and Sayles had no intention of wasting more time and wearing himself out trying to dig three holes in the frozen ground.

CHAPTER SIX

※

Listening to the winches worked by crewmen directly overhead on the main deck of the riverboat *Mustang*, Malvern Litchfield watched the gangplank being lowered by two stout ropes. The gangplank was quite long, and needed to be, since the Brazos River was very shallow in places, filled with snags and shifting sandbars, so that even a stern-wheeler like this one, which drew no more than fifteen inches at around a hundred tons, usually could not venture very near the bank. In this instance, though, a large and ramshackle dock jutted out from the bank.

Boats had always fascinated Mal. Growing up in Whitechapel, he had frequented the docks along the Thames to watch boats great and small ply the mighty river, his boyish imagination embarking him on fits of reverie that usually involved being a daring sea captain during the Age of Exploration. Many was the poor boy in the East End who wanted to escape a future of dreary poverty by sailing the high seas. Being a seaman was a life of risk and hardship, but at least there was the allure of the unknown, the adventure that might await just over the horizon. That was more than could be said for wasting away in some workhouse your entire life, knowing that every day would bring the same misery as the day before.

Mal could be a friendly, charming sort when he wanted to be, and he had cajoled this stern-wheeler's skipper— with a bottle of gin as an accomplice—into telling him a great deal about the history and hazards of navigating the Brazos. This river ran through some of the most fertile land in Texas, and prior to the war numerous steamboats had carried mercantile goods up the river from the port of Galveston and cotton, hides, corn, and pecans back down. The postwar railroad boom threatened to diminish the river trade, but the financial crisis had led to the abandonment of some unfinished iron roads and the failure of some newly completed ones. So there was still a commercial need for a few riverboats.

There were two men standing on the dock. The bigger of the pair was still holding the lantern he had used to signal the stern-wheeler. The signal light was used day or night, to distinguish the people who loitered on docks or riverbanks to watch the big boats pass by from those who sought passage. The two men's horses were tied near a small, run-down shack behind them. Time had taken its toll on the structure. The roof had caved in and the brush had grown up around and within it. The dock was sizable, with plenty of room for stacking barrels, crates, or cotton bales. Mal had an agile mind and a vivid imagination, and he could visualize this dock twenty years ago, bustling with slaves carrying cotton up the gangplank and crates and barrels of goods back down. There had probably been a plantation or two in the vicinity, but now the shack was the only sign of civilization in the thick woods that lined the Brazos on both sides. There had to have been a road at one time, wide enough for a wagon, but all Mal could see was a narrow trail wending out of the thicket to the dock.

A quarter of an hour earlier Mal had been in the cabin he shared with his brother Lute, reading a dog-eared version of the Edinburgh Edition of the *Reliques of Robert Burns*. He was chuckling as he read aloud a verse from his favorite poem, the irreverent "Holy Willie's Prayer" . . . *O Lord! yestreen, Thou knows, with Meg / Thy pardon I sincerely beg; / O may it ne'er be a living plague / to my dishonour, / And I'll ne'er lift a lawless leg / again upon her* . . . when he felt the vessel lurch and begin to slow. By his estimation they had been making about fifteen kilometers an hour, a fair clip up a river that ran as strong as the Brazos. He had swung off his narrow bunk when he felt the slowing boat veer to starboard. It was then that he suspected something might be wrong. By his calculation it was too early to have reached their destination, a place called Port Sullivan, which was the end of the line when it came to navigating this particular river. It struck him as a little odd that an inland town would be called a port, but then this was America.

He donned his heavy wool peacoat. A Gasser Model 1870 army service revolver was secured under his belt in back and brass knuckles were stowed in one coat pocket with the book of verse in the other. Only then did he venture out to investigate. This took him through the boiler deck saloon aft of the cabins, and here he found his brother playing poker with two other men. Lute was gloating, and called him over to see the size of his winnings, but Mal ignored him and went out on deck. In his single-minded pursuit of entertainment, be it with the ladies or a deck of cards, Lute sometimes seemed to forget that they were fugitives on the run from the law.

A glance confirmed they weren't anywhere near Port Sullivan, since the *Mustang*'s captain had mentioned the town was located on a bluff just downstream from giant limestone boulders. There was no town, no bluff, and no boulders—just two men on a weather-warped dock flagging down the stern-wheeler. Mal felt the deck beneath his feet shudder as the paddle wheel began to revolve counterclockwise, churning up the brown water. The crew threw bow-, stern-, and spring lines as far as the dock so that the two men there could secure them. A moment later the gangplank touched the dock and one of the men proceeded to board, while the other remained where he was.

"Bloody hell," muttered Mal. He had a nose for coppers, and he would have bet his last farthing that these two were lawmen. No longer talking to his associate, the man left standing on the dock was scanning the ship from stem to stern, and he gave Mal a long look. Mal flashed his teeth in a grin, gave a jaunty salute, hoping to pass himself off as a man without a worry in the world, who didn't care if he attracted the attention of a lawman, then turned to hasten back inside the saloon. He went straight to the table where his brother was playing five-card stud and clamped a hand on Lute's shoulder while flashing another one of those disarming grins at the other two players.

"Begging your pardon, gents, but I need to speak to my brother for a moment."

"You two don't look like brothers," said a stout, florid man whose surly expression, Mal surmised, had something to do with the fact that Lute was a skilled broadsman—or cardsharp as they called such players over here. Most of the greenbacks on the table were piled up next to Lute's arm.

"You have a keen eye, sir," said Mal, pleasantly. "Our mother, God rest her soul, was a ladybird and quite popular with the gentlemen, two of whom, apparently, were our fathers." Indeed, he and his brother bore precious little resemblance to each other physically. Lute was slight, slender, devilishly handsome, and clean-shaven, with straight black hair and very striking light-blue eyes. Mal was a tall, brawny man with curly auburn hair, thick and unruly. He sported Newgate knockers—bushy side whiskers—swept back over his ears. His hair resembled a lion's mane.

"You know," said Lute, mildly, "I really would rather you didn't tell *everyone* that we are sons of a whore." He was studying the three upcards in his hand, the upcards of his opponents, and the size of the pot.

Mal leaned down and whispered, "And I really need to talk to you . . . now!" emphatically enunciating the last word.

Lute sighed, turning up the corner of his hole card. "Would you walk away from that?"

Mal looked at his brother's hand—and saw that Lute had nothing. With one card still coming, the best he could do was a pair, and a low one at that. He glanced at Lute, whose face was serenely inscrutable, then at the other players, who were staring at him, trying to read his face for even a hint that Lute had a hand to be worried about. Mal's nape hairs were rising because there was a copper aboard the *Mustang* and there was a chance that he and Lute were the reason. Yet the fact that Lute was bluffing seduced him, because in his experience there was hardly anything better than separating a mark from his money under false pretenses.

"No," he said, straightening. "No, I can't say I would. Just hurry."

The florid man produced a sigh of resignation and turned his cards over, folding. "I'm done for anyway." The other man folded as well. Lute exultantly added insult to injury by showing his hand and then provided a free lesson. "Never fold if you don't see at least one pair on the table, gents." He swept the winnings into the crown of the flop-brimmed hat he had stolen in Galveston, bade the glowering men farewell, and followed his older brother out of the saloon. Once they were on deck, on the port side of the *Mustang* and out of the sight of the man on the dock, Mal turned angrily on his brother.

"What did you do, eh? Back in Galveston? Besides steal that hat? Did you kill the poor sod who was under it, you bludger? I swear to Almighty God I ought to give you a good anointing!"

Lute was startled at first, but by the time Mal's tirade ended his pale-blue eyes were like chips of ice under lowering brows. He resented Mal for undermining his short-lived glee at having outplayed and then bluffed those two dupes. "What the hell are you talking about? I didn't do nothing."

"There is a copper who just came aboard, and another ashore. Figure they are looking for someone and makes sense they either come up from Galveston or word was sent ahead."

Lute waxed indignant. "You just know these crushers are here because of something I've done!"

Mal thought it over and nodded. "Yes! Exactly." He looked anxiously up and down the deck. He was counting on the man who had come aboard to observe the age-old custom of informing the skipper as to the purpose of his visit. If indeed he was looking for them then by now he was aware that there were a couple of Englishmen aboard the *Mustang*. He had to assume that their nationality, made evident by their accents, would be one of the primary identifiers used by lawmen to track them down. The riverboat captain knew Mal was British from their conversations. Mal thought that he and Lute had, at best, a few minutes to get off the *Mustang* before they were discovered. As riverboats go this one wasn't very large, 120 feet in length. Searching it stem-to-stern would not take long. The weight of the German-made barker in the pocket of his peacoat was a comfort, as he fully expected to be confronted at any moment. "You can tell me later. We would do well to get off this bloody boat."

Lute dubiously studied the murky brown water about fifteen feet below where he stood, and shivered. The north wind coming right down the river channel numbed and reddened his cheeks, ruffling his thick black hair since he still clutched his winnings-filled hat to his body. "It's damned cold here, Mal," he whined. "I thought it would be warmer over here than it was back home."

"We went west, not south, numskull. It be winter anywhere north of the equator."

Lute's brows knit, as he wasn't sure what the equator was exactly, or what it had to do with warm and cold weather. "I'm not about to go over the side. I don't swim that good anyway and I got maybe one hundred dollars, mostly coin, to weight me down. How much is a hundred dollars in pound sterling, Mal?"

"About twenty quid."

Lute grinned. He was in a good mood again, even if there was a lawman on board hunting them. Lawmen worried Mal a lot more than they worried him. "Ah, a good day's haul, then! Both those gents were merchants, which means they're bigger criminals than I'll ever be, so I'm happy to relieve them of their ill-gotten gains."

Mal had long ago given up trying to follow his brother's twisted logic. "Shut your bone box and listen, if you don't want to be pegging out today. Go to our cabin and get our belongings and meet me at the stern. I'll keep an eye out for the law."

Lute was still worried about the possibility of having to go over the side. "How are we going to get off this boat, Mal? You know I'm not much of a swimmer . . ."

"Just go fetch your dunnage and your weapons and do it on the fly," said Mal. "We're going to disembark like proper, law-abiding blokes."

Relieved that he wasn't going to risk drowning in the Brazos River, Lute smiled and began to take the coins and greenbacks out of his hat's crown by the fistful, stuffing them into his trouser pockets, as he walked past his brother with the intent of doing as Mal had said. He was the first to see a tall, broad-shouldered man in a brown greatcoat and hat appear near the bow of the stern-wheeler, striding toward them. The man saw Lute at the same time, and grimaced beneath his thick mustache as he lengthened his stride. Lute stopped and turned back to his brother.

"Mal, I think . . ."

Mal had already spotted the man—the one he had seen boarding the *Mustang* moments before. "That's the copper," he muttered and was already moving past Lute as though to confront the lawman, shoving his hands into the pockets of his peacoat. "Five and follow," he muttered over his shoulder to Lute. "Five and follow."

Lute nodded, counting Mal's strides as he firmly tugged his hat down on his head so the blustery winter wind gusting over the river didn't carry it off. They had established a verbal shorthand over the course of pursuing their criminal livelihood in the streets and alleyways of Whitechapel. *Five and follow* meant he was to wait until Mal took five steps and then follow. What he didn't know was that Mal had decided on five rather than six or eight strides because with five Lute could use the fingers and thumb of a single hand to keep count, which he often had to resort to since even the most basic mathematics had been a struggle for him. Ordinarily the brothers employed this technique when closing in on a mark. One of them would take the lead, distract the mark, and try to turn him so his back was to the other, who closed in from behind. Lute checked his coat pocket. His garrote was in his left pocket, his gull—a folding knife about the size of a barber's razor and just as sharp—in the other.

As Lute went into motion, he watched Mal admiringly. His brother tried to avoid danger whenever possible, but when it couldn't be avoided he faced it head-on. Lute experienced a tingle at the base of his spine. It was anticipation rather than apprehension. Long ago, when they were hardly more than boys but had already committed all manner of crimes, he and Mal had made a pact, sealed with a blood handshake, that they would never be taken alive. At the time it had seemed quite daring, even moving.

Seeing both of the Litchfield brothers moving toward him, the man in the greatcoat no longer strode so swiftly and with as much swagger as he had been, slowing down with brows furrowing. He was accustomed to guilty parties taking flight when they saw him coming. "You two!" he said gruffly, gesturing for them to stop. "Hold it right there." His other hand began to pull back his coat which, Lute noticed, was buttoned only from the waist up.

Mal had been walking with his head down, looking at the deck, appearing for all the world like someone deep in thought and in no big hurry, almost as though he hadn't even noticed the big man or, if he had, didn't think a thing about him. When the man spoke, Mal looked up, then over his shoulder, like he thought the man was addressing someone behind him. Still walking, he passed the man on the right with a nod and an amiable smile. The man half turned, his back to the railing, keeping a wary eye on Mal. His coat was pushed back enough that Mal could see the holstered Colt revolver as the man took hold of it and began to pull it. As Mal turned to his left, he took the Gasser out of his right coat pocket, and the man didn't see it until it was aimed at his face. The *clickety-click* of the Gasser's hammer being thumbed back froze him in place with the Colt half drawn.

Mal still wore an engaging smile. "We're the Litchfield brothers from Whitechapel, by the way," he said affably, and the man's expression told him all he needed to know. He didn't look perplexed, as one might who did not recognize the name or could not fathom why this information would be provided. Instead he looked angry—and afraid. This convinced Mal that he had been correct—he and Lute were the ones this lawman was seeking.

Mal's Gasser held the lawman's attention just a little too long. He reasoned that Lute was coming up on his right and he was just looking that way when the garrote wire came down and around his neck. The man was taller, bigger, and stronger than Lute, but that didn't matter. Lute knew how to use a garrote on a victim larger than himself, since most men *were* larger. The lawman clawed at the wire embedded in his throat, then groped blindly behind him in an effort to grab Lute, wasting the few precious seconds during which he might have employed his pistol to good effect because the garrote induced panic like almost no other killing device.

All of this moved the lawman away from the rail, giving Lute the opportunity to get directly behind his victim and push a knee into his lower spine. As soon he had the lawman bent over backward the deed was as good as done. A few seconds later he sat down and pulled his victim down with him. The lawman's eyes bulged in a face going purple, blood pouring from the gaping wound as

Lute kept sawing on his neck, and then a geyser of bright-red blood marked the severing of the carotid, followed by a sucking sound and a froth of bubbles signifying the fracture of the larynx. Lute sat there cross-legged and covered with blood with the man's head in his lap, blithely sawing away as his victim went into his death throes, his boot heels beating erratically if briefly against the deck before his eyes glazed and his body went limp.

Taking a step back as soon as he was sure the man wouldn't draw his pistol, Mal lowered the Gasser and looked toward the bow and then the stern while Lute committed the murder. When he heard the death gurgle, he sat on his heels beside the body and quickly but thoroughly searched the dead man, getting his hands bloody in the process. He didn't mind. Lute sat there a moment, panting, flush with excitement. He had once explained to Mal that it was the palpable fear in his victims that excited him so. Garrotes were a common weapon in the London slums, easy to make and cheap to acquire. They were a quick and relatively quiet way to kill when used by someone who knew how. London bobbies had taken to wearing wooden stays in high collars to help protect them from being garroted, and more than once Lute had laughingly taken credit for the "new fashion of the London constabulary"—at least those assigned to the East End. Until recently, the garrote had even been used in the execution of criminals in Spain.

Mal found the folded wanted posters stuffed under the dead man's vest. After perusing them for a moment he muttered, "Bloody hell" and looked sternly at Lute. "You just had to kill the Badham girl didn't you! The daughter of an MP, no less!" Disgusted, he showed his brother the notice for one Luther Litchfield.

Lute studied it a moment while he detached the garrote from his victim's neck, pulling the wire free of the mutilated flesh. "A bloody poor likeness if you ask me."

"Are you nicked?" asked Mal, incredulously. "This is Scotland Yard's work, and it got halfway 'round the bloody world before we did. Probably on a China clipper to Boston or New York, then on around the coast, to Charleston, New Orleans, Galveston." He was thinking aloud. The China clippers were the fastest sailing ships the world had ever known. They were used to import silk, tea, and opium to Britain. Opium dens were everywhere and laudanum, made from opium, was widely used as a painkiller. On the way back to China they would carry other goods, including mailbags. Some passed through the new Suez Canal, but there was profit to be made by carrying goods to the United States.

Lute was on his feet, bending down to take the dead man's pistol before rolling the corpse over and working the blood-splattered greatcoat free. A shout from the front of the steamboat made him look up. One of the *Mustang*'s crew had appeared near the bow and seen them. Mal stood and turned, raising the Gasser, but the crewman vanished and began shouting—what exactly Mal couldn't tell.

"Let's go!" Mal shouted. A few long strides brought him to the port-side door of the saloon. He threw the door open and strode in, ready to shoot if anyone tried to get in his way. But there was no one in the room so he continued across to the starboard door.

"What about my things?" asked Lute, following close behind his brother.

Mal didn't care too much about their dunnage. They had their weapons, and he had his Burns. He went through the doors onto the starboard deck and saw a crewman running toward him, and noticed too that the man who had been waiting on the dock was now striding up the gangplank, pistol drawn. Someone in the pilothouse was ringing the ship's bell in a frantic way that made clear it was an alarm being sounded. Seeing the brothers emerge armed from the saloon, the crewman blanched, turned, and ran back towards the bow. Since he was unarmed Mal didn't waste a bullet on him. He moved quickly toward the gangplank, reaching it when the man coming up was ten feet shy of the top, He caught a glimpse of a young, scared face, and then saw the blossom of flame and puff of acrid gray smoke as the man brought his pistol up and took a shot. Mal didn't flinch or hesitate. Shooting from the hip, he put two bullets dead center in the man's torso, his primary aim to stop him from getting off a second round.

Realizing he was unscathed, Mal glanced back at Lute to make certain his brother was unharmed as well. The man he had shot was sprawled on his back across the gangplank, wrapping his arms around his midsection and producing wheezing grunts. Mal paused, looking down at him. He felt no animus toward this young lawman, who in the grip of fear had rushed his shot and missed his mark. Lute tried to push his brother on down the gangplank but Mal brushed him off, standing over his gunshot victim.

"Please!" wheezed the man. "Don't . . . don't kill me!" Tears were welling up in his eyes. "I have a family! I have a son! I—I told him I would be b-back for Christmas . . ."

Mal shook his head. "You're not going to make it," he said, and there was a trace of regret in his voice. He thumbed the hammer of the Gasser dangling in his right hand.

A rifle barked from somewhere in the vicinity of the pilothouse. "Bloody hell!" shouted Lute after he heard a sound like an angry hornet close to his ear. It wasn't that he thought he would die today, but getting shot hurt like hell and could make you wish you were dead. He reached down, grabbed the dying man by his lapels, grunting with exertion as he lifted him and then threw him headfirst over the gangplank's rope railing. The man uttered a strangled cry, flailing as he tried—and failed—to grab on to something. Mal caught a glimpse of the horror on his face as he went over.

"Come on!" Lute shouted, trotting down the gangplank, firing twice in the general direction of the pilothouse on the way.

Mal followed, walking with long, angry strides, glancing down at the muddy brown river, knowing he would not see the young lawman surface. A gut-shot man wasn't going to come back up. He didn't break into a run when he reached the dock, either, even though a bullet splintered the weathered gray wood a few inches from his boot. Up ahead, Lute hurriedly shrugged off the greatcoat and muttered another heartfelt curse as a bullet plucked at one of the coat's windswept tails.

The horses of the two dead lawmen were fiddle-footing, made nervous by the gunfire and the smell of blood that Lute carried on him. Lute had some trouble getting into the saddle of a blaze-faced sorrel, and did some more swearing. He didn't know much about riding, being a denizen of Whitechapel streets and alleys, and he envied his older brother because Mal swung aboard the other horse and sat there like he'd been born in a saddle. Mal was focused on the steamboat, scanning it from the stern wheel forward past the forty-foot smokestacks billowing gray-black smoke to the pilothouse. Whoever was shooting at them with a long gun had stopped now, and now nary a person on board was visible. He presumed they were hiding, waiting for him and his brother to ride off before coming out from behind cover.

He looked around at Lute, who was finally perched precariously in the sorrel's saddle. "Where are we going, Mal?" asked the younger Litchfield as he yanked on the reins, trying to bring the horse beneath him under some semblance of control. Despite the difficulty the horse was giving him he seemed quite cheerful. You could not have known by his demeanor that he had just killed two men.

"Wherever we want," said Mal flatly. He could not get the face of the wounded man Lute had thrown off the gangplank out of his mind. "You know," he muttered, "they say whatever bad you do to people in this life, it will be done—and worse—to you in Hell, for all eternity." He glared at Lute a moment before kicking his horse into motion, up the narrow, overgrown trail and into the thicket covering the riverbank.

"Little late for getting religion," commented Lute, following.

Day Three

CHAPTER SEVEN

It was snowing again when Bill Sayles arrived in Cameron with Jake Eddings in tow. Even the occasional Christmas trees visible through windows, and doors adorned with wreaths made of evergreen boughs and colorful ribbons could not dispel the day's gloom. Due to the weather the wide rutted streets and warped gray boardwalks were almost empty when they arrived, but before long people began to appear at the windows or emerge from the doors to get a look at them. Sayles had a hunch their interest wasn't solely the result of curiosity about two men traveling in such inclement weather conditions. Cameron was a pretty small community, but not that small. It seemed more likely that their arrival had been expected. The word had gotten out somehow that the local boy turned outlaw and prison inmate was coming home to bury his son. Sayles wondered if the lawyer, Hanley, had anything to do with it. He had never had much use for lawyers. In his opinion they just complicated the law, and sometimes even thwarted justice.

Occasionally he looked back at Eddings. The prisoner had scarcely uttered a word since the confrontation with the three road agents yesterday. Chatting with a captive was sometimes useful in determining the other man's state of mind and perhaps even a clue as to his intent. But as a rule Sayles had never been much for small talk, and that conversation he and Eddings had engaged in the first night out of Huntsville had conjured up more than enough bad memories. So he was glad there hadn't been much chatter since then. Besides, he didn't need a verbal exchange to figure out what was bothering Eddings.

Checking his timepiece, he noted with satisfaction that it was midafternoon. They were on time based on the schedule he had imposed on himself before leaving Waco bound for Huntsville. Despite the snowfall, the gunplay on the road, and a delay at the ferry over the Brazos, they had made good time.

He thought about the ferryman's news of a shooting on a riverboat the day before. Two lawmen from Washington-on-the-Brazos had been killed, one with his throat cut ear-to-ear. The other had been shot to pieces and then thrown into the river to drown. The killers had escaped into the brush. It was the kind of crime that would be the topic of conversation among the local folk for months to come. Having seen worse, Sayles was too jaded to get excited or overly concerned about running into the pair of cold-blooded killers during his travels in the area. He woke up every day expecting trouble and was always prepared to deal with it.

Dismounting at the Cameron jail, Sayles saw a tall, skinny man with a thick mustache looking out the window and glimpsed the glint of lantern light on the tin star pinned to his shirt. It was midafternoon but almost dark as dusk thanks to the steady snowfall, so windows all along the town's main street glowed with yellow lamplight. The man studied Eddings and then gave Sayles a nod of acknowledgment before moving away from the window. When he came outside he had a jacket on and a flop-brimmed hat pulled down around his jug-handle ears. Sayles had tethered the coyote dun to the hitching post, with the bay's lead rope secured around his saddle-horn, and was in the process of bringing the sorrel that had once carried a knife-wielding black outlaw up to the post.

"You must be the Ranger," said the thin man, hugging himself against the wind that came whipping down the street to blow snow in his face. "Lawyer Hanley told me you were coming. You might have sent me a telegram about it."

Sayles reached down and pulled the Sheffield bowie from his boot. "You just said you knew I was coming—and without getting a telegram," he observed.

The lawman's eyes widened when he saw the bowie's twelve-inch blade, and he muttered, "Just sayin' it's a simple courtesy between officers of the law." His tone carried a trace of resentment still, but was not nearly as officious as before. He was pretty sure Sayles didn't mean him harm, but then he *was* a Texas Ranger, and they were known to be unpredictable and violent.

Sayles turned and employed the bowie knife in cutting Eddings free from the bay on which he had come all the way from Huntsville Prison. Eddings couldn't seem to swing his leg up and over the cantle to dismount, so Sayles helped him down, noticing his body was rigid and shivering. His legs seemed to give out when he finally got his feet on the ground, and Sayles hooked one of the prisoner's arms over his shoulders and helped him to the jail.

"What's wrong with him?" asked the sheriff, primed to become even more resentful if it turned out the prisoner was injured, since that could well inconvenience him. "He hurt?"

"He's froze up. Move aside," said Sayles gruffly. Noticing the door was ajar, he kicked it open and proceeded on into the jail's office.

He sat Eddings down in the nearest chair, poured a cup of java from a blackened coffeepot on a potbelly stove, and put it in the prisoner's hands. The sheriff closed the door and walked around his cluttered kneehole desk but didn't sit down. He felt a little better with the desk between him and the Ranger with his bowie knife. Crossing his arms, he cast a disapproving look at Eddings, then snatched up a pair of wanted posters and thrust them in the Ranger's direction.

"This is not a good time for me to have to deal with this," he complained. "Looks like we have a pair of real hardcases in the area."

Sayles looked at the posters of two men named Litchfield, noting that if they were related they didn't look it.

The sheriff handed him a telegraph. "Came this morning. Most likely those two will head west, and that means they could come through here."

The telegram didn't tell Sayles anything the ferryman hadn't already told him about the killings on the riverboat. He looked up from the telegram and studied the Cameron sheriff for a moment, trying to figure out if the man was just annoyed or anxious. "Wouldn't worry too much," he said, putting the posters and the telegram on the sheriff's desk. "They don't know this country, or the people. They wouldn't know what they were riding into. Reckon they're just looking for a hole to crawl into for a while."

The sheriff didn't like that the Ranger had made light of the threat he'd hoped to use as an excuse to get out from under taking care of Eddings. He flared at the prisoner. "Didn't think I'd lay eyes on you again for many a year, if ever." Eddings didn't give any indication he even heard. He sipped the hot coffee, then held the cup up close to his face, for the warmth. The sheriff looked askance at Sayles as the latter opened a door and inspected the cell block—four small, windowless cells and a back door securely barred. "I'm Tom Rath, sheriff of Cameron for going on six years now. That's my jail," he added, possessively.

"Gathered as much. Be needing you to lock this feller up, and I'll be sleeping in one of the empty cells."

"This isn't a hotel. Got one of those down the street. I can keep an eye on your prisoner just fine without your assistance."

"Reckon you can. But I don't fancy wasting money on a room when a cot in one of them cells back there would suit me."

Sheriff Rath scowled. He had already told the Ranger that his jail was not a hostelry, but Sayles was either thickheaded or dim-witted as he obviously wasn't going to be swayed from his intent to use the jail like one. Feeling territorial and imposed upon, Rath was about to argue the point when the door opened and Temple Hanley entered.

The lawyer quickly shut the door, rubbed his gloved hands together, and stamped his feet, flashing a big smile at Rath. "Colder than I can ever recall, Sheriff!" he said, cheerfully, noting the lawman's frowning features. That wasn't unusual, Rath being a rather dour man. Hanley just naturally tended to counter truculence with pleasantness. He moved nearer the potbelly stove, where Sayles was helping himself to Rath's coffee. "You must be the Texas Ranger, Bill Sayles." Hanley stripped off a glove and offered his hand. "Temple Hanley is the name. Just got word you had arrived. Right on time, too. Couldn't have been a very pleasant trip, the weather being what it is."

Sayles shook the proffered hand. It was soft and fleshy. "Mr. Hanley."

Hanley turned his attention to Jake Eddings, huddled in the chair with his head down and by all appearances unaware of or completely indifferent to what was transpiring around him. The lawyer's smiled faltered. This was the first time in two years that he had set eyes on Jake, and the changes that prison life had wrought were startling. Where once had been a strong, robust young man was someone gaunt, hollow-cheeked, and much older looking. Not since his youth, watching his own father die of consumption, had Hanley seen such a distinct transformation occur in such a short span of time. He gently put the ungloved hand on Eddings's hunched shoulder and bent over slightly. "Jake, do you remember me? Temple Hanley, I represented you in court."

Eddings looked up. "Purdy," he said, his voice hoarse. "How is Purdy?"

Having already given considerable thought to how to answer that question, Hanley smiled reassuringly. "She is holding up, Jake. As well as can be expected under these circumstances. I will go out to your place first thing tomorrow and let her know you've arrived."

Rath spoke up. "Sooner his boy is buried and he's hauled back to Huntsville Prison, the better."

Hanley was perturbed by Rath's callous disregard for Jake Eddings's suffering. He knew Rath to be a lazy, ambitious, and self-centered man. He was not so much an officer of the law as a bureaucrat who viewed the position of sheriff as a springboard to higher office—and the respect he desperately sought but could not earn by dint of his personality or character. Since acquiring the office had been Rath's sole objective, the duties that came with it were usually nothing more than an annoyance to him. Having to deal with Eddings—and Sayles—put him out. During his tenure as Cameron's sheriff Rath had earned a reputation as a man who was perhaps a little too quick to resort to gunplay. He had shot several men to death, and Hanley had wondered in every case whether it was because disposing of a dead man was easier than having custody over a living one. Or, perhaps, Rath had a sadistic nature. Whatever the truth, he did not treat the men in his charge very well at all.

"I will put everything in motion," Hanley assured him, his disapproval of Rath effectively masked by a broad and disarming smile. Digging in a pocket, he produced a handful of silver dollars, which he placed on the sheriff's desk, leaning forward to pitch his voice low, as though about to share a confidence. "I realize it isn't always easy to effect reimbursement for your expenses here, Tom. So permit me to defray the cost of housing this man."

Rath looked at the coins, somewhat mollified, then remembered Sayles. "The Ranger, too. He seems to think my jail is a hotel."

Hanley glanced at Sayles, who now was leaning against a wall, still close to the potbelly stove for warmth's sake, drinking his coffee and seemingly paying no attention to the conversation, instead casually looking at an old map of Texas, from back in the Republic days, that decorated one of the office walls. Hanley was relieved to know that Sayles would be around. That boded well for Eddings. Having brought several more silver dollars in case Rath was inclined to haggle, he added these to the pile on the desk. "That should cover it."

Rath quickly gathered up the coins, as though afraid Hanley might change his mind and take them back.

As soon as Rath appropriated the silver, Sayles emptied his cup, put it down, and fastened his gaze on the sheriff. "You want to lock this man up so's I can go tend to some business?"

Rath took offense. "He's not going anywhere," he said curtly.

"I'd like to be sure."

Hanley intervened. "Ranger Sayles is here by order of the governor, Tom. It's understandable that he doesn't want to misplace his prisoner, as he would he held responsible."

Rath fumed. Hanley's logic was unassailable. The sheriff got Eddings to his feet and took him into the cell block, securing him in the first cell on the right. The sheriff then unlocked the first cell on the left and opened the door, glancing at Sayles, who had strolled into the cell block. "Your room," he said, the words laden with sarcasm.

Sayles turned, nodded at Hanley, and left the jail. He led the horses down the street to the livery, where he sold the sorrel and the dead outlaw's cross-draw rigs for ninety dollars after some haggling. From the proceeds he paid to have the coyote dun and the bay stabled and fed. Carrying his Winchester and the carriage gun, he made his way to the nearest saloon and bought a bottle of Old Overholt. There were half a dozen men in the place, three of them playing poker over in the vicinity of one of the two stoves, and two more jawing with the barkeep at the long mahogany bar. The men stopped talking and playing and gave him a long look, as they would anyone who was a stranger to them, especially someone carrying so many weapons. As the bartender produced the bottle and a reasonably clean glass, he asked Sayles if he was the Ranger who had brought Jake Eddings to town. Sayles grimaced and without replying took his whiskey to a table in the back. One of the men bellying up to the bar drawled, "Unsociable cuss, ain't he."

He had knocked back just one shot when Temple Hanley walked in, spotted him, and, with affable greetings to the other men, made his way to the back.

"May I join you, Mr. Sayles?"

Sayles gestured at an empty chair while pouring himself another glass. The first shot had been an explosion of liquid warmth in his belly that took some of the aches and pains out of him, and he was thirsty for more. For the first time since Superintendent Goree's office at the prison he was starting to feel warm. "Seems like everybody in this town knows my business."

Hanley sighed as he sat down across from Sayles, putting his hat on the table and running fingers through his thick matted hair. "I am ashamed to say that is my fault, sir. I let it slip to a local newspaperman."

Sayles wasn't one to cry over spilled milk—or to berate the one who had done the spilling. What was done was done. "Eddings have many friends in Cameron?"

The lawyer shook his head, brushing snow off the shoulders of his buffalo coat. "He kept to himself for the most part. The few who might have called him friend before the robbery have washed their hands of him now. Kill a man in cold blood, or even be party to the killing, and you become a pariah." He put his arms on the table and leaned forward. "And even worse, so do your own people. In this case, his poor wife. I cannot seem to find a single woman in this town willing to go out to the Eddings place and help Purdy get through this terrible time. Though to be honest that may not be entirely due to Jake being an accomplice to murder." He paused, looking at Sayles expectantly, but when the Ranger didn't ask what he meant, he sighed, looked around, then spoke in barely more than whisper. "You see, rumors are going around that before her son became ill Purdy Eddings had taken up with another man. A farmer named Norris, a widower whom she allowed in her bed in return for helping her with the planting and harvesting."

Sayles looked up from his whiskey then. "Be best if Eddings doesn't find out about that. Seems to me he's pert near the end of his rope. That kind of news might make him plumb loco and then he could get himself kilt."

Hanley nodded. "Tom Rath wouldn't hesitate. Killing Eddings is more convenient than taking responsibility for keeping him. That's how the sheriff would look at it. I suppose you wouldn't hesitate either."

"Reckon not." Sayles knocked back the second shot of who-hit-john, gasping as the liquid fire chased away the last of the winter chill out of him and let him relax.

"It would save you the trouble of hauling him back to Huntsville."

Sayles fastened his steely gaze on the lawyer. "I don't have a problem doing my job," he said, curtly.

Flustered, Hanley felt a tingling anxiety at the base of his spine. "No, no, of course not, Mr. Sayles, I wasn't implying that you would actually . . ."

"So the boy can be buried tomorrow?"

"I will go out to the Eddings homestead first thing in the morning and take a couple of hired men with me, as Purdy insisted on keeping her son's body close at hand until time came. Poor woman sits in her rocking chair on the porch with a shotgun, watching over the casket." Hanley sighed. "Hobbes was right. Life is nasty, brutish, and short. Especially out here on the fringe of civilization. In the meantime, I will hire other men to dig the grave in the Cameron cemetery. At first Purdy insisted her son be buried at their farm, but I talked her out of that. I mean, realistically there isn't much chance of her holding on to that land. Barely made enough from the last harvest to pay the bank."

Sayles had no idea who this Hobbes feller was but decided that he was right about at least one thing. "You do this sort of thing for all your clients?"

"No. But I find it difficult to think of Jake Eddings as just another criminal. Yes, he was involved in a robbery. Yes, a man was killed in the commission of the crime. I understand that the dead man deserves justice done. That the law-abiding in society should be protected from the scofflaws. But I also believe justice must be tempered by mercy. Jake made a mistake. He didn't pull the trigger that ended the victim's life. An eyewitness even testified to that fact. He had a family, a wife, to take care of. I believe the sentence of fifteen years was excessive, considering the circumstances. I know of cases where men were incarcerated for that length of time and even less for shooting someone. The law out here is very . . . unpredictable." He studied Sayles's craggy features a moment. "I suspect you don't agree. My hunch is you have an Old Testament view of things."

The barkeep brought a clean glass to the table for Hanley. Sayles poured two fingers of whiskey into it. "What does that mean?"

"Eye for an eye, tooth for a tooth." When it came to strong spirits, Hanley preferred brandy, but he tentatively sipped the whiskey since the Ranger had been kind enough to share. "The problem is, what you do to one person usually affects other people as well. In this case, Purdy Eddings. You've seen Jake. Probably talked to him. You think he has been punished after two years in prison? Do you think he will be any more chastened and remorseful after thirteen additional years behind bars? Or will be become embittered, violent, desperate?" He held up a hand. "Rhetorical questions. I am just saying, Jake Eddings was not a hardcase outlaw. But he might well be one thirteen years from now when he walks free. As for Purdy, if she thought her husband would be free and in her arms in a year or two she might be able to hold on to hope. But fifteen years, Mr. Sayles? That's a lifetime out here."

Sayles sipped his third dose of whiskey. He wasn't sure what *rhetorical* meant but it was clear the lawyer didn't expect him to express an opinion. "Well, speaking of hardcases, two such killed a couple of lawmen on a Brazos riverboat yesterday. From what I was told they headed east, but they might have doubled back, crossed the river, and gone west, where there's less law. Either way, they're somewhere in these parts, and if that Purdy Eddings is alone . . ."

"My God!" exclaimed Hanley, an expression of horror on his face.

". . , you might want to go fetch her, and the boy's body, today."

Temple Hanley was not a brave man, and he didn't delude himself into believing otherwise. A quick calculation of time and distance convinced him that even if he left right away he could not be back in Cameron before nightfall. But knowing that Purdy was potentially in great peril, waiting until the morning was out of the question. "Yes, yes, of course." He put his hat on, rose from the chair, and then, as an afterthought, picked up the glass and downed the rest of the liquid bravemaker it contained. The expression of high anxiety on his face made it possible for Sayles to anticipate what was coming next. "Mr. Sayles, could I . . . could I trouble you to come with me?"

The Ranger grimaced. He had been looking forward to enjoying his bottle of Old Overholt and then laying his weary body on something besides the hard cold ground. He knocked back the third shot and corked the bottle, stuffed it under an arm, and rose, picking up the Winchester repeater and the sawed-off 10-gauge shotgun. "Go get yer wagon, Mr. Hanley," he said, without enthusiasm. "I'll fetch my horse."

CHAPTER EIGHT

Jake Eddings lay on his side on a narrow bunk in the Cameron city jail cell, knees pulled up as if hugging himself against the cold; the thin, musty brown blanket he had been provided wasn't sufficient to keep the bitter chill at bay. There was no heat source in the cell block. The sheriff kept the door closed to trap the warmth produced by the potbelly stove in the office. After two years in prison Jake was accustomed to having his health and well-being disregarded. He understood that as a consequence of his crossing the line and breaking the law he no longer warranted any consideration from others.

In a way he wished he was back in prison. At least there, among men and women who through their actions had become outcasts like him, he hadn't felt as ashamed as he did now that he had come home. Even though he remembered Tom Rath all too well from the weeks during which he had languished in this very jail before and during his trial, the sheriff's contempt drove home an indisputable truth—that he was a loser. He'd had a loving wife, a beautiful child, land to call his own as long as he paid the banknote. He had been on his way to becoming a respectable member of the community. That had always been of foremost importance to his father, but Jake really hadn't given it much thought. He had been wrapped up in his family, not his self-image. Now his son was dead, and he blamed himself, even though it was unlikely his presence would have changed anything where Joshua's sickness was concerned. Without their son's help, how was Purdy going to be able to hold on to the farm by herself? She certainly couldn't afford to hire any help. But the most troubling question of all was—How could he expect Purdy to spend the next thirteen years of her life waiting for him to serve out his sentence?

For the past two years he had longed to see his wife again, an agony that was like a knife in the heart. Every single day he woke up with it, tried to get through the day with it, and then went to bed and tried to sleep despite it. Now, though, he didn't know how he could face her. He had let her down, had ruined her life. She had been forced to watch their son die all by herself and he had not been there to even attempt to comfort her. Even so the painful longing to see her was stronger, now that he was only a few miles away. It made his eyes burn with tears to think of her out there, alone and hurting. Angry and bitter, he cursed himself for being such a worthless husband and father.

When he heard the door to the street open and close, Eddings forgot about breathing, wondering if it was Purdy come to see him. But it wasn't Purdy, and the mind-numbing sorrow that had resided in him for two years felt like an invisible fist squeezing his heart. He was so close to her in terms of physical distance and yet she felt so far away. Tom Rath was conversing with another man whose voice he didn't recognize. The latter wanted to see "the prisoner" and Rath was reluctant to accede to the request. The other said, "This is very important to me, Tom. I would be willing to make it worth your while. And be sure, I will mention you often in whatever I write as a result of the interview." A moment later the cell block door creaked open and Rath preceded a slender young man wearing a straw boater, yellow duster, and mud-caked boats. Eddings sat up.

The young man smiled brightly and stuck a hand between the bars of Eddings's cell. "Mr. Eddings, my name is Emmett Placer. How are you today?"

Incredulous, Eddings stared at Placer, then at the proffered hand. He didn't bother getting up to shake it. "Is that some kind of joke?"

Placer suddenly looked flustered. "My apologies. I am a newspaperman and would just like to ask you a few questions, if I may."

"Don't stick your hand in there," barked Rath. "They call men like him desperadoes for a reason, Placer." His tone dripped with sarcasm. Stepping into the front room, he returned a moment later with a wooden chair, which he set with its back against the door of the empty cell across from the one occupied by Eddings. "You sit in this chair and don't get any closer, you hear? I'll be right outside."

Placer nodded meekly. He didn't want to do anything that might set off the mercurial sheriff and cost him this one chance to talk to Cameron's most notorious son. He sat in the chair and waited until Rath had left the cell block before leaning forward, one arm draped over the other with elbows on his knees, peering through the bars with keen interest. "So tell me, Mr. Eddings, *are* you a desperado?"

Eddings shrugged. "Does it matter what I think I am?"

"Indeed it does, indeed it does. Mr. Eddings, you may not be aware of it, but this is a rare opportunity for both of us."

"An opportunity to do what?"

"For you to tell your side of the story. About the crime you committed, your capture, the trial, your incarceration, all of it. And for me to write it all down and present it to the public. Now, I would never be allowed to enter the prison at Huntsville to listen to your story. But as luck would have it—here you are." Placer paused to study the expression on Eddings's face. "Of course one would wish it had happened under happier circumstances. I am truly sorry for your loss, sir. Truly sorry." He paused, giving Eddings a chance to speak, but the prisoner sat there silently, staring morosely at the floor. Placer decided to try a different approach, hoping to coax at least an opinion from Eddings. "Temple Hanley rode all the way to Austin to make the case for you. He's a good man, Lawyer Hanley. But Governor Coke?" Placer shook his head. "Never met him but from what I've heard he is a hard man. Maybe he was susceptible to Lawyer Hanley's oratorical skills, which are considerable. Or maybe he was moved by the spirit of the season. Christmas is just a few days away, you know. Regardless, you must be grateful."

"Sure," said Eddings, flatly." It's always nice to be treated like a person and not an animal. You talk a lot."

Placer chuckled. "Yes, yes, that's true. Words are my stock-in-trade." He had been willing to rattle on until he struck a nerve, or at least found something that animated the prisoner. Sensing that he had succeeded, he leaned forward a bit more. "Do they treat you like an animal in prison, Mr. Eddings?"

Eddings sat there a moment, brooding, then got to his feet without a word, letting the blanket slide off his body onto the bunk. He unbuttoned his shirt to shrug it down off his shoulders, revealing a webbing of scars on his back.

"Jesus," muttered the newspaperman.

"They like the whip," said Eddings, matter-of-factly.

"What did you do to warrant such punishment?" Placer assumed the scars were the result of multiple whippings. He didn't think any man could survive taking all that punishment at one time.

Eddings buttoned up his shirt, draped the blanket back over his shoulders, and sat down. "Didn't move fast enough. Didn't get enough work done in a day. One time I got sick, puked in a basket of raw cotton. Couldn't help it. But that cost them so they made sure it cost me too. They put us to work in there, you know. Dawn to dusk, seven days a week, unless the preacher from town came in to hold services on Sunday. Then you could get out of working until noon. Some prisoners were taken out to work as lumber crews, or to lay rail for a railroad. Or they used to. Lay rail I mean. Seems hard times have hit the iron roads too. Me, I usually worked in the prison textile mill, and sometimes on the farm."

Placer nodded. "The idea, I suppose, is that you have to earn your keep."

Eddings smiled bitterly. "Yeah, we earn a lot more than our keep. That company, Ward-Dewey, makes a tidy profit off what we make inside that prison, or the work we do outside of it."

"Well, that's as it should be, don't you think? Ward-Dewey is not a charitable institution. Besides, it's generally believed that giving prison inmates work to do keeps them healthier and makes the time go by faster for them. Some might even learn a trade that will stand them in good stead once they get out." He studied Eddings's expression. "You don't agree?"

"They treat us like slaves. Worse. Slaves were an investment. Inmates, well, they don't care if we live or die. Not really. Always new labor being brought in." Eddings sighed, thinking he was wasting his time complaining to this wordsmith, who didn't know what a hard day's work was anyway. "Point is, we're treated like . . . like . . ." He couldn't think of the word.

"The dregs of society. At least you're still alive, Mr. Eddings. You are better off than your partner—what was his name? Underhill?"

"Am I? I wonder sometimes."

Placer had hoped to get a different response from Eddings on the topic of his imprisonment. Instead of the defiant, unrepentant rogue shaking his fist at society and vowing vengeance for all his suffering, which he thought would make good copy and titillate his readers, he had a broken and embittered man on his hands. He tried a different approach. "When you've served your sentence, what do you intend to do? Do you think you will return to a life of crime, as so many others do?"

Eddings sat silent for a moment, elbows on knees, hands tightly clasped, head down. He tried to see himself thirteen years into the future, walking out of Huntsville Prison's West Gate a free man. But he couldn't. Some things he *could* envision. "I don't know," he muttered. "Thirteen years from now that farm won't be mine anymore. I don't expect Purdy will be mine anymore either." He paused and cleared his throat. "But then, in thirteen years I'll probably be eating dirt in the prison cemetery anyway."

Tom Rath had kept the door to the office open so he could keep an eye on Placer and listen to the conversation between the newspaperman and his prisoner. Eddings was grateful for that, since some of the warmth previously confined to the front room had begun to permeate the cell block. But now Rath appeared in the doorway, leaning with arms crossed against the frame, chuckling as he looked at Placer while directing his comment at Eddings.

"I think Mr. Placer here had hopes you'd turn out to be Cameron's very own version of Jesse James, or some such—instead of a man with no gumption who's just waiting to die."

Even though Rath was right, Placer waxed indignant. "That's uncalled for, Sheriff. I simply wanted to interview one of Cameron's own, a man who has gone astray and is now paying the wages of sin. I think this man's story is a cautionary tale my readers will appreciate and perhaps benefit from." He stood and looked at Eddings, trying to think of what to say in parting, and settling on, "I would pray for you, sir, except that I don't believe there is a God. I have heard and read and seen with my own eyes too much senseless tragedy to believe that a caring God watches over us. But I digress. Thank you for your time, Mr. Eddings."

"He's got time," said Rath, chuckling. "That's one thing he's got plenty of,"

Placer smiled faintly—clearly he wasn't as amused by Rath's attempt at humor as the sheriff himself was—and quickly left the jail.

Rath remained in the doorway for a moment, staring smugly at his prisoner until finally Eddings looked up. "I could use some food and water," he said.

Rath shrugged. "Maybe in the morning. If you're still around."

"Seems like I recall Mr. Hanley paying for some food and water for me."

"Stop your whining. Hanley likes to throw his money around. Makes him feel important. Truth is he's weak. Soft. That you're even here and not still behind bars in Huntsville Prison where you belong is proof of that. What I can't believe is that the governor turned out to be soft too. Maybe the next one will be made of sterner stuff when it comes to dealing with no-account vermin like yourself."

Eddings sighed and resumed his inspection of the cell floor. There was no point in debating with a self-centered man like Rath, who not only wasn't interested in another person's opinion but didn't really listen to what others had to say anyway. But his silence failed to get rid of the sheriff, who settled into the chair recently vacated by the newspaperman.

"You know," Rath drawled, "you're right about your farm. And your woman. Neither one is going to belong to you by the time you get out of prison, if you ever do."

Eddings didn't look up. He knew from previous experience that the Cameron sheriff was a bully with a sadistic streak who enjoyed goading people. Some of the guards at the prison fit the same mold. The best course of action was to ignore them, or just take it and keep your mouth shut. Rath's comment cut him deeply, and he bristled, but he let a bitter retort die stillborn on his tongue.

"Your wife paid the banknote last year," continued Rath. "Brought in a crop with a little help from your neighbor, that fellow Norris. Maybe you knew about that. Maybe she wrote you about it. She does write you letters, doesn't she? By all accounts he stays over at your place from time to time, if you know what I mean." He chuckled. "My guess is now that she's all alone, and him being a widower, they'll get joined up in more ways than just under a blanket one of these days."

Eddings's hands curled into fists. The sheriff's words seemed to knock the wind out of him. He pressed those fists against his temples while slowly leaning forward until he was doubled over at the waist. The anguish he experienced at that moment made all the other pain and misery he had endured these past two years pale in comparison. It was like a white-hot blade twisting in his heart. Hot tears brimmed in eyes he squeezed shut. His guts were tied up in an excruciating knot so intense it made him gasp for breath.

The thought that Purdy might take up with another man while he served his time *had* crossed his mind. One of his greatest fears had been that she would not wait for him. Was it even fair to expect her to? But he had hoped. That fear had really come home to roost when her letters stopped coming. She had written a few, in response to his. He had asked how she and Joshua were doing, how they were faring with the farm, had begged for forgiveness, had pleaded for patience, had told her how much he loved and needed her. Her letters answered his questions. She had forgiven him. She promised she would wait. She told him that she loved him. But there was something missing. The Purdy who was so full of the joy of life had not written those letters. Even her "I love you too"s had been perfunctory and rather lifeless responses. No *I love you so much* or *I will love you forever.* He had tried to convince himself that it was only because writing letters under the circumstances was difficult, if not gut wrenching. This he knew from his own experience.

When her letters stopped coming he told himself it must be because writing had become simply too painful for her to endure. That she had met someone else and did not love him anymore was a possibility he couldn't bring himself to accept or even think about. Then he had received word from Temple Hanley that his son had died. Purdy had not even written him to tell her Joshua was ill. He decided she had kept quiet to spare him the anguish of being unable to be with Joshua in his son's time of greatest need. More and more he wondered if Purdy would ever be able to forgive him.

Eddings remembered all too well how the widower had looked at Purdy. Norris had come by the farm quite often—*too* often, in Eddings's book. Purdy was indulgent, reminding her husband that Norris was just a very lonely man, with no offspring and a wife who had died in childbirth. Horribly, the baby she carried died with her, strangled by its umbilical cord.

That another man lusted after one's wife fed the egos of some men and the self-doubts of others. Eddings fell into the latter category. He had always wondered how it was possible that the most beautiful and alluring girl in Texas could have fallen in love with *him*. After letting the problem fester for a while, he called Norris on it. Norris deflected his anger and avoided a confrontation with assurances he meant no harm, and then, in a good-natured way, chided Eddings for his jealousy since it was obvious Purdy loved him and only him. Eddings derived some solace from the knowledge that his wife didn't care for Norris—this she had made abundantly clear on more than one occasion and with such sincerity that he never had cause to doubt her. Purdy didn't have a deceitful bone in her body. She could not tell a lie without him knowing.

Even so, Eddings believed that what Tom Rath told him about Purdy and Norris was true. Maybe that was why she had stopped writing. So that she didn't have to lie. He drew a ragged sigh. He wasn't angry at Purdy. He couldn't blame her. How could he? It was his fault. Like Ranger Sayles said, he'd made a choice, the wrong choice, and everything that happened as a result of that was on him. He hadn't always thought that way. At first he blamed God, had started blaming God during the hard times that led him to take the outlaw trail out of desperation. What had he done to deserve all that had befallen him? It was a question he asked countless times, at least as many times as he cursed the Almighty for all these unfair afflictions that had been cast upon him. Over time he changed. Self-recrimination rather than self-pity seemed a better fit in his case. He realized now that it wasn't God who had done this to him. Instead, God had simply abandoned him.

The jangle of keys, the rasp of metal against metal, the clatter and clunk of a lock being unlocked drew him out of his grim reverie. He looked up. Rath was at the cell door, was opening it an inch, leaving the key in the lock, the big ring of keys to which it was attached chiming as it bounced off the stout iron bars of the door. The sheriff had a pistol in his right hand, held down at his side as he took two steps back.

"I take it from the look on your face that she neglected to write you about all that," murmured Rath. His eyes were gleaming "Guess maybe she was trying to spare you." He shrugged his indifference.

Eddings sat up, looking at the door, then at Rath. "What are you doing?"

"I'm doing you a favor, though you don't deserve it."

"You're not letting me go," said Eddings, skeptically.

Rath smiled. "Not exactly. I'm giving you a choice. It's been a while since you've had one, hasn't it? Don't ask me why, but I feel like you should have the right to die a free man. To be buried here at home and not in that prison cemetery you mentioned when you were talking to Placer. All you have to do is step out of that cell. Then you'll be free. All you got to do is step through that door and your troubles are over. It's that or just sit there, and spend the rest of your life in a cage. Because we both know you won't walk out of prison alive. You don't have the grit to live through an ordeal like that. And why should you? What have you got to live for now?"

Eddings stood there, staring at the floor just outside the

cell, at the spot where he would place his foot if he stepped out. He tried to sort through his thoughts. The space outside the cell held a very strong allure, even though he knew it contained the bullet that would end his life. He didn't believe for a minute that Tom Rath really cared if he died a free man. Rath was a cold-blooded killer. He got something out of taking another's life. There had been incidents in the past involving Rath and the death of men held in one of these jail cells. A crotchety old local drunk who always gave the sheriff what-for ended up hanged in one of them. A two-bit rustler who threatened Rath in the presence of others ended up being shot to death "trying to escape" that very night. Eddings had never given much thought to those events, but now he was on the verge of becoming the next prisoner to die in this cell block.

What Tom Rath wanted to do now was nothing short of murder, but because of the badge he wore he wouldn't lose his life or freedom or even his job for committing it. Eddings didn't waste time speculating on what story the sheriff would concoct to justify the shooting. It didn't matter. What mattered to Eddings was that he had just been offered a way to escape the pure misery and heartbreak that resided like a big cold black aching hole in the middle of him. He had just been envying Underhill for spending the last two years in a grave rather than prison, and here was his chance to join his former partner in crime. The only reason he hadn't wanted to die in prison was the hope of one day being reunited with his family, and then, after Joshua's death, with his wife. But now that hope seemed to have been taken from him too.

"Make up your mind," said Rath, impatiently. "This is your last chance to die a free man."

Looking at the pistol Rath held down at his side,

Eddings gauged his chances of reaching the sheriff and wrestling the smoke-wagon out of his grasp. The hammer wasn't cocked, he noticed. Rath didn't look concerned, though. He didn't look at all like a man taking a chance, and Eddings had to concede that he wasn't. And why would he want to escape? To be on the run, hunted like an animal? He wouldn't be able to restore his good name, or hold on to his farm, or be with Purdy. Ranger Sayles had said that there was nothing after death. That you wouldn't even know you were dead. After two years of unremitting misery he found the concept of nothingness to have a certain appeal.

But there was one problem. He didn't believe what Sayles had said about dying. He couldn't believe that his son had never been anything more than flesh and bone, now lying lifeless in a pine box. What had become of his soul? It still existed. Even the Indians—which his own kind considered heathen—believed in spirits and a life beyond the grave. And so did he. His father had not been a churchgoing, God-fearing man, and Eddings could count on the fingers of one hand the number of sermons he had heard in his lifetime. He hadn't bothered attending the Sunday-morning services at the prison. But he believed in an Almighty God, which meant there was a life after death, a Heaven and a Hell. Joshua resided in the former. And even if he didn't see his son again in the next life, he couldn't shake the feeling that his son could see him in this one. So the question was, Did he want his son to know he had taken the coward's way out? Because that was what Tom Rath was offering him.

In this moment of clarity, Eddings became reacquainted with self-respect. He raised his head and looked squarely into the glittering eyes of Tom Rath. "I'm not going to take the easy way out. Not this time. Not going to play your game. You're a cold-blooded murdering snake, Sheriff, and I've seen better men than you'll ever be in Huntsville Prison. As for me, I have to say good-bye to my son, I have to tell him how sorry I am." He sat down on the bunk. "And while maybe I wasn't much of a father to him when he was here, I still have a chance to be."

Rath angrily slammed the cell door shut and locked it. "You're just a yellow coward," he sneered, keenly disappointed. "You deserve to rot in that hellhole of a prison."

Eddings nodded. "Yeah," he said softly. "I do."

He leaned back against the wall and closed his eyes.

CHAPTER NINE

After escaping the lawmen on the *Mustang*, Mal Litchfield led the way north along the east bank of the Brazos.
He was always the one who led the way. Lute was content
to let his older brother make the decisions, especially the
hard ones. In his opinion there were too many idle plea-
sures available in life to waste time anguishing over
choices to be made. He just took what came his way and
let Mal decide which direction afforded them the best
chance to avoid the law.

Mal had spent the few days he and Lute lingered in
Galveston listening and chatting, on docks and street
corners, hotel lobbies and watering holes, learning a lot
about Texas. They had fled England on a ship bound for
Galveston because that seemed the most direct route to
what, as Englishmen, they believed was the lawless frontier, a vast stretch of sparsely populated and poorly
policed territory located between the Mississippi River
and California, where men such as themselves could do
what they wanted with little fear of consequences. That
included Texas, or so he had thought. For this reason, Mal
wanted to get across the Brazos and head west. Coming

from a place like Whitechapel, which was crawling with bobbies, a place where a person rarely saw a badge struck Mal as being the closest thing to paradise he would ever experience.

They spent the night in a dilapidated shack deep in the woods and overrun by brush. It was a sleepless night for Mal, who thought there was a fair chance that posses were already out searching for him and his brother. He stood guard, because it was too risky to rely on Lute with the stakes so high. Giving the town of Port Sullivan a wide berth, they came. at midmorning, upon a ferry where what appeared to be a well-traveled east–west road crossed the Brazos. Lute assumed they were going to take the ferry but Mal informed him otherwise, as they sat their stolen mounts close enough to get a clear view of the ferry but not so close they risked being seen. The raft was halfway across the river. An older man and a big strapping youth were manning the stout rope, taking two men and two horses to the other side. The horses blocked his view of the two passengers.

Mal had already discovered that people out here were curious about strangers, about where others had been, where they were going, what they had seen along the way, and their reasons for traveling. In a country where telegraph stations were few and far between, and newspapers were just as scarce, news largely traveled by word of mouth. For this reason, he and Lute needed to stay away from the ferry.

"We don't want anyone knowing we headed west," he explained.

Peering after the ferry, Lute said, "So, they take us across and then we drown them. People will assume it was the river that did them in."

"Two men killed on a riverboat. Two more disappear just upstream. A smart copper would draw the right conclusion."

"Then how the bloody hell do we get across this bloody river?" asked Lute with a petulant scowl. He was sick and tired of being so cold it hurt. "I want walls and a roof—and maybe a ladybird to warm me up."

Mal scanned the bleak overcast sky, blinking at the snowflakes that fluttered down into his eyes. It was difficult to tell the time of day with any precision, but he calculated they had roughly an hour or two of daylight remaining. It was impossible to know with certainty whether their wanted posters had reached this far inland, or even how long it would take for word of what had transpired on the riverboat to reach the settlement. But if men weren't scouring the countryside for them now, they soon would be. He realized they needed to cross the Brazos soon.

"We'll go upriver until we find a likely spot and swim our horses over."

Lute was aghast. "What? Have you ever tried to swim one of these bloody animals across a river?" He stood in his stirrups to get a better look through the brush at the surface of the Brazos. "And I can't swim, in case you had forgotten!"

"You don't have to. Your horse will. You just hold on to the saddle."

For once Lute decided to balk at one of Mal's decisions. "I say we take the ferry. I'll kill those two. It's no problem."

Mal sighed. No problem. That was what worried him. The more dead bodies left in their wake, the less likely they would make it into the wild country. He shook his head. "That we don't take it—that nothing happens to those two blokes down there—will cause anyone who might be on our trail to think it's likely we've remained on *this* side of the river. And that's what we want them to think."

Lute looked at his brother and fumed. He knew it was pointless to argue with Mal. Sometimes he did anyway, just to get his opinion and objection on the record, but he realized that whether he wanted to or not he was going to have to risk swimming across the river. "Fine," he muttered. "But if I drown you'll never forgive myself."

"It will be one more thing added to the list," murmured Mal.

They continued upstream for about an hour and then Mal saw what he was looking for. A small wooded island hugged the western bank of the Brazos. This far inland the river was considerably narrower than it was where they had boarded the *Mustang*, and the presence of the island meant they would only have to swim two-thirds of the river's width. Between the island and the western bank was a narrow channel clogged with debris and a fallen tree, the river tumbling over these obstacles like a staircase of small waterfalls. While Lute stared apprehensively at the expanse of slow-moving brown water between him and the island, Mal sat his saddle on the verge of the thick brush on the eastern side and took a long look up and down the river. He saw no road or farm or structure of any kind, nor pasture or fence line, either.

"We'll cross here," he said, dismounting. "Strip down to your long johns. Bundle up your clothes and use your trouser legs to tie it all together. Boots come off too."

Lute stared incredulously at his brother. "Are you off your head? That water must be freezing cold."

"Soaked clothes will make you colder still and weigh you down. Your boots will fill up with water and do the same." Mal was already stripping.

Lute sighed. Mal knew a lot about many more things than he did, so he was willing to give his brother the benefit of the doubt in most instances. That included crossing a river in the dead of winter, but he didn't have to like it. He pulled off his mule-ear boots and put his gull and garrote in one, into which he also stuffed his shirt. The boots were wrapped up in the greatcoat that yesterday had been in the possession of the lawman he had garroted aboard the riverboat. He tied this bundle up with the legs of his trousers, which he knotted, and then knotted again at the bottom, fitting the saddlehorn through the space between the knots. His poker winnings had been transferred from the crown of his hat to a coin pouch that resided in a saddlebag, the flap of which he checked to make sure it was securely tied down. But this time he was shivering uncontrollably, and his ordinarily nimble fingers had become clumsy.

Mal was barefoot and in his long johns and back in the saddle. "Ride your horse into the water," he told Lute. "If he doesn't like it when he loses the river bottom give him a good kick and make him swim, and when he starts, slip off to port . . . the downstream side . . . and hold on to the saddle." That said, he urged his horse into the river.

After the fact, Lute decided that the next ten minutes were the most harrowing of his life—ten minutes during which his youthful sense of invincibility abandoned him entirely. He was afraid of the water, and thought for sure something would go wrong and he would end up drowned, and since God had a sense of humor, he imagined his waterlogged corpse would be carried all the way down the Brazos until the river spit him out into the sea, where sharks would feast upon his remains. His horse balked momentarily when it reached deep water, lunging and snorting, and no sooner had Lute slid off the saddle than he came perilously close to losing his grip. Now it was up to the horse. His life depended on the blaze-faced sorrel's strength, stamina, and survival instinct.

Mal's horse made for the nearest land—the island—and Lute's followed. After what seemed like an eternity of fear combined with a cold so severe that he was shivering uncontrollably even while every muscle, tendon, and ligament in his body seemed to be tied up in knots, the horse dragged him onto dry land. He had gripped the saddlehorn so tightly it took him a few tries to make his fingers work so that he could let go and collapse in the snowy muck. Mal got him under the arms and stood him up, helping him stay upright until he could be sure his legs would support him. Teeth chattering violently, Mal told him to shed the long johns, which clung to Lute's lanky body like a cold wet second skin, before putting on the rest of his clothes.

Their horses stood nearby. They were shaking, too. The island was small, hardly more than a sandbar overgrown with brush and a few young trees. With the water rushing on all sides the horses were not inclined to wander far. Peeling off the long johns, Lute got his clothes bundle off the saddle and on the ground. His fingers still didn't want to work properly but he finally clawed the bundle open and thanked God that his shirt and trousers, wrapped tightly in the greatcoat he had confiscated, were fairly dry. The greatcoat itself was soaking wet and quite heavy as a result, but he donned it anyway, since the north wind was blowing steadily. It felt like the marrow in his bones was turning to ice. He retrieved his weapons from his boots and shoved them in his pocket, then had to struggle mightily to get his boots on. Taking up his horse's reins, he led the animal to the center of the island before huddling miserably in the lee of both the horse and the trees that grew in a clump there.

Once dressed, Mal took a closer look at the jumble of timber debris that had collected in spots and at varying heights between the island and the western bank of the river. He returned to Lute and said, "I think we can lead our horses across," clenching his teeth to keep them from chattering.

"We better," moaned Lute, hugging himself tightly. "I end up in the river again it will be the death of me for certain."

Mal took a long look around, grimacing as the raw winter wind seemed to cut right through his damp clothes and freeze his flesh. He was willing to concede that crossing the river in this way had been ill advised, because if they didn't find shelter they would be in a bad way come nightfall. A deep thicket where they might find enough dry wood to provide kindling for a fire, and dense enough to hide the glow of said fire—that would do, since finding an empty place with a roof on it was unlikely.

He coaxed Lute to his feet and urged his brother to keep moving, to keep the blood circulating in his limbs. He then turned to his horse, took up the reins, and ventured out onto a natural bridge formed by the trunk of a large oak that had not too long ago been swept downriver and become lodged between island and riverbank. The upper branches had become entangled with the brush on the island, while its roots were anchored in the muddy western bank of the Brazos, so that the portion of the trunk that traversed the swift narrow channel was for the most part clear of limbs. Ten feet below him the water rushed and tumbled violently over other, submerged debris.

Lute waited until Mal had successfully crossed the

natural bridge and then, with a tight grip on the sorrel's reins, followed in his brother's wake. The snow and ice on the top of the tree trunk had been broken up by Mal's booted feet and the iron-shod hooves of his brother's horse, and when he didn't lose his footing after the first half-dozen tentative steps Lute began to relax and think he might actually make it safely across. He was glancing at the torrent of water below when his left foot found a patch of ice and shot out to the side. With a strangled shout, he tottered precariously for a heart-stopping instant, a flailing arm catching the wide brim of his hat and knocking it off his head. He tried to steady himself by climbing the reins, but that pulled the horse's head down sharply and then the sorrel lost its footing and went into the water on its back. Lute clung to the reins almost too long, as though he thought he could keep a thousand pounds of horse from being swept away. But he let the leathers slip away and, still teetering on the trunk, arms windmilling, watched in dismay as the wild-eyed horse whinnied and struggled and careened violently from one tangle of debris to another before being carried out of sight beyond the southern tip of the island.

"Get down on your hands and knees and crawl!" shouted Mal, then muttered a curse as he looked downriver, hoping to catch sight of the sorrel. He was already in the saddle by the time Lute had crawled across, impatiently extending a hand. "Come on, come on! Get up behind me!" Lute wasn't even settled astride the cantle of Mal's saddle before they were off at a canter. They traveled about half a mile downriver before Mal, muttering more epithets, gave up. There was no sign of the sorrel in the water or on the eastern bank. It had either been swept away by the quick currents or managed to clamber up on the west side and elude them.

"Wasn't my fault," muttered Lute. He could tell his brother, sitting there stiff and silent in the saddle, was angry. "Just lost my balance, is all. We'll find another horse." He sighed. "But now we're broke. Every bit of what I won on the riverboat was in the saddlebag."

Mal shrugged. "Since when did you ever *pay* for something instead of just take it?"

The day was drawing to a close, night shadows gathering under the trees, when Mal found a deadfall in a deep thicket a few miles from the river. As he had hoped, he salvaged some wood dry enough to start a fire while feeling fairly certain that the thicket was so dense no one would see the firelight from a distance. Once the campfire was going, Lute got on his knees and curled his trembling body right over the flames. Mal erected makeshift tripods using limbs from the tangle of deadwood caused by a tree that had fallen and crushed other foliage. On these tripods he hung his brother's greatcoat and the blanket roll that had been tied behind the saddle on the stolen horse. He kept feeding the fire for a couple of hours, sitting there with his eyes peering into the pitch-black night, his hand resting on the comforting shape of the pistol in the pocket of his peacoat. Finally thawed out, Lute fell asleep sitting up, and Mal laid him on his side and covered him with the blanket once it was reasonably dry.

Mal sat there throughout the night, contemplating the future and dwelling on the past. All in all it had not been a very good day. The previous night, in the cabin aboard the *Mustang*, he had slept quite well, excited by the prospect of arriving at Port Sullivan, acquiring a couple of mounts by fair means or foul, and then heading westward, a stranger to all who came upon him and his brother. Possibly because he was on the water—albeit a river rather than the ocean—he had dreamed of being on a clipper ship plying the seven seas, a dream that left a smile on his lips when he woke. His good mood had been short-lived, since a few hours later he discovered that wanted posters originating in England had caught up with them. Worse still, they had snuffed out the lives of two lawmen. The situation had become considerably more perilous in a very short period of time.

His goal was to get as far west of the Brazos as possible without being seen. But they wouldn't get far with just one mount. Acquiring another, regardless of the means they employed, increased the likelihood of being spotted and then identified. Although he had been in plenty of tight spots before, thanks to the life he led and to his careless brother's proclivity for violence, Mal still tried to maintain some semblance of order and routine in life. His hope had been that they could travel upriver without incident, disembark at Port Sullivan, and strike out west. Out where there was so much unpopulated territory they could live by their own rules and still avoid dying young, as most wanted men did, if they were smart. But so many things could go wrong—and might have already. He thought about the horse swept downriver. If it was found west of the Brazos, and somehow traced back to the dead lawman . . . Mal shook his head.

Even if they made it to the wild country, they would not be leading a life of ease, but then Mal wasn't deterred by the prospect of hardship. He and his brother had grown up in one of Whitehall's workhouses and there were few greater hardships than that fate. The Poor Law provided London's underclass with food, clothing, and shelter. In return, the destitute were put to work. In theory this seemed a compassionate response to the plight of the poor in England. In reality, it punished them. They were worked hard, for long hours, and in return got to live in a small room in a rat-infested hovel and were given rations that barely kept them alive. A cup of gruel and a piece of bread with a dab of butter morning and evening was the usual food allowance. There might be a little meat once or twice a week. A cup of tea was a rare treat. Their mother had been abandoned by their seafaring father before Mal was old enough to remember him, and life in the workhouse had taken their mother fifteen years later. Languishing on her deathbed, she had made Mal promise to always watch out for his brother. Mal had been eighteen years old at the time, his brother two years younger.

But for that promise, Mal was certain he would have followed in his father's footsteps and gone to sea. Instead, he and Lute turned to a life of crime, which seemed a better choice than spending their years in a workhouse. They began with petty theft but quickly graduated to more serious crimes—mugging and armed robbery. A phenomenon that came to be called slumming worked in their favor. Middle-and upper-class people began to frequent the East End. Some of them were artists, writers, missionaries, and social workers. Others were just tourists, curious to see how the poor lived. Mal concluded that this made those who were better off feel superior to the denizens of Whitehall, Spitalfield, and Bethnal Green. It became commonplace for gentlemen and their ladies to don coarse clothes and venture into these districts. Many gentlemen, married and single, also went there seeking sexual pleasure, as the East End was full of young women who sold their bodies for money enough to buy food, drink, and opium.

These gentlemen, and sometimes their ladies, became the targets of the Litchfield brothers. Mal devised a number of schemes to coerce them into parting with their coin. One such caper involved an association with a prostitute—a ladybird, as women of ill repute were called in the East End. There were thousands of such women, many of them concentrated on Flower and Dean Streets, either in brothels or working out of rented rooms. A pretty French girl named Sylvie became a willing accomplice in the extortion of dozens of her well-to-do customers, with Mal and Lute taking care of the blackmailing details. This turned out to be profitable for all three of them. But then Lute's prodigious sexual appetites ruined everything. Disregarding Mal's orders to leave her alone, Lute turned his attentions to Sylvie, who was quite a toffer, but who soon balked and ended her partnership in crime with the Litchfields. A few days later she was found knifed to death in an alley. Lute swore to Mal on their mother's grave that he had not done the dirty deed. Mal didn't believe him. He had been more than a little fond of Sylvie himself, but had never touched her. Her murder turned out to be a harbinger of things to come.

Lute's skill as a cardsharp inspired Mal's next scheme. Cheating at cards was problematic when trick-taking games like whist and hearts were in vogue. But the growing popularity of poker—first stud, then draw—changed that. It wasn't that Lute had to cheat, since he was one of the most astute card players Mal knew. But when cheating was called for, few excelled at it like Lute Litchfield. Best of all, this new enterprise took them out of the slums and into better society. They had become known to the constabulary that tried to keep the law in the East End, which made plying their trade there ever more difficult, since the bobbies never hesitated to roust them or even throw them in jail for "cooling off." Putting Whitechapel behind them, the brothers became accomplished at passing themselves off as gentlemen of means. Mal took the role of shill, and for over a year they did quite well for themselves.

Then they sat down to a game of stud poker with one Sir Charles Badham, a prominent member of the Tory Party and illustrious member of Parliament. Badham fancied himself a good card player while in truth he was atrociously bad. But the brothers let him win—just not quite as often as he lost. They played regularly and in the process Lute made the acquaintance of Sir Charles's beautiful raven-haired daughter, Barbara, nicknamed Babs. Convinced that Babs was as innocent and naive as she was pretty, Lute relished seducing her. This went so well that he came up with the notion of marrying the girl, thereby gaining access to the incalculable wealth of her father.

Being an astute judge of character, Mal was skeptical. He saw Babs in an entirely different light than did his brother. He suspected that she was playing Lute every bit as skillfully as his brother was trying to play her. Why was easy to guess. Though hardly more than twenty years old, Lute Litchfield had established a reputation for sexual prowess. Mal was convinced that Babs was playing the innocent to keep Lute interested. Their trysts occurred in an abandoned cottage tucked discreetly away in a forest near the Badham estate. This went on for a couple of months and Mal saw no harm in it. That changed when Lute informed his brother of his plan to marry Babs. He was going to propose. Then he and Mal would be set for life. Mal failed to talk him out of it, since Lute was convinced that Babs was madly in love with him, and Sir Charles liked him immensely.

Mal turned out to be right about Babs, as Lute discovered when he proposed marriage. Babs spurned him, having known instinctively that he was not highborn despite his acting skills. She had been meeting him for one thing and one thing only, and love had nothing to do with it. Lute was stunned. She haughtily informed him that while he was good for a roll in the hay he would not share her marriage bed. No, that honor would be reserved to a young man of means, no doubt the scion of a well-to-do and important family. Lute was angry but he let Babs go that time, then talked her into meeting at the cottage just once more, telling her that he and Mal were leaving Britain forever. Mal could only assume that she couldn't resist the idea of Lute dabbing her once more, but carnal desire proved to be the end of her. Barbara Badham's body was found the next day, her father having mobilized a small army of constables and citizens to scour the countryside. For those accustomed to reading between the lines when it came to Victorian news accounts of violent crimes, it was clear she had engaged in sexual intercourse before being brutally murdered, stabbed multiple times in the heart.

This time Lute did not proclaim his innocence. He quite calmly informed Mal that if he couldn't have Babs, no one would. It was at that moment that Mal realized his kid brother was insane. Lute had always had a mercurial temper and been prone to violence, but now it was clear that the life of any woman Lute took a fancy to was at risk. Other men might have walked away, brother or not. But Lute was the only family Mal had left. And there was that solemn promise he had sworn to his mother on her deathbed. He suspected that Mother had long feared Lute would come to a bad end and that only Mal could save him. Mal had been trying to do so ever since.

Lord Badham was a man of tremendous wealth and influence, so remaining in England was not even an option for the Litchfield brothers. Mal managed to get them on a ship even though, as luck would have it, Babs had confided to one of the chambermaids in the Badham house all about her trysts with Lute Litchfield. The two young women had enjoyed sharing details of their sexual adventures, whispering and giggling with heads together, eyes bright and cheeks flushed, which the distraught chambermaid divulged following her friend's horrific death. That Lord Badham's reach extended to the Americas didn't surprise Mal—the wanted posters he carried in a pocket were proof. The only place he could think of where they might be able to disappear was the wild frontier. The sooner they put the Brazos behind them, and the fewer the people who saw them, the better.

Day Four

Day Four

CHAPTER TEN

Mal dozed off shortly before daybreak. When he woke it was impossible to tell the time of day with any degree of certainty. Last night's fire was dead, coated with a layer of snow, but it was beyond him to calculate how much time had to pass before the embers of a fire like the one he had built were cooled enough to allow snow to collect on them. None of that mattered once he realized Lute was nowhere to be seen. At first he thought his brother might be in the brush relieving himself, but privacy wasn't normally a factor between brothers when it came to pissing and shitting. The horse was present and it whickered softly when it saw Mal get up, so wherever Lute had gotten off to it had been afoot.

"Lute?" He spoke loudly but didn't shout. The air was quite still. The snow had stopped falling. There was no wind. The only sounds he heard were made by him and the horse. When no reply came he tugged furiously at his bushy auburn side whiskers, rasped an exasperated "Mary Mother of God," and told the horse, as he shook a fist, "I swear I'm going to give him a bunch of fives when I see him." The horse whickered in response.

He noticed then that the greatcoat was gone. Circling

the camp, he found boot prints in the snow. Struggling through the thicket, he picked up the sign again once he broke out into the open. He caught a whiff of wood smoke then, and spotted a dark-gray plume rising above the trees on the other side of a large meadow. It seemed to him that his brother's boot prints were aimed directly at it.

"Ah, Lute," he muttered. "New trouble for a new day, no doubt."

He went back to the camp to collect the blanket and horse. He was in a hurry and didn't waste time rolling the blanket and securing it to the saddle, but tossed it across the horse's withers and then led the animal out of the thicket on foot, climbing into the saddle once they had emerged into the open.

He kept the horse to a walk and his hand in the pocket of his coat, the one that contained the revolver, as the foot-prints in the snow led him across the meadow. Beyond was a narrow strip of timber, and once through that he emerged into another, larger meadow and saw the cabin. Mal checked his horse, curbed his impatience, and sur-veyed the scene. The plume of smoke he had spotted earlier rose from the cabin's stone chimney. Nearby was a small barn, and between this and the cabin, a corral. One of the barn doors was open, presumably to allow the animals housed within to venture out into the corral, and there were two mules visible within the confines of the latter. On the other side of the cabin was what Mal took to be an outhouse and another small structure made of stone, which he surmised might be either a springhouse or an icehouse. No one was in view but he noticed that the door of the cabin was ajar, which seemed odd considering the bitter cold of the morning. Even more curious was the chestnut horse standing some distance from the buildings, a lead rope dangling from its bridle. It pawed at the new snow, seeking something edible beneath.

It was quiet. Almost too quiet, and Mal's concern for his brother quickly trumped his innate caution. Pulling the revolver from his coat pocket, he thumbed back the hammer and held it on his thigh as he kicked his mount into motion and rode up past the loose horse and on to the corral, keeping his eyes on the cabin door and the single shuttered window. Dismounting, he tied his horse to one of the corral posts. Approaching the door warily, he used his foot to push it open wider. Rusty hinges creaked and then the door thumped against something and began to swing closed. Mal tried pushing it open but an obstacle of some sort prevented it from opening enough for him to pass through, so he put his shoulder against the door and pushed harder, budging the obstacle just enough to make an aperture for him to slip through.

His heart lurched when he saw the dead man on the floor, even though it only took him a split second to realize it wasn't his brother. It was the corpse that had blocked the cabin door. To his left a curtain moved—he caught the movement out of an eye corner and whirled, bringing the Gasser around at shoulder level. Lute was standing there, shirtless and bootless, an arm hooked around the throat of a woman and aiming the gun taken from the lawman he had killed aboard the *Mustang* at Mal. There were specks of dried blood on one side of his face and neck. The woman clutched a tattered old quilt to cover herself, as though modesty was still a priority in a situation where two men were aiming pistols at each other.

The brothers lowered those pistols simultaneously. Mal started breathing again as he glanced at the man lying facedown in a pool of blood, then at the frightened woman, and finally at Lute and muttered, "What the bloody hell have you done this time?"

The centerpiece of the cabin was a rough-hewn table with a bench on one side, and Lute made the woman sit on it. She was staring at the dead man, silent tears running down her cheeks. Lute seemed not to notice the tears. He cupped her chin and turned her face toward Mal. "Isn't she a pretty one, Mal? So sweet and wholesome."

Mal thought she was rather plain. It was sometimes hard to gauge the age of woman who had lived a hard life, but he guessed she was closing in on thirty. Her skin was very white, her long tangled hair a nutmeg brown, and her eyes—her most striking feature—an emerald green. Perhaps, he thought, she might be pretty under better circumstances, but it seemed unlikely she would ever luck into those.

"Get dressed, Lute," snapped Mal. His tone was brusque, and Lute could see the cold rage in his brother's expression. He looked rather petulant as he turned and swept aside the curtain and Mal glimpsed a space barely large enough for the bed it contained. Once he had his shirt on he came back to sit on the bench beside the woman and pull on his boots. She had wrapped the worn quilt around her like a makeshift sarong. Mal took a wary look outside then shut the door and leaned against it to glare at Lute.

"I guess I didn't make myself clear. We're trying to get out of this part of the country without anyone else seeing us."

Lute could tell his brother was agitated, and he adopted a supplicant's tone. "I couldn't sleep much. It was too cold. At daybreak I smelled wood smoke. When I spotted this place I saw the horse in the corral. I decided we needed it worse than he did." He glanced at the dead man sprawled on the blood-splattered puncheon floor. "I was going to just slip away with it but one of the donkeys started braying as I began to lead the horse away. Then I heard noise from inside the cabin. It's so quiet out here compared with London, you know? You can hear the smallest of sounds. Anyway, I couldn't run for it, Mal. I knew if he had a rifle and was any kind of marksman he would have me dead to rights before I reached the bushes. So I rushed the door and got there right when he started out. He had a pistol in his hand, so I stabbed him in the neck a few times " The woman sitting beside him covered her face with her hands and sobbed quietly. Lute patted her on the shoulder. "Then this lovely girl came out from behind the curtain and, well . . ." He glanced apologetically at his brother and shrugged. ". . . you know me, Mal. I felt like I should comfort her."

Mal was silent for a moment, mulling things over and considering options. For one, Lute had mentioned his name not once but twice, so if they left the woman behind, the death of the man on the floor would certainly be laid at their door. Even if they silenced the woman permanently, once the bodies were discovered assumptions would eventually be made that the men who were responsible for the killing of two lawmen on the Brazos were in all likelihood the ones who had killed two more people a half day's ride away. His goal of putting the Brazos far behind them without leaving any sign as to the direction they were taking had just been made more difficult, if not impossible, thanks to Lute.

"Stay put," he told Lute curtly. He started to go out the door then turned back and added, "Don't let her out of here." He left the cabin, shutting the door behind him and walking out to retrieve the chestnut, who stood right where he had first spotted it. He counted it a much-needed stroke of luck that he was able to walk right up to the horse without it bolting. It looked to be a nag, rather old and swaybacked, so he assumed it was so accustomed to humans that running away from one was too great an effort.

Taking the lead rope, Mal walked it back to the corral, where he tied the rope to the top pole and went into the barn, emerging a moment later with a worn-out old hull. He had never put a saddle on a horse before, but he had seen horses put into the traces of various conveyances so he was able to figure it out. Back inside the cabin he found the woman hadn't moved. She sat there staring at the dead man as though under some sort of spell, a stunned expression on her tear-streaked face. Lute was transferring cans of food from a wooden crate nailed to a wall to a burlap sack. Mal went to the fire to stand with his back to it, looking at the woman so intently that something primal, perhaps nape hairs rising, made her glance apprehensively at him.

"You going to kill me too?" she whispered.

Lute stopped looting and looked at his brother in time to see Mal shake his head. "What's your name?"

"Alise. Alise Graham."

"Is that your husband?"

Alise nodded. "He wasn't much of nothing, But he was mine." She covered her mouth with a hand as she strove to hold back another rush of tears.

"How far to the nearest village?"

"Village?" She blinked, perplexed, like she didn't know the word. "Oh . . . I guess the nearest *town* would be Cameron, about a half day's ride west."

Mal nodded and made up his mind. "Get dressed. You're coming with us."

"Coming with you?" she whispered. "Where?"

"Do what I say."

She rose and walked unsteadily toward the sleeping area. When she got there she started to close the curtain but Mal told her not to. Turning her back, she let the quilt drop around her ankles and rushed to put on a dress of faded brown gingham. Mal looked at Lute, who stared at Alise for a moment before joining his brother by the fireplace.

"Why are we bringing her along, Mal?" he whispered.

"Because I'm not a cold-blooded killer." The tone of his voice made clear he thought that only one of them wasn't.

Lute could tell his brother was very angry. Mal didn't like it at all when his plans went awry. "I didn't want to kill him," he muttered, nodding at the dead man. "But it might have been me lying on that floor all shot to hell instead of him."

Mal leaned forward and rasped, "Would you like to put a bullet in her bloomin' brainpan, then? Is that what you want, now that you've had your fun?"

Lute frowned but didn't say anything. His brother rarely lost his temper, but when he did it was a frightening thing to behold. He had once seen Mal beat a man to a bloody pulp in a quarrel over a prizefight wager at a pub on Little Paternoster Row, one of Whitechapel's seedier streets. This had led one of the local slum landlords to recruit Mal for some organized fights, a career that proved short-lived. It seemed Mal Litchfield was not a pugilist so much as a brawler, and wasn't devastating with his fists unless he was madder than hornets. Like he was right now.

"She comes with us," said Mal, taking his temper in hand. "It's possible they might think she killed him and then ran away. Depends on how much time passes before that body is discovered, and whether the winter will be obliging and cover our tracks before that happens."

Lute shrugged. "Well, I suppose there is something to be said for having her along. You go on about how there aren't many people out there on the frontier, so I suspect women will be hard to come by. Might as well bring our own." A slow smile curled his lips. "And while she may not be a raving beauty, she'll look better and better as time goes on, right?"

Mal noticed that Alise was emerging from the sleeping area and knew she had overheard. She stood there forlornly, barefoot in her worn dress, and he didn't even ask if she had shoes or boots. He instructed Lute to get the boots off the dead man and onto her, and to collect as many supplies as he could carry in one sack. He noticed that the pistol still clenched in the corpse's beefy hand was an old black-powder pistol, what he knew as a dragoon revolver. He decided it wasn't worth taking. But he pried it out of the dead man's grasp anyway, and took it outside and threw it as far as he could. It was impossible to say what Alise Graham would do if she suddenly decided she didn't want to be abducted, with the prospect of being raped repeatedly in the bargain.

He sighed. They had killed three men in three days, and the third day was far from over. "Hurry up!" he called out, and climbed into the sorrel's saddle, casting an anxious look around. He was in a hurry to go, because the farther west they got the longer they would live, and Mal Litchfield wanted to live a very long time, since he knew where he was going when he died. Lines from "Holy Willie's Prayer" came to mind—*Lord in Thy day o' vengeance try them . . . And pass not in Thy Mercy by them . . . But for Thy people's sake destroy them.*

CHAPTER ELEVEN

"Moreover, brethren, I declare unto you the gospel which I preached unto you, which also you have received, and wherein you stand; By which also ye are saved, if you keep in memory what I preached unto you, unless you have believed in vain. For I delivered unto you first of all that which I also received, how that Christ died for our sins according to the scriptures; And that he was buried, and that he rose again the third day according to the scriptures . . ."

Bill Sayles wasn't listening to the Cameron preacher who stood at the head of Joshua Eddings's grave while reading solemnly from the Bible, and it didn't seem to him that many of the other people present were paying much attention either. About twenty were congregated in the town cemetery under the skeletons of old oaks stripped bare of their leaves. Some of them were staring at Purdy Eddings, who stood arm in arm with Temple Hanley, and Sayles was glad the lawyer had persisted in hooking the woman's arm under his because she looked none too steady on her feet.

Sayles had seen plenty of grieving women in his time on the Texas frontier, women who had lost loved ones to sickness or violent death at the hands of Indians or bandits. Some were made of stern stuff, had been forged in the crucible of frontier life—a life of privation and danger. It bred a stubborn resolve seasoned with fatalism that left them as prepared as a person could possibly be for the loss of someone dear to them. But others were destroyed by such tragedy.

He knew one such woman quite well. Ellen Carnaby had been the pretty young wife of an acquaintance and fellow Ranger who, along with Sayles and about eighty more Rangers, had followed Captain Rip Ford on an expedition into the heart of Comancheria to pay the Indians back for incessant raids that had left the frontier a bloody shamble. Accompanied by nearly a hundred Tonkawa Indians, mortal foes of the Comanche for generations, they struck the village of the legendary Comanche leader Iron Jacket, who wore a Spanish coat of mail and was thought to be invincible. Iron Jacket had certainly thought so; he rode out to meet the oncoming attackers alone, taunting them. A Tonkawa marksman took the chief down with an old black-powder buffalo gun. Sayles figured that maybe in the past the chain mail might have deflected a bullet or two fired from an ordinary rifle, which could have lulled Iron Jacket and his warriors into believing he was invincible. But no suit of armor was going to save the Comanche chief from a buffalo gun.

Fierce fighting raged in and around the village in what came to be known as the Battle of Little Robe Creek. As was the case in the Comanche wars, no mercy was asked for or received by either side. The Comanches routinely slaughtered men, women, and children along the frontier, occasionally taking women and children as slaves. Ford's orders, written by Governor Hardin Runnells, instructed him to inflict the most severe and summary punishment on the Comanches, and this the Rangers and their Indian allies were more than happy to do. Such was the way of war on the frontier. It wasn't enough to kill the men who did the fighting. One had to kill the woman who could produce another fighter, and kill the children who would grow up to be a fighter or a producer of fighters. There weren't many in the ranks who had not lost a loved one to the Comanche scourge. Most of Iron Jacket's people were killed that day, with a mere handful managing to escape. The Tonkawas, who were cannibals, ate some of the dead and enslaved a number of Comanche women.

Reinforcements from a village farther along the Canadian River arrived, led by a chief named Peta Nocona, whose wife was a captured white girl named Cynthia Ann Parker. The Comanche kept their distance, hurling challenges at the Rangers and their Tonkawa allies to fight in one-on-one duels. Some of the Tonkawas accepted and usually paid the ultimate price for doing so. Ford finally put a stop to that and charged the Comanches in force, but the elusive Nocona kept falling back and a running fight commenced that took up most of the day, continuing for several miles. Eventually Nocona's braves slipped away, but not before several Rangers lost their lives. One of them was Jubal Carnaby, and the unpleasant task of carrying word back to his young widow fell to Sayles. Carnaby's body had been carried away from the site of the battle and buried in a shallow grave without marker of any kind, so that it would not be discovered and the body defiled by the Comanche scouts who were sure to shadow Ford's expedition.

The news of her beloved husband's death sucked the life right out of Ellen Carnaby. For a short while she lingered at her place on the outskirts of San Saba. Sayles and a few other Rangers dropped by to check on her whenever they were able. Then she disappeared, leaving all her belongings behind. No one knew for certain if she was the victim of foul play or had just wandered off to die. For years there were rumors that a crazy woman—some were convinced it was a ghost—roamed the woods near San Saba. Some people swore they heard her wailing in the distance, calling to someone, but no one was ever close enough to tell who or what she was saying. Sayles had decided if it wasn't a ghost he could track the woman down. In the end he decided against trying, knowing that if the woman turned out to be Jubal Carnaby's widow there was really nothing he could do for her.

Looking at Purdy Eddings as they laid her only son to rest that morning, Sayles didn't think there was much anyone could do for her either.

"Now if Christ be preached that he rose from the dead, how say some among you that there is no resurrection of the dead? But if there be no resurrection of the dead, then is Christ not risen and if Christ be not risen, then is our preaching vain, and your faith is also vain. Yea, and we are found false witnesses of God; because we have testified of God that he raised up Christ: whom he raised not up, if so be that the dead rise not . . ."

Others were staring at Jake Eddings, who stood next to Sayles with his hands shackled behind him, on the other side of the grave from Purdy and Hanley. The lawyer had argued that binding Jake Eddings's hands behind his back wasn't necessary, but Sayles disagreed. "I've seen grief make men do crazy things," he said. It was something he knew from personal experience, but he hadn't elaborated and Hanley hadn't pressed the issue. He already knew Sayles well enough to know that the Ranger wasn't going to enter into a debate once his mind was made up.

The prisoner wore a suit of plain brown wool, courtesy of the lawyer. He had washed and brushed his hair and shaved the stubble from his cheeks, courtesy of Bill Sayles. Tom Rath hadn't approved of what he described as mollycoddling a prisoner, and assumed that the hair washing and the shaving had been Hanley's doing and the Ranger was just seeing it done. In fact, it was a decision made by Sayles before Hanley even had an opportunity to bring it up.

Eddings didn't seem aware of the attention he was getting. He had stared at Purdy when he arrived at the cemetery on the outskirts of town. Sayles made sure they stood on the opposite side of the grave, something Hanley had suggested and which the Ranger had agreed to. When the preacher began to speak, Eddings seemed to forget about his wife and from that point on stood there with a blank expression on his face, his eyes riveted to the pine box that had already been lowered into the grave by the laborers the local undertaker had paid, with Hanley paying the undertaker's bill. Sayles tried not to think about the body in the coffin, or listen to the preacher recite the Gospel, or look at Purdy's grief-stricken face. He tried to distract himself by consulting his timepiece and looking at the sky, wondering if it was going to snow again, and calculating how many miles he could carve off the long road back to the prison at Huntsville before sundown.

He was anxious to get this job done. It was turning out to be a good deal more unpleasant than he had anticipated. Not on account of anything that had happened. It was the constant threat of old wounds being opened. Seven days to Christmas, and he had to hurry if he wanted to get home to Mrs. Doubrett's boarding house in time, sipping brandy while sitting in one of her comfortable, upholstered chairs, warmed by a crackling fire in the parlor's hearth and by the landlady's relentless good cheer. He would sop a brandy, since Mrs. Doubrett lifted her ban on strong liquors for Thanksgiving and Christmas. He tried not to think about Jake Eddings spending that same day in a prison cell, or Purdy Eddings sitting alone in a dark and empty house.

He had traveled with Temple Hanley to fetch Purdy and the body of her son the day before. They had talked on the way there, though were silent on the way back to Cameron, since Purdy accompanied them. He had watched the lawyer with the distraught young woman. Hanley was gentle, compassionate, and at the end of the day Sayles found that he had a large measure of respect for the man. Hanley had handled everything, had paid the coffin maker, the gravediggers, and the undertaker. He had paid for the simple headstone, already in place. He had provided for the suit Eddings wore, as well as a new black-and-gray woolen scarf and a pair of gloves for Purdy. He had carried food for Purdy to the Eddings place. At first Sayles had wondered if the lawyer did all this because he had failed to do the impossible, to successfully defend Eddings at his trial. And while guilt might have been a factor, to think it was the lawyer's only motivation did an injustice to the man. Temple Hanley was just a genuinely good and decent fellow.

"Jake should have been convicted of robbery but not murder," Hanley had told him during the ride to the Eddings farm. "He and his accomplice were starting to leave the scene of the crime when the stage driver made his play. If anything, he was shot in self-defense. It certainly wasn't a cold-blooded killing. If he'd had better aim he would have shot Jake in the back." All that Sayles had offered in response was that it seemed to him that the driver had just been doing his job, which was to prevent anyone from making off with something that belonged to another. Realizing that he wasn't going to lure Bill Sayles into a discussion on the logic and temperance of the law, Hanley had sighed and simply added, "Perhaps one day this land will be more civilized, and the law will be, as well."

Sayles had pondered Hanley's last comment for a spell, arriving at the conclusion that he had no interest in living in a world so civilized. As far as he was concerned, if a man rode with an outlaw he was himself an outlaw, and if one committed a crime the other was equally guilty. Once a man took that path he surrendered any right to fair play at the hands of others. The law was not about fairness, but rather about justice, justice for the victim of the crime or for society as a whole, but not for the one who committed the crime. In Hanley's perfect world the motivation of a criminal would also be taken into account. True, a person might make a mistake or be a victim of circumstance. From what Sayles could discern, that had been the basis of Hanley's defense of Jake Eddings. In the Ranger's view, only one person could know with complete conviction why a crime had been committed, and that was the person who committed it. The law had to focus solely on the facts because the facts didn't lie. That made for justice swift and sure. But Sayles knew better than to argue with a lawyer because it was as much a waste of time as would be arguing with a woman or a mule.

"Awake to righteousness, and sin not; for some have not the knowledge of God: I speak this to your shame. But some man will say, How are the dead raised up? And with what body do they come? Thou fool, that which thou sowest is not quickened, except it die . . ."

Sayles scanned the faces of the men and women who had come not as friends and neighbors in support of the couple who had lost a son, but rather as spectators to gawk at the homegrown outlaw and the Texas Ranger who had him in custody, or to whisper behind their hands about the young mother who, according to rumors, had sought comfort in the arms of a man other than her husband. Hanley had warned him on both counts—about the rumors regarding Purdy and the widower named Norris, and about the newspaperman named Placer and the article he had written that had gotten the whole community in a buzz about the return of Jake Eddings. While his creased and leathery face was a stoic mask, as usual, Sayles met every set of eyes that came his way, and he stared at each and every one of them until they looked away. He felt sorry for Jake Eddings. At least Eddings was so consumed with grief that he didn't seem aware that people were looking at him.

Though he wasn't paying attention to the preacher, Sayles caught a line here and a word there and knew the end of First Corinthians 15 was drawing near. He checked his keywinder again. He had learned to read with the Bible, which was just about the only book one was likely to find on the frontier. It wasn't that he wanted to learn what the Bible had to say, but on occasion he had been embarrassed by his lack of schooling, his inability to read or even write his name. He had plenty of time to school himself, sitting under the stars in countless lonely night camps, miles from anywhere that had a name. He had taught himself by reading out loud, phonetically, but the first time through he wasn't able to comprehend much, since so many of the words remained stubbornly incomprehensible to him. With subsequent readings, though, he began to match what he heard people say to the words he read out loud, and eventually he not only could read and write but knew the Bible backward and forward.

Standing there watching a boy being buried, Sayles couldn't help but think about his own mortality, and how imminent his own death had to be. He was old and didn't have many years left. Most people, especially those who lived on the frontier, didn't survive as long as he had. Long ago he had made up his mind that he didn't want to be buried like this. No pine box planted six feet into the cold and quiet earth of some crowded bone orchard. No preacher reading scripture. It wasn't like he had anyone who would weep over his passing. Mrs. Doubrett might show up for his burying, but he doubted she would shed a tear. Behind all her compassion and concern she was made of stern stuff. She would be sorry to see him gone, and not just because he had been a boarder who paid her regularly, but she wouldn't be reduced to weeping and the gnashing of teeth.

His Captain would make an appearance, and maybe say a few words about how fine a Ranger he had been, and how he had served the state of Texas with distinction, but only if there were other people there to hear him speechify. Sayles respected the man's rank but The Captain was a new and different breed of Ranger, one dedicated as much to politics as he was to duty. He was certainly no John Coffee Hays or Bigfoot Wallace or Rip Ford, all men who didn't hesitate to do what was called for, come hell or high water, and damn the consequences. Sayles got the impression that his superior considered him a man whose usefulness had waned now that the frontier was safe from rampaging Indians.

Sayles had never been a very sociable man. He tended to keep to himself, so he could count true friends on the fingers of one hand. There was Newt Pellum, but Newt had gone north to become the marshal of some trail town when he realized the halcyon days of warring against the

Comanches were coming to a close. After having survived countless scrapes with Indians, Pellum ended up being shot in the back by a drunken cowboy after just a few weeks wearing the tin star.

Then there was Mateo Morado, a half-breed, whose father had been a Tennessean come to Texas to fight for its independence from Mexico and whose mother had been one of the camp followers accompanying Santa Anna's army, a girl who had been captured after the Mexican army was routed at San Jacinto. According to Matty, as his fellow Rangers called him, his father had forced himself on his mother, and then, out of remorse, had made her his bride. Despite such an inauspicious beginning, the couple had gotten along pretty well for the short time they were together, just long enough for Matty to be born. Then Matty's uncle rode up from Mexico, having heard of the fate that had befallen his sister. He had shot Matty's father six times and carried mother and infant off.

Matty's father didn't die but was crippled in both legs for life. It was not certain whether the uncle's intent had been to kill his victim or cripple him. Sayles was of the opinion that Mexicans were pretty poor shots for the most part, faring much better with blades than bullets. Matty's mother married again—in fact, her union with his father was not recognized, much less spoken of, but when Matty began catching hell because he clearly had gringo blood in him, he convinced his mother to tell him the truth. He rode north to Texas to find his father, and ended up staying a while, becoming one of the best trackers the Rangers ever had and one of Sayles's best friends.

One day Matty had received a letter from down Mexico way, a letter that informed him of his mother's death at the hands of her husband. Matty rode south and killed the man. Rumor had it the man had been on his knees begging for mercy when Matty shot his eyes out. Then he vanished into the Sierra Madre. Sayles figured his friend, who was as slippery as an eel and knew as much about covering tracks as finding them, might still be on the loose in the wild country of those mountains.

"In a moment, in the twinkling of an eye, at the last trump: for the trumpet shall sound, and the dead shall be raised incorruptible, and we shall be changed. For this corruptible must put on incorruption, and this mortal must put on immortality. So when this corruptible shall have put on incorruption, and this mortal shall have put on immortality, then shall be brought to pass the saying that is written, Death is swallowed up in victory. O death, where is thy sting? O grave, where is thy victory?"

The preacher closed his Bible and looked at Jake, and then at Purdy. Sometimes the bereaved wanted to say a few words or put something in the grave, but a single glance convinced the preacher that neither of the dead boy's parents was so disposed, and he nodded to the two gravediggers who stood nearby. As the first shovelful of dirt thumped against the coffin Purdy sobbed quietly and turned away, burying her face in Temple Hanley's buffalo coat. Sayles took a close look at Jake, and the expression on the prisoner's face made him wonder if it might have been more compassionate on the part of the governor to deny Hanley's request that Eddings be allowed to attend this ceremony. Meanwhile the preacher concluded the service with "In sure and certain hope of the resurrection to eternal life through our Lord Jesus Christ, we commend to Almighty God the child Joshua Eddings; and we commit his body to the ground; earth to earth; ashes to ashes, dust to dust. The Lord bless him and keep him, the Lord make his face to shine upon him and be gracious unto him and give him peace. Amen."

The onlookers began to disperse. Sayles caught Hanley's glance in his direction, and nodded. The lawyer would take Purdy home, while Sayles intended to waste no time in starting on the road back to Huntsville. Hanley's glance was a silent query, asking if it was time they went their separate ways. He had suggested letting Jake and Purdy speak but Sayles was opposed to the idea. "Won't do either one of them any good," he opined. Now he reached out to take Eddings by the arm. "It's time we got going."

Eddings looked at him. He was deathly pale, with a blank look on his face. Sayles had seen that look before, the look of a man who had been so traumatized that he had momentarily taken leave of his senses. He didn't seem to grasp the meaning of the Ranger's words and Sayles sighed and said, "Come on. Nothing more you can do here." Eddings's arm still in his grasp, he started to turn toward the horses beyond the crumbling stone wall that marked the cemetery's perimeter.

Seeing that Hanley was already leading Purdy away from the grave site, Eddings suddenly wrenched his arm free and half ran, half stumbled after them. "Wait!" he called out. "Purdy, wait!" Sayles muttered a curse under his breath and went after him, but he wasn't much of a runner anymore and the prisoner's legs were a lot longer than his horse-warped ones, so that Eddings reached his wife and the lawyer with the Ranger still a step or two behind him.

Startled, Hanley pulled Purdy closer and held out an arm as though to fend off Eddings. "For the love of God, Jake! Calm yourself!"

Eddings didn't even look at the lawyer. His eyes were riveted on his wife. "Purdy, I-I am so *sorry*. Please, *forgive* me! Please . . . *wait* for me, I . . . I love you! Please don't stop loving me!'" He was trembling with emotion, his voice strident with desperation.

Sayles latched on to Eddings's arm again, bracing for a struggle. But Eddings didn't seem to notice him any more than he noticed Hanley. He was focused completely on Purdy, who stared at him with eyes that brimmed with tears. Sayles didn't think she was going to say anything, or was even capable of speech, until Hanley tried to lead her away.

"Wait!" she gasped, directing this at Hanley. "Wait, it's all right." She looked at her husband again, and finding the right words seemed a struggle. "Jake," she whispered, and dragged a ragged breath. "Oh, Jake! The last words Joshua said to me . . ." There was a catch in her voice, and she had to compose herself. ". . . He said he was so sorry . . . that he and his father had left me alone."

Eddings made a sound like like he had just been gut-punched. He wrapped his arms around his midsection and dropped to his knees in the muddy snow. He leaned forward until his head touched the ground and made a hoarse wailing sound filled with despair. Hanley looked horrified as he bore witness to this emotional disintegration. Still gripping the prisoner's arm, Sayles felt his nape hairs rise, a primal response triggered by the sound his prisoner made. He noticed that most of the spectators were still around, and all eyes were glued to Eddings. Sayles leaned down a little more and in a fierce whisper said, "Get up! For God's sake, man, get off your knees. Stand up!" while putting all he had into trying to haul Eddings upright.

Aware that Hanley was hurrying Purdy away, making for his buggy, Sayles looked at the other people standing about—and lost his temper. "Clear out!" he rasped. "Get on home! You had no business being here in the first place." Seeing some resentment flash in one man's face he reached into his coat pocket and brandished the Schofield and snarled "Git!" That did the trick. The resentment was replaced with fear and the man hastened away, along with all the others. They scattered like sheep who realized there was a wolf in their midst. Letting go of Eddings's arm, Sayles straightened and pocketed the six-shooter. His lips pursed, he exhaled slowly then took a deep breath, smoothing down his hackles. It was rare that he lost his temper. Having seen capable men bested and sometimes killed because they lost control, he had trained himself to keep his head.

Eddings was getting on his feet. The fact that the Ranger had stood up for him penetrated the fog of intense misery that enveloped him. "Thanks," he mumbled.

"Eh." Sayles made a dismissive gesture. "Just remember. There's only one thing that can't be taken away from you, son. Your self-respect. That you have to *give* away."

"I almost did yesterday. Rath unlocked my cell door, said he was giving me a chance to die a free man. We both knew if I made a break for it I wouldn't get far. I almost did it anyway."

The Ranger's squinty eyes glittered. "That man is no-account," he murmured.

Eddings looked morosely at Hanley's buggy, which was already rolling down the road back to Cameron, taking Purdy away, and he felt sure he had seen her for the last time. When he spoke it was with the voice of a man who had lost all hope. "Rath told me that Purdy is letting our neighbor, George Norris, in her bed. I don't blame her. I mean, she can't hold on to the farm without some kind of help. I guess it makes sense, in a way. Norris is a widower. She never liked him but . . . well . . . I can't expect her to wait for me for thirteen years. Can I?"

Sayles figured Eddings wanted him to lie and tell him he could in fact expect that. "No, I reckon not."

"For better or worse. Through sickness and health. Nice words, but hard to live by sometimes." Eddings's voice was shaky. He glanced at Sayles. "Ever been married?"

Sayles turned away, making for the cemetery gate and the horses beyond, but he didn't turn fast enough. Eddings saw him wince.

"Let's get going," said Sayles gruffly.

Eddings spared his son's grave a glance. It was now completely filled in, and the gravediggers were hiking back to town. Back to a drink at the saloon, or back to their families. A wave of self-pity overwhelmed him as he turned away and followed Sayles through the gate. He was alone. He had no one left. He noticed that Sayles was unlashing the coiled rope from his saddle.

"You don't need to tie me up like you did on the way here," said Eddings, after Sayles had helped him up into the saddle on the sorrel horse, since his hands were bound behind his back. "I won't run. I give you my word."

Sayles looked him in the eye a moment, then without a word returned to the coyote dun, tied the rope back to his saddle, and climbed aboard. Taking up the lead rope attached to the sorrel's bridle, he led the way down the road east, away from Cameron.

As they drew near Cameron, which was no more than a quarter mile from the cemetery, it occurred to Temple Hanley for the first time that perhaps Purdy wouldn't want to go home now that she was truly alone. With everything else that had been on his mind with respect to the burying of Joshua and the business with Jake, he hadn't had time to consider the aftermath. He slowed the horse in the buggy's traces to give himself a little more time to think how best to phrase the question. He had put her up in a room at the hotel the previous night, and could continue to pay for that room if she so desired. His first impulse had been to offer her the spare room in his own house, and that option crossed his mind again—as did the reasons why it might not be a good idea. In addition to their lack of Christian charity when it came to helping Purdy in her time of need, the good people of Cameron would be quick to judge both Purdy and himself if she were to spend any time at all under his roof. That he paid for her room at the hotel in itself might stir up some mean-spirited gossip. Hanley shook his head and sighed. Despite all the possible pitfalls, though, he had to do what he thought was right.

"Perhaps you would like to stay in town for a little while, my dear," he murmured.

Suddenly the thought of ever seeing Cameron again made Purdy sick to her stomach. After thinking about it a little longer she realized she didn't want to be anywhere to see anyone in particular. But especially not Cameron or, more precisely, the people who lived there. She had been lost in a fog of grief and exhaustion for weeks, but she remembered that Hanley had promised to find someone to come help her, and while she hadn't really wanted anyone around she was aware, now, that he had failed. She knew he wasn't one to say such a thing just to say it, that he had no doubt made an effort to do it, and he hadn't told her why he wasn't able to find anyone but she *knew*. It must be because the word was out about her and Norris, and for that and that alone she had been ostracized.

She pasted a wan smile on her lips. "Thank you," she murmured, her throat hoarse from all the crying she had done. "But you can just take me . . ." She almost said *home*. And right then she realized the farm no longer felt like home. ". . . take me back to the farm." There wasn't a trace of enthusiasm in her voice because she didn't want to go back there either. The problem was that she had no other place to go.

Hanley gave her a sidelong glance and noticed she was crying again, quietly. He had never seen anyone so lost, and he wanted more than anything to ease her suffering but was powerless to do so. "Don't give up, Purdy," he said finally, using her given name for the first time.

They passed through Cameron in silence. There were a few people on the streets, and Hanley glowered at each and every one of them. Had anyone spoken to him they would have discovered a Temple Hanley they had never known existed. A very rare thing had happened—he had lost his temper. He was angry at his neighbors and ashamed of them at the same time. These people who considered themselves good Christians. Where was the charity? Where was the forgiveness? Where was the helping hand? He wanted to confront them as Jesus had confronted the mob that wanted to stone a woman accused of adultery in John 8:7—"Let he who is without sin among you cast the first stone."

Approaching the Eddings farm, Hanley was struck by how desolate it seemed. The fact that the day was overcast, as it had been for many days now, didn't help matters. He longed to see the sun break through the clouds. The only color in the scene was provided by the occasional pine tree nestled in the leafless oaks and sweet gums. The snow-covered fields were white and black, the farmhouse with his shuttered windows a dull, weathered gray. As he stopped the buggy in front of the house his instinct for survival had him looking around for the big yellow dog. Then he remembered that Purdy had tied Buck to a stout length of rope on the porch, afraid the dog might try to follow her to town the day before. But Buck wasn't on the rope, and the rope was half as long as he remembered it being. On closer inspection it was evident that the rope had snapped in two.

Purdy was distraught. She searched the house, the outbuildings, ran out into the fields in one direction, then another, calling out the dog's name. Hanley was no tracker but he managed to pick up what he thought might be the dog's tracks in the snow. They were headed north along the road in the direction of Cameron. When he showed Purdy this, she became frantic with worry.

"Someone might shoot him! Please, please take me back to the cemetery. Perhaps he followed us." She clutched at his arm. "I can't lose him!" she cried. "I can't lose Buck too!"

Hanley was exhausted, but he didn't hesitate to comply with her wishes. They rode back through Cameron to the cemetery and searched all around, to no avail. The snow within the low stone wall that marked the cemetery's perimeter was churned up by the twenty-odd people who had attended Joshua's funeral hours before. Once again Hanley circled outside the wall, looking for sign, but this time he failed to find any. He urged Purdy to come back to town with him. Together they would keep an eye out for Buck. There was no point in going to Tom Rath for help. Rath would shoot the dog even if he knew it wasn't a stray. Purdy's reaction to this new crisis concerned him. She was crying inconsolably. He wondered how much more she could take.

"Try to calm yourself, dear," he said. "In all likelihood your dog will find his way home. That's what dogs do, isn't it?" He made it a statement of fact rather than a question.

Purdy grabbed that thread of hope and clung to it, asking him to take her home again. On the way back to the Eddings farm Hanley found himself offering up silent prayers to God that they would find Buck waiting for them. But there was no sign of the dog and Purdy sat on the porch steps, head in hands, and sobbed. Hanley went inside the farmhouse, made some coffee, and carried two pewter cups out to sit beside her, offering her one. He was relieved that she had stopped crying, but it was short-lived relief. Her expression worried him. In his line of work he had seen utter hopelessness before. Now he saw it in Purdy Eddings and was at a loss what to do about it. What cruel twist of fate, he thought, that she would lose her dog on this day, of all days. His own helplessness frustrated him.

"I'll go back to town and look all over for him until it's too dark to see," he promised. "If I find him I know some people who will help me get a rope on him, and he won't be harmed, I assure you." He rose and looked down at her. Staring blankly across the dead fields at the line of trees that marked the course of the Little River, she gave no sign that she even heard him. He hated to leave her, but there was always the chance that Buck would come home. Hanley sighed. This was one of those moments when there were simply no good choices. He went back inside, built a fire in the fireplace, took Purdy by the arm, and led her inside, seating her in a rocking chair near the hearth and finding a blanket to drape around her shoulders. He promised to return first thing in the morning and then laid a comforting hand lightly on her shoulder. "Don't cry, Purdy. You've shed enough tears to last a lifetime. Things will get better." When she didn't respond he sighed again and left her there, leaving the door slightly ajar so that Buck could enter if he did return. Reaching the buggy he cast one last hopeful look around and then glanced skyward, shaking his head. "Sometimes I just don't understand why You let so many bad things happen to good people," he confessed, then climbed into the rig, took up the leathers, and started back to Cameron.

Day Five

CHAPTER TWELVE

Purdy sat by the fire all night long. There were a few pieces of wood left in the stack by the hearth, but she didn't bother adding any to the fire when it died down. She slept fitfully, but even so she dreamed. Dreamed of a happy and carefree childhood as a tomboy who spent much of the time on her father's riverboat. Then she would dream of sitting by her father's deathbed, and that moment when the life had gone out of his eyes and his grip loosened as they held hands. She dreamed of the day when she and Jake had been married; outside the church on the edge of Cameron because it had been such a bright spring day, sunny and warm, with a cooling breeze making the limbs of stately oaks sway with every leaf dancing, the day as exceptional as their future seemed to be. That had been the happiest moment of her life—up until the day Joshua was born. Life had been so utterly perfect after that. For a while. Even when they fell on hard times, she was profoundly content with her situation. But then there came that fateful day in the courthouse when the judge sentenced Jake to fifteen years in the state prison. She had never forgotten the devastated look on her husband's face as their eyes met in that moment when everything changed irrevocably for them both.

As night fell she began to drift in and out of a troubled sleep. She lost count of how many times she woke. Once she thought she heard a baby cry. Once she thought she heard the heavy thumping associated with a hundred pounds of dog walking across the floor planking. But most of the time she heard absolutely nothing, and the weight of the silence was crushing, compounded by the nearly total darkness in which she sat. It was like the whole world had died and there was nothing left for her to hear or see. She wasn't frightened, though. There was nothing to be afraid of, since everything that had mattered to her had been taken away. What else did she have to lose? Her life meant nothing now. Jake was being taken back to prison for thirteen more years. That seemed like more than a lifetime to Purdy. She thought she was all cried out, feeling dead inside, but that night she did weep once more, when she recalled how Jake had looked and sounded at the cemetery, begging her to forgive him and to wait for him. To see the man she loved reduced to such a state had been gut wrenching. She regretted not telling him that she had already forgiven him. But waiting for him, for thirteen years? Thirteen years of emptiness and despair? That was something else again. She didn't want to face the morrow, much less thirteen years, so how could she promise to wait?

The grayness of dawn began to leak in around the window shutters, and through the door that Hanley had left ajar when he departed. It provided just enough light for her to look around the room and ascertain that Buck had not returned, and she sighed and felt like crying again but she just didn't have the tears. Hope soared when she heard a thumping on the porch and then the squeaking of hinges as the door swung open. But it wasn't Buck. The figure of a man was silhouetted in the doorway. She was too emotionally numb to be afraid. "Mr. Hanley?" she asked softly.

"It's me, George," said Norris, as he stepped to the table that was the room's centerpiece. There was a candle there, and he lit it with a match. He looked around for Buck, and was relieved not to see him. "Where's that big yeller dog of yourn? Usually the bastard comes out to bark and growl at me."

"Gone," she said, her voice sounding hollow. "Run off."

"Really. Well now, ain't that a shame." He didn't even try to sound sincere as he turned and shut the door, then went back to the table to sit down. He was greatly relieved. The yellow dog had always been aggressive around him, and he figured the only reason he hadn't been attacked was because Purdy had never fought him when he had made advances toward her. When he demanded that Buck be put outside and the door closed she had complied. His wife had fought him, at first, but a few beatings had brought her around, had made a good woman of her. He hadn't had to beat Purdy yet, but he wouldn't hesitate if he needed to.

"You expectin' that lawyer to come a-callin' then?" He felt a stab of jealousy when he thought about Temple Hanley and it made him angry. He didn't believe any man would do all the things the lawyer had done without an ulterior motive. Considering how attractive Purdy was, there could be only one possible motive as far as Norris was concerned.

"Just to check on me. To make sure I'm all right."

"Well, he don't need to worry about that any longer. I'll take care of you from here on."

Purdy glanced at him apprehensively but said nothing.

George Norris was a tall, stocky man, a strong man honed by a lifetime of farming, with black curly hair and small, piercing blue eyes in a weathered, square-jawed face. From the first day she had met him she hadn't liked him. She had taken a homemade pie to the Norris farm to introduce herself shortly after marrying Jake and moving in, and she had been shocked by the way Norris treated his wife, like she was little more than a slave. She had liked him even less a year later, when his wife died in childbirth and Norris blamed her for the death of their baby, who died with its mother. Hugging herself tightly, she stared at the dead fire in the hearth, anxiety creeping through her. She could well imagine how horrible it would be to have to take that poor woman's place.

"So you buried your boy yesterday. About time. And your no-account husband is on his way back to prison. Now your dog is gone too. I'm all you got left, I reckon." He paused, watching her intently, wondering what her reaction would be, and he frowned when she didn't react at all. This was the day he had been waiting two years to come. Finally, nothing stood between him and making a claim on this woman. It had been a long campaign. At first he had come over as a friend and neighbor, helping her till, plant, and sow, and asking for nothing in return. But he kept a mental ledger of what she owed him for every little thing he did. When Joshua Eddings fell ill he had kept his distance, checking by only occasionally, gauging how far the sickness was progressing, estimating how much longer it would take the boy to die.

His intent had been to leave Purdy be until her boy was gone but his lust had gotten the better of him. He had his way with her several times before Josh breathed his last. She had tried to fight him off the first time, but he had taught her a lesson, forcing himself on her after Buck was put outside. It didn't bother him too much that her son lay in his bed in the same room as the four-poster where, in his mind, he staked his claim to this auburn-haired beauty. As far as he was concerned she owed him for his help. Without him she could not have grown enough crops to give the bank the annual payment owed on the loan that Jake had inherited. Purdy was better off with him than Jake anyway, he thought, since he considered himself to be a much better farmer. Now he intended to take her as his own, to join the two farms together. She would bear him sons to help him work the fields. He didn't ask her what she wanted because it didn't matter. She was a woman alone and her purpose in life was to please her man and to bear his children. That she was young and attractive, probably the prettiest woman in the county, was a bonus.

"You just been sittin' there all night, then?" he asked. "It's a shame about your boy but what's done is done. Pull yourself together. It never does a damned bit of good feeling sorry for yourself. Stir up that fire and make me some coffee."

Purdy got up slowly, letting the blanket fall from her shoulders to drape across the rocking chair. Norris admired her slender frame, evident beneath the plain gingham dress she wore as she sat on her heels to stir into life the embers of last night's fire. She added another piece of wood then carried a wooden bucket outside to fetch some water from the well. Norris remained at the table. She didn't look too enthused about doing for him but he didn't demand enthusiasm. He wasn't worried that she would run off. Where would she run to? Besides, he was confident that she already knew better than to cross him.

Back inside, Purdy poured some water in a kettle, which she hung on the iron crane in the fireplace. She hadn't paid much attention to the stores that Temple Hanley had brought her these past—how many days had it been since Joshua died?—so it took her a moment to find the bag of Arbuckle's pre-roasted coffee beans. As she began grinding the beans using a mortar and pestle, she glanced over her shoulder at Norris and then quickly away because he was staring at her, though not at her face. She found herself hoping that Lawyer Hanley would show up soon, and then dreaded that he might. There was no telling what Norris might do if another man showed up, especially one as attentive as Hanley.

"Just cause or good provocation," said Norris. "Your husband being off in prison for—what is it, thirteen more years?—well, that's one or the other. That's all you need to get a divorce out here. Good thing we don't live back east. You might be expected to go without a man for that long." He grinned, admiring the flare of her hips as she stood with her back to him, the process of grinding the beans making her body move in a slight and rhythmic motion. "Out here, though, it's about what's necessary to survive, and the way I see it all you got to do is ask the judge for a divorce and you'll get it."

"But I don't want a divorce," she said softly, not looking around.

Norris shook his head as he got up and moved over to her. He saw her shoulders bunch as he drew near and smiled coldly. Planting his big meaty hands on the kitchen cabinet to either side of her, he leaned in close, looking over her shoulder. "It don't really matter what you want, Purdy, now does it?" She stopped grinding the coffee and stood as still and silent as a statue. Being so close to her unleashed his lust and he grabbed her, his fingers closing like a vise around her arm, digging into her soft flesh, making her wince in pain. He dragged her into the small adjacent room where the beds were and threw her roughly onto the four-poster. She lay there, her heart racing, her stomach churning, and she covered her face with her hands as he hastily worked on his belt and the fastenings of his trousers. An instant later he had thrown her dress up and then his weight was pinning her down and she felt like throwing up but didn't. Turning her face away from his hot gusting breath, she saw Joshua's empty bed and closed her eyes and kept them closed while Norris had his way, and it hurt a little because he was rough. She didn't fight him, she didn't cry out, she didn't do anything but lie there, keeping her eyes closed, feeling ashamed, empty, and lost. She had resisted the first time and he had punished her, tying her to the bed and using his belt on her until he drew blood. She didn't resist after that.

When he was done he lay sprawled on top of her for a few minutes, minutes that seemed to her like hours. He finally rolled off her and off the bed too, getting his pants back up and belt buckled. "Tomorrow you're coming home with me," he said flatly. "Gather up anything you want to take and be ready by first light." He looked around at her. "You hear me?" She hadn't moved, hadn't even pushed her dress back down, just lay there, eyes closed, and he growled, "When I ask you a question you answer me, woman!"

She opened her violet-blue eyes then and looked at him. "I don't want to leave this house," she said quietly. There was no defiance in her tone, and no grief; it was merely a statement, devoid of emotion.

Norris chuckled. "Didn't we just talk about that, woman? Don't matter what you want. Says it right there in the Good Book, doesn't it. Eve was made to do for Adam. To make his life better, easier. More pleasant. You'll be a good wife, and my sons will learn what kind of woman to get for their own when they grow up. You're coming home with me tomorrow. And I'm going to burn this place to the ground just to make sure you get it through your thick skull that you belong to me now. You're going to cook for me, work for me in the fields, and you're going to bear me a passel of sons. That's what you were made for and that's what you're going to do." He grabbed her dress and pulled it down over her legs. "Don't just lie there like a whore," he snapped, and left the room.

Purdy heard his boots thumping on the floorboards and then on the porch, and it was so still she even heard the crunch of snow under his weight as he walked away. His farm was about half a mile along the river, and he had always made the journey on foot. She lay there awhile longer before rising and walking unsteadily into the main room. The kettle on the crane over the crackling hearth fire was putting out a lot of steam. She ignored it and stepped out onto the porch and saw Norris striding across the field in the direction of his place. Going back inside, she emerged a moment later with the shotgun, and sat down in the rocking chair, laying the gun across her lap. Norris was just then disappearing into the scrub oak thicket that separated his place from hers, so she scanned all the fields around, and the edges of the woods along the Little River, and sighed despondently because she didn't see Buck. For a while she sat there, not thinking about anything, or seeing anything either, feeling numb, her mind empty. Eventually she realized her skin was crawling. She had Norris's smell and his sweat on her, and his seed was inside her. She had felt the same way when he had covered her before, and she had drawn water from the well and washed herself on the porch. This time, though, she laid the shotgun down beside the rocking chair then stood and headed across the fields toward the river. She walked slowly, stumbling at times. The field beneath a foot of snow wasn't easy to walk on when you couldn't see the furrows.

Halfway to her destination she looked up and spotted a single buzzard circling in and out of errant gray wisps that whirled and dangled like lost ghosts beneath the thick layer of the cloud stretching from horizon to horizon. Reaching the tree-lined embankment, she looked up and down the Little River, which was about forty feet across here and running strong. The corners of her full pale lips moved in a melancholy smile as she remembered strolling along the bank with her husband, making love now and then beneath the stars on sultry spring evenings. She remembered too that special day when Joshua had caught his first fish. She settled down on the log she had often sat on when she came down to the river to cool herself in the shade on hot summer days and listen to the song of the river. She did that now, hugging herself against the bitter cold that cut right through her. In no time at all she was shivering violently.

Her mind went blank and she sat there for quite some time until she remembered why she had come. She unlaced her shoes and took them off. Then she rose and pulled the dress off over her head and draped it across the log, wrapping the new black-and-gray shawl around her shoulders again before turning and stepping into the shallows. The shock of the frigid water rushing over her feet made her gasp, but her feet numbed almost immediately and she took a few more small steps. When the water was halfway up her calves, she squatted down and gasped again as the frigid water rushed over her hips and thighs. The water was cold, painfully cold, but she felt cleansed where it touched her, and she wanted to be cleansed all over. All she could think about was the river, how breath-takingly cold the water was, because it made her numb, and she found the numbness comforting, so she stood up and walked in up to her waist, hugging herself tightly, teeth chattering, body twitching involuntarily. The she spread her arms out and lay back, letting the strong current pull her off her feet and carry her downstream.

Her pulse was a loud and rapid drumbeat in her ears and she was breathing high and fast, coughing and spewing up water now and then when the river pulled her under and she bobbed back up to the surface again. She was very dizzy and, oddly enough, felt hungry for the first time in weeks. She decided she really needed to find something to eat and tried to swim to shore, but she couldn't feel her arms and legs anymore. She flopped and flailed and didn't make much headway. As the current slowly spun her around and around, she caught an occasional glimpse downriver and saw that she was being swept swiftly closer to a bend where a large tree had fallen a few years before, extending halfway across the river. A few of the major limbs jutted down into the water. She couldn't decide whether she needed to swim to the left to avoid the tree or to the right to get within reach of one of those limbs, and before she knew it she had reached the tree, and the river was carrying her at a much greater velocity as it narrowed at the bend. Her fingers grazed the smooth, slick surface of a limb but she couldn't grip it, couldn't seem to get her fingers to work properly, and in an instant she was past the tree.

Too fatigued to try to swim against the current and make the riverbank, she lay back and let the river carry her away. More and more water sloshed over her face. She tired of trying to spit it out her mouth and started swallowing. Then the shawl was swept over her face like a dark shroud, making it even harder to breathe when she bobbed to the surface. She kept her eyes closed. She was beginning to feel warm. The pounding of the pulse in her ears slowed. That was when she heard the barking, and it animated her. She raised her head and the current rolled her over and took her under and when she came back up she didn't hear the barking anymore. She looked around to see Buck running full-stride along the bank abreast of her before leaping into the river. She was so happy and relieved to see him, and just wanted to wrap her arms around him and hug him tightly The dog swam strong and true toward her, and as she called out his name the river pulled her down. She came up spluttering and gasping and tried to swim again but couldn't make her arms and legs do what she wanted them to do. Then Buck was within reach and she clutched at him and instantly the dog began swimming back to shore. Purdy could feel him lunge and strain and even go under a few times and then she felt alarmed. They were both going to drown if she held on, and as soon as she realized this she let go of him. "Go home, Buck! Go home!" she cried as the river reclaimed her and began carrying her downstream again. Then she saw the rope, the one she had tied him to when Hanley had taken her and Joshua's body to Cameron. About four feet of it was still attached to the loop around the dog's massive neck and lay on the surface of the river like a tawny snake. She clutched it and instantly Buck, who had managed to get turned around and was heading for her, began swimming for shore again.

When Buck pulled her out of the river Purdy was limp and still. The yellow dog stood with head down and tongue lolling, his legs trembling from exertion. He had been pushed to the limit of his strength and beyond. He barked, but this elicited no response from her. He licked her face, and her head rolled limply to one side. Her eyes remained closed and she lay unmoving, sprawled on her back in the muck of mud and snow and small debris that marked a river's edge. Buck whined and draped his hundred-pound frame across her. His weight forced water from her lungs and out through her mouth.

He lay his massive head on her shoulder—and waited.

CHAPTER THIRTEEN

When they came to the edge of the big clearing Bill Sayles took one look at the homestead out in the middle of the wide-open space and knew something was wrong. The door was open. There was no wood smoke rising from the chimney. This was not a good day for having no fire in the hearth and the door open. The corral gate was open, and the corral itself was empty. There was something else too, something he could not have put into words had his life depended on it. Call it instinct, intuition, a gut hunch. He felt a tingle at the base of his spine. In his years as a Ranger he had come upon many a place that had borne no overt sign that something was amiss, but upon closer look proved to be an ambush site, or the scene of a tragedy. He glanced behind him at Eddings, who was also gazing at the cabin and who, when he realized Sayles was looking at him, said, "Maybe they can spare some coffee. I'm frozen clean through."

"You just had coffee," drawled Sayles.

"That was at least three hours ago."

"Like I said, you just had some. You'll get more tonight."

Yesterday they had traveled no more than half a dozen

miles after leaving the Cameron cemetery. Someone like
Temple Hanley would have argued that it made more
sense to spend the night in the shelter of the jail and get
an early start in the morning. But Sayles figured it was
better for Eddings if they put some miles between them
and his son's final resting place. Besides, he didn't like
burning daylight. If he pushed hard he might get Eddings
back to prison in two days, and he was eager to be done
with this job. For that reason he decided not to investigate the homestead. With a cluck of the tongue and a flick
of the reins he got the coyote dun moving again, with the
bay that bore Eddings trailing along behind on the lead
rope. They began crossing the clearing, angling east by
south, on a bearing that would not take them any closer
to the cabin. For a moment there was only the crunch of
snow under iron-shod hooves, the creak of old saddle
leather, the breathing of the horses to break the stillness
of the winter day. But before they got halfway across Sayles suddenly pulled rein and muttered "Goddamn it." He
crossed his arms on the pommel of his saddle and turned
his squinty eyes to the cabin again. The coyote dun whickered softly. "I know," he said. "Curiosity killed the cat."
Then he straightened, sighed, and changed course, making
straight for the cabin.

He checked the dun about thirty feet from the cabin,
dismounted stiffly, and ground-hitched his horse. He
knew from experience that the dun was steadfast even
when there was gunfire. He pulled his Winchester from
the saddle boot and slanted it over a shoulder while he
gave the place a careful survey. Then he proceeded to
study the tracks in the snow. There was plenty of sign.
With no snowfall in the past two days and no sun either,
the footprints were virtually pristine. He looked at the
trees to the west and then the trees to the east, in the di-

rection of the Brazos. He suspected the river was not more than a mile or so in that direction. When you had spent a lifetime tracking Comanches across the plains of West Texas for hundreds of miles, you became adept at remembering landmarks and determining the distance between them. He finally walked back to the bay and looked up at Eddings.

"You make a fine target sittin' up there," he remarked.

"And if someone shot me dead this minute you'd probably haul me back to Huntsville anyway, wouldn't you."

"Thought we'd hashed that out. Yes I would, although I believe Superintendent Goree would rather you be alive, so as you could make more shoes or whatever it is you make for the law-abiding. So get on down, now."

Eddings threw a leg over the saddlehorn and slid off the rig, landing unsteadily. Once he had his balance he looked about uneasily. "What is it? Why'd you decide to stop after all?"

"Reckon the answer's inside." Sayles turned his steps toward the cabin's doorway, certain that Eddings would follow. The prisoner wasn't foolish enough to run, and with his hands shackled behind him he couldn't get back in the saddle.

The door was only halfway open and Sayles paused briefly just outside, tilting his head, listening intently. Then he tried to push the door all the way back with the barrel of the repeater but it was blocked by something, so he shoved his hand in the pocket of his coat where the Schofield revolver rested and slipped inside. Stepping to the left, keeping his back to the wall, he looked down at the body that had prevented the door from opening fully. His steel-cast eyes swept the room, and then he moved abruptly to the curtain that partitioned the main room from the sleeping area and swept it aside, bent over to peer under the bed; only then did his hand emerge from the coat pocket. His nostrils flared as he moved to the table at the center of the cabin. He could smell blood, and he smelled a woman, too. He had already known a woman had been here thanks to the tracks in the snow outside, but now he believed that she had lived here. Eddings stood just inside the door, staring at the dead man, and Sayles asked, "Any idea who that jasper was?"

Eddings shook his head. "No. I never came down this way."

Sayles used a foot to roll the corpse over. "Throat cut," he murmured and instantly he thought about what the ferryman had told him a few days before, how two lawmen had been killed on a riverboat, one of them with his head nearly severed. "Stay right there until I get back," he told Eddings as he went out the door.

"Where are you going?" asked Eddings.

Sayles didn't answer. He untied the lead rope from the pommel of his saddle and led the coyote dun by rein leather toward the woods to the east, following one of the two sets of prints that came from that direction. The bay stood right where he left it, watching them go. Sayles was fairly certain whoever had killed the man in the cabin was long gone—and headed west, not east—but he wasn't one to take unnecessary chances, and if trouble waited for him behind that eastern tree line he didn't need a second horse to worry about.

Once he reached the trees it didn't take him long to find the Litchfield brothers' night camp. Two men, one horse. That was immediately obvious. One of the men had walked across the clearing to the house and the other had led the horse to the same destination, but far enough away from the first man's tracks to make Sayles surmise that they had not made the walk together. He went a little deeper into the woods and before long heard the unmistakable murmur of the river. He didn't need to see it to know it was a river and not a creek, and since it was a river it had to be the Brazos. He estimated that the ferry was less than half a day's ride south.

Sayles grimly thought it over, re-creating the past in his mind's eye based on what he had seen and smelled. Two men had killed those lawmen on a riverboat not too far south of the ferry, and two men had been here, leaving a dead man in their wake and in all likelihood riding off with a woman on a stolen horse. They had crossed the river, but not on the ferry. There were plenty of men capable of murder in this country, but it was entirely possible that the same pair had done all three killings.

Retracing his steps, he checked inside the ramshackle barn and found it empty before going back inside the cabin. Eddings hadn't moved and even as he opened his mouth to ask the obvious question, Sayles answered it. "Two men with one horse camped in the woods to the east. They come up here, went inside. Came out with a woman and rode west on two horses. More tracks around the barn, probably two mules. They come out of the corral and one headed due north while the other headed for the river."

"How do you know they were mules?"

Sayles looked at Eddings with mild disbelief, wondering how a man, a farmer at that, wouldn't know enough about mules that he would need ask such a question. "Well, for one thing, they walked, they didn't run. A mule won't run 'less it has to. And they struck out in different directions, since mules don't get attached to one another. Horse tend to stick together. Now, a mule might have a fondness for his mother if it's a horse, which it usually is. But generally it's just not very sociable."

"Like some people I know," said Eddings.

Sayles nodded and scratched an itch on his beard-stubbled jawline. "Yeah, well, some people don't have the luxury of being sociable. Also, they weren't shod—the mules, I mean. It can be a struggle putting a shoe on a mule. It don't like nothin' between its feet and the ground. And finally there's the fact that the two men who killed this feller and took his woman didn't take 'em. It's not that a mule can't run. In fact they're as fast and sometimes faster than a cowpony if they got good reason to be. But they can be troublesome and I don't reckon men on the run would want to bother with 'em."

Eddings looked embarrassed and said, defensively, "I had a mule . . . for plowing. I already knew . . . most of your lecture on mules." Having heard more than enough on that subject, and having had plenty of time to study the interior of the cabin, he changed topics. "Maybe they killed this man for the woman. Maybe she wanted to run off with them."

"Maybe. But most likely those two jaspers are on the run. They come here with just one horse and they didn't go back the way they came. So not likely they come to fetch a woman and took her back home. They're heading west, and the farther west you go the less law you find." Sayles sat on the edge of the plank table in the middle of the room and lit a cheroot with a strike-anywhere, drawing the smoke deep into his lungs and letting it trickle out through his nostrils as he surveyed the room carefully. Meanwhile Eddings thought about Purdy, alone at the farm. If the two men who had done the killing here passed that way.

"Just because they rode west doesn't make them outlaws."

"Well, no, I reckon not. They could be mustangers.

More of them going out that way now that the Comanches are dealt with. But a mustangin' crew is usually more than two and they would have a pack animal with them. No buffalo to hunt anymore. You can take a westward-bound stage line from points south of here—and points north too—all the way to Tucson and whatever's beyond so you don't need to ride across the desert unless you're just fond of sand, rattlers, and alkali water. Homesteaders would be in a wagon. So I don't know. You tell me what two men who took another man's woman with them, and left the man dead, might be."

Eddings just shook his head and moved over to the fire, kicking at the pile of ashes with his toe. There was nothing to be gained by arguing with Sayles, especially since he was usually right.

The smoldering cheroot dangling from his lips, Sayles eventually stood up and moved toward the door. "I'll send a wire to Tom Rath about what we've found here, once we get to Huntsville."

"That's two days from now!" exclaimed Eddings. "Whoever killed this man will be long gone by then."

"Maybe so."

"And what about the body? Oh, yeah, I remember. Critters got to eat, right? Isn't that what you said after you killed those three men on the road?"

"You ever dug a grave in frozen ground? We'll close the door on our way out. Weather being what it is, he won't get too ripe." The Ranger went past Eddings and out the door.

Eddings followed, unwilling to let it drop. "I don't understand you. You gunned down three bandits who were ready and willing to ride off because, you said, if you didn't deal with them they might rob someone else. But you're going to let the killers of that man in there get away with it. What if these are the same two who killed those lawmen on the riverboat? You know, the ones that ferry-man told you about?"

Sayles looked at the lead-gray sky and grimaced as he produced the Elgin keywinder. When the sun was out he could calculate time about as well as a watch could, even a timepiece as fine as his, but there was no sign that the sun was going to make an appearance anytime soon. The thought had crossed his mind. "I have a job to do. I told Superintendent Goree I'd have you back at the prison in six days or a week. That's tomorrow or the next day. Don't have time to go chasin' after a couple of bad eggs."

Eddings stared at him in disbelief. "So what you're saying is the only reason you killed those three men was because they were on our way to Cameron. Had you needed to go out of your way to get them you wouldn't have bothered. If I didn't know better I'd think you were afraid. The men who did this are cold-blooded killers. They probably kidnapped the woman who was here. They'll probably rape her if they haven't already. And what do you reckon the chances are that she'll live to tell the tale? "

Sayles looked at him with eyes that were every bit as cold as the day. He took one last long draw from the cheroot and flicked it away. Eddings's heart was galloping in his chest. He had just suggested that Bill Sayles was a coward, and that was something you were wise to think twice about doing to any man out here, much less *this* man. But Eddings was tired and angry and worried, and he often spoke before thinking. And since he had already crossed the line, he had more to say while he had the chance.

"Truth is, you don't care," he said grimly. "You don't care what happens to the woman they took. You don't care if they kill a few more innocent people. You Rangers are supposed to be the brave and noble defenders of the frontier but looks to me like you're just heartless killers, not much different from the two men who came through here. Big talk about all the people you saved but you don't give a tinker's damn about how many died. They just justified you killing others. In fact, I doubt you ever cared about anybody your whole life."

"Turn around," rasped Sayles.

Eddings had the sensation of the blood running cold in his veins. He hesitated, staring at Sayles in fear and then disgust. "Could at least give me a gun," he said, his tone bitter, his voice hollow.

Sayles walked around Eddings, stowing the watch back in a coat pocket before producing the key to the shackles on the prisoner's wrists, which he unlocked and stuffed into the same pocket. Eddings slowly turned to face him, certain that he had said too much, pushed too hard, and that Sayles was going to kill him for it.

"Go ahead," he said. "Not like I have much to lose anymore."

"Just get on the damned horse," said Sayles.

Eddings glanced at the bay, then down at his wrists, and then at the Ranger.

"We travel faster if I don't have to lead that bay. I assume you know more about horses than you do mules. Need to make better time than we have been if we're to have a hope of catching up with those two jaspers. If you get it in your head to try to ride away I'll just shoot you dead and take you back to Goree and you can do the rest of your time six feet under in the prison boneyard."

Without saying another word, and feeling he was lucky to be alive, Eddings went to the bay and climbed up into

the saddle. Sayles moved to the coyote dun and put boot
to stirrup and hauled himself up onto his rig. Every time
he climbed aboard the dun it looked to Eddings like it
would be be the last time he would be able manage it. And
yet the old man, for his stiffness and groaning, was all grit
and gristle and just kept going on. Sayles settled into his
rig and sat there a moment, looking around like he had
suddenly forgotten where they were. Then he reined the
dun around and pulled up alongside Eddings,

"Haven't had many people to care about," he said flatly.
"My mother and father died of cholera when I was a
young'un. Don't know why it didn't kill me too. And I had
a wife and daughter once. They were killed by Comanches. Thirty-five years ago. That was during the Great
Raid led by Buffalo Hump. It wasn't his bunch that done
it, though."

Eddings was visibly taken aback by these revelations.
It was hard to imagine Bill Sayles as a family man. He
didn't know what to say, so he settled on asking a question. "That was because of the Council House Fight,
wasn't it?"

Sayles nodded. "I still don't know why they done it. I
mean those thirty Comanche chiefs who rode right into
San Antone to talk about a peace treaty. Foolish thing to
do. See, back then, the Comanche nation was something
to be reckoned with. I don't think they were ever as strong
as they were back in those days. They had been raiding deep
into Mexico and all along the frontier from the Red River
to Matagorda Bay. They took a good many captives back
in those days, both Texan and Mexican, and tempers ran
hot when the meetin' took place in San Antone's Council House. When the Comanches didn't agree to release
all the captives they'd taken, the effort was made to grab

them and then trade them for the captives. But a Comanche don't surrender. The chiefs put up a fight and lost. About twenty or thirty Comanches were killed that day too. A few months later Buffalo Hump did what no other chief had ever been able to do, before or since. He got all the bands to join forces. He put together an army of about four hundred warriors. There were a hundred or more women and children who went along too." Sayles paused, staring off into the distance, and Eddings sensed it was not the distance of space but rather of time. "It was a sight to behold, I'm telling you.

"I reckon Buffalo Hump didn't want to waste such a force on the small towns along the frontier, and even four hundred Comanches weren't going to attack a city the size of San Antone. So they rode all the way across Texas, down to the coast. Showed up first at Victoria and killed about a dozen people, then moved on to the port of Linnville. Only thing that saved the people of that town was all the ships out in the harbor. You see, Linnville was a busy port in those days. Lot of sailing ships from all over the world. The people got on those ships and watched the Comanches loot and burn their town. There was a lot to loot in the warehouses along the docks, including a small fortune in silver bullion. They spent three whole days there. By then the word was out. Volunteers from Bastrop and Gonzales headed that way, and every Ranger who could ride was in the saddle too. I was at home with my wife and daughter when my company showed up. See, the captain was in such a hurry he just mounted up and rode around and collected the men one by one." After a long pause, he added, "That was my old captain, Jack Hays. Usually, Captain Hayes would send a messenger ride out to tell you to report. When that happened I always took my family into town before I lit out. But this time I had to settle for telling them to go to town and then I rode away. That was the last time I saw them . . . alive."

He paused, took off his battered hat, ran gloved fingers through his thinning hair, then untied his canteen from the saddle and took a drink. His throat was dry, and not entirely because he hadn't said so many words all at once since . . . he couldn't remember when. For once he regretted the decision he had made years ago not to carry a flask of whiskey with him while on the job. That was because ever since the event he was now revealing to Eddings he had developed a tendency to drink a little too much on occasion, and he didn't want to go out falling off his horse in a drunken stupor and breaking his neck. That was no way for a Texas Ranger to die. But he sure needed a drink now. He had never told anyone this story and he wasn't exactly sure why he was telling it now. Jake's assertions that he was a cold-blooded killer who didn't give a tinker's damn for anyone or anything didn't bother him. Many worse things had been said of him, though usually by people who knew to say them behind his back rather than to his face. Maybe he was doing this because everything about this job, from the moment The Captain had given him his orders in Waco, had conspired to bring these painful memories to life and he had to talk about it, just had to get it out. He drew a long, somewhat ragged breath, and let the past take hold of him again.

"Thirty-five years, and I still remember how my daughter's tears tasted. She had just learned to walk, and when she came to me that day she fell down and started crying. Remember how my wife felt in my arms when she hugged me good-bye. She was the prettiest woman I ever seen. She smelled like . . . wildflowers. We caught up to Buffalo Hump at Plum Creek. For once the Comanches were travelin' slow. They'd found so much loot they had hundreds of pack mules. Had more than a thousand stolen horses with 'em too, as I recall. We killed about eighty in a running fight that lasted a whole day, daybreak to sundown. Got most of the loot back and most of the horses too. We should have kept after them but the militia had gotten hold of the bullion and they forgot all about the Comanches and started divvying up the treasure. Then they just went home. Our captains called it quits after that. I should have headed straight home myself but some of the men in my company wanted to pay a visit to the saloon in Lockhart and I went along. When I did get home I found it was burned to the ground. My daughter's skull had been crushed. My wife had been . . ."

He made a sound like something was caught in his throat. Eddings saw his Adam's apple bobbing and muttered, "I'm sorry." That hardly seemed adequate but he couldn't think of anything else to say.

Sayles was silent a moment, still looking away. When he continued his voice was husky, flat, and devoid of emotion. "Was five or six bucks from what I could tell. They hit other places nearby. Guess they thought it was a good time for a little raiding of their own, with every able-bodied man out after Buffalo Hump. I just missed them too. See, if I had gone straight home from Plum Creek . . ." He shook his head. "The burned my house. The smashed my little girl's skull in. And they raped my wife then cut her throat. I've always wondered which one had to watch the other die."

"My God!" Eddings was horrified.

"After I buried my family I lit out after that raiding party but I lost the sign in a storm. Real fence-lifter, that storm was. But it didn't really matter. I spent the next thirty years killing every Comanche I could find. Men and women, old and young. Just couldn't kill the children, though. Kept seeing my own daughter. Thing is, no matter how many I killed it didn't make me feel a damned bit better. Maybe I was just trying to get myself killed." He drew a long breath and looked at Eddings, his creased, sun-dark face seemingly etched in stone. "I made a mistake, and people I loved died. I've lived with that mistake. But you get tired of hurting. It's a hurt that doesn't seem to get better. But then you know all about that kind."

Eddings nodded and looked off into the distance himself, bleakly aware that at that moment his resolve to do his time like a man should, like his son would want him to, began to waver. Could he endure thirteen years of the hurt that Sayles had just described? He doubted it.

"I'm sorry," he said, again. "And sorry for what I said before."

Sayles nodded. "Let's ride." He kicked the coyote dun into a canter, heading west.

Day Six

CHAPTER FOURTEEN

Temple Hanley drove the buggy out to the Eddings place early in the morning on the day after the funeral. It was bitterly cold, as it had been for weeks now, weeks that seemed like months. At least it hadn't snowed in two days. He had seen quite enough snow to last him a lifetime, or at least that was how he felt now. When the Texas summer came he supposed he would wish for cold weather again, since summers in these parts were hellish. Back in the Reconstruction years General Phil Sheridan had famously said that if he owned Texas and Hell he would live in Hell and rent out Texas. Hanley was of the opinion that Sherman was not so much slighting Texas weather as showcasing his dislike for Texans—a feeling that was mutual. But anyone who had endured a Texas summer could be forgiven for wondering at times if Hell might not be a little bit cooler.

He had spent a troubled and mostly sleepless night worrying about Purdy, so he was motivated to venture out as soon as there was enough light to travel by. Seeing the front door of the farmhouse wide open when he pulled up out front caused his concern to spike. He called her name as he climbed down out of the buggy and then again as he clambered up onto the porch, pausing to cast a quick look across the fields as he rapped on the door with his knuckles, which pushed it further open. He ventured inside, experiencing a sense of dread, worried about what he would find. The fire he had started for Purdy the day before was dead, the ashes cold. He checked the bedroom and then went back outside. Brows furrowed with concern, he shouted her name at the top of his lungs and listened to . . . a deathly stillness. Venturing away from the house he saw three sets of footsteps in the snow. Two came from the west, and crisscrossed each other. The third headed north, across the field to the line of trees that marked the course of the Little River. Hanley was no tracker, but even he could tell that the southbound sign had been made by smaller feet than the other two, so he struck out in that direction.

When he reached the trees and saw the dress draped over the log his heart lurched in his chest. He called out her name again several times, and now there was a frantic edge to his voice. "What have you done?" he cried out. "What have you done?" He was chastising himself for leaving Purdy alone, for not insisting that she come to town, even stay in his house, propriety be damned. He ran clumsily through the snow, heading downstream. A man unaccustomed to physical exertion and with too much meat on his bones, he was quickly winded. His legs were burning. He wasn't paying attention to the ground in front of him, instead scanning both banks of the river, and he stumbled several times. Once he pitched facedown into the snow. For once, though, Temple Hanley wasn't concerned with appearances.

He slowed down at the bend in the river, checking the limbs of the fallen tree that went down into the water, where a body might be snared. Then he stumbled on, the breath rasping in his throat, but he didn't have to go much farther. He saw the big yellow dog first, lying on the river's edge, and then he saw Purdy's naked body beneath the dog, and an anguished cry escaped his lips. Knowing how devastated she had been, he cursed himself for leaving this poor woman alone. He stood there a moment, trying to cope with gut-wrenching dismay. There didn't seem to be a need for urgency anymore. Purdy Eddings was dead. A suicide. He advanced slowly, warily, holding out his hands as the big dog lifted his massive head and watched his approach with those gleaming eyes—one bright blue, one golden brown. Since Buck didn't lunge at him, or even produce one of those bloodcurdling growls of his, Hanley wondered if somehow the beast could comprehend his gesture. He took a few more cautious steps and then, overwhelmed with emotion, dropped to his knees in the snow, tears burning his eyes.

The dog rose, standing over Purdy's slender white body, head down, tongue lolling, watching Hanley a moment before stepping back and dragging his tongue over his owner's face. He whined and licked her again and it was then that Hanley saw her head move, heard the faintest of sounds well up from her throat and emerge from her slightly parted, bluish lips. "Purdy!" gasped Hanley, and crawled on hands and knees to her side. The dog backed away a little and watched him as Hanley touched her face. She was so cold, so pale! She looked so lifeless. But her head moved again, and he hastily took off his buffalo coat, laid it out on the snow, and gently, if clumsily, lifted her onto it and wrapped it over her. Brushing tendrils of auburn hair off her face, he talked to her . . . "Purdy. Purdy, it's me, Temple Hanley. Can you hear me? Purdy?" until she moaned and moved again and this time the tears escaped his eyes and he sobbed, "Thank you, Lord!"

He sat up and looked at the bruising and punctures on her upper arm, and then at the dog. One thing Temple Hanley was good at was looking at evidence and putting two and two together. "Good dog!" he said. "Good dog!" The dog, seemingly satisfied that Hanley had come to help, not harm, his owner, lay his long body right next to Purdy's and rested his head on her shoulder. Even then he kept his eyes glued on the lawyer.

Glancing over his shoulder, Hanley tried to calculate just how far he had come from the Eddings farmhouse and whether or not he could make it back there while carrying Purdy. He couldn't see the place anymore and figured it was farther than a man in his condition could carry someone, even someone as slender as Purdy, but he knew for certain that he had to try. He got on his feet, which was a monumental effort in itself, but nothing like the effort he had to exert getting her cradled in his arms. He trudged along the river, going upstream. The big yellow dog followed. Eventually, as exhaustion loomed, Hanley began to stagger. He stopped once, dropping to his knees and sitting back on his heels. But he didn't dare put Purdy down, afraid that if he did he might not be able to lift her into his arms again. The dog circled around and sat on his haunches in front of him, watching him and his burden intently.

Hanley could piece together what had happened. Purdy had gone down to the river to drown herself. The missing dog had appeared as if by magic at just the right time, jumping into the river, latching on to her arm, and somehow getting her to shore. It was an extraordinary display of courage and devotion, nigh on unbelievable. What were the odds that the runaway canine would show up at just the right moment to save his owner? And what were the odds that the dog would know to lie atop Purdy and keep her alive with his own body heat through the bitter-cold night? Maybe the best and certainly the easiest explanation would be that it had been a miracle. He stared at the dog in awe, and the dog stared at him with great intensity, then stood up and barked. It wasn't a menacing sound, but still it made Hanley jump. "All right, all right," he said, and groaned and grunted his way onto his feet and continued to plod through the calf-high snow with his precious burden.

When at last he reached the farmhouse his legs and arms and back were aching fiercely, and he tottered up onto the porch and through the door and laid Purdy gently on the floor right next to the fireplace, still wrapped in the buffalo coat. While he built a fire he watched the dog sniffing around in an agitated way, first in the main room and then in the bedroom. Once he had the fire going strong he went into the bedroom and grabbed a blanket and draped it over Purdy. He noticed that the kettle on the crane in the fireplace was full of water, and that there was fresh-ground coffee. Having forgotten the other tracks in his concern for Purdy's whereabouts and well-being, he remembered them now. Someone had walked to the farmhouse and then walked away, and he had a feeling it was George Norris. The Norris homestead was in the direction from which those tracks came—and went.

Settling down at the table, he sipped hot coffee and began to thaw out. The yellow dog was curled up near the crackling fire and his owner, eyes shut, and sleeping. In stark contrast with how he had always felt before, Hanley felt somehow comforted by the dog's presence. His anxiety had something to do with Norris. Purdy's neighbor was an unpleasant and potentially dangerous man. Norris had never done anything to him personally but there were rumors, most particularly about the way Norris had treated his wife. After meeting the man, Hanley had not doubted the rumors were true. The lawyer prided himself on being a good judge of character, and there was just something about that man that put him ill at ease. There was an ugly rage simmering just beneath the surface in Norris; one could see it in his eyes and expression, and hear it in his voice.

The question now was when Norris would return. Hanley considered putting Purdy in the buggy and heading for Cameron. He could take her to the doctor. But he worried about exposing her to the elements. Torn by indecision, Hanley looked around, and saw the shotgun propped up in a corner of the room. He fetched it and sat back down at the table. Having done a little hunting as a youth, he knew something about shotguns, and determined that both barrels were loaded—powder, wadding, shot in equal measure to the powder, and more wadding. With the weapon laid across the top of the table, he checked on Purdy again, laying the back of his hand against her cheek. She was no longer cold as ice, and seemed to be breathing normally. Further relieved, he sat at the table and gave in to exhaustion, laying his head down on his arms. He passed out right away.

He woke with a start, when something soft and cool touched his cheek, and found Purdy standing beside him. There was some color in her cheeks now, and her lips as well. She had put on faded blue gingham dress and draped the buffalo coat around his shoulders and then touched his cheek. "I made you some hot coffee," she murmured, and he looked at the cup of steaming java on the table in front of him. He looked back up at her and for once found himself at a loss for words. What did you say to someone who had tried to kill herself?

She smiled pensively. "Did you save me?"

Hanley sipped the coffee while he collected his thoughts and carefully considered his words. "Your dog saved you. I found you both on the bank of the river. He was lying across you. It seems somehow he knew you needed the warmth of his body to stay alive." He shook his head. "One hears about such tales, but I never expected to see such a thing with my own eyes."

Purdy was looking at Buck, who sat on his haunches by the fireplace, watching her. "I guess that's how I got these," she murmured, touching the bruises and punctures on her upper arm. "I don't remember much of anything." She stepped closer to Buck, then sank to her knees and wrapped her arms around the beast.

Deeply moved, Hanley cleared his throat and drank some more coffee. He decided not to ask her why she had gone into the river. Considering the ordeal she had been through, the reason seemed obvious enough. "That's not surprising. I expect you were freezing to death. I've read of people becoming confused, dizzy, incoherent, as their body temperature drops."

Her face buried in Buck's thick mane, she murmured, "I'm sorry, Mr. Hanley." She sounded ashamed.

"No, no, my dear, no need to be." He rose and draped the buffalo coat around her shoulders again, relieved when Buck made no show of aggression. It seemed the dog was convinced that he meant Purdy no harm. Hanley had proven himself and no longer had to fear for life and limb. He added wood to the fire, and the cheerful red-orange light produced by the flames permeated the room, a marked improvement over the gloomy and lifeless gray of the farmhouse in weeks past. "Perhaps you should come to town with me. Let Dr. Crighton take a look at your arm. You can stay at my home."

Purdy rose and shook her head. "I can't. My arm will

be fine. I don't mind the pain. It's a reminder that I'm . . . that I'm alive. And besides, you know how people would gossip. Especially if you put me up in your own house."

"That doesn't matter."

"But it *does* matter, Mr. Hanley. You have been so kind to me. I'm not going to be a party to ruining your reputation. They must think me some shameless Jezebel. And I suppose I've brought that on myself. But no, I won't go with you." She looked around the room. "George Norris is coming here today and he said he was going to burn the house down." Her gaze returned to Hanley's face. Even though her eyes were filled with apprehension, she uttered her next words quite resolutely: "I'm not going to let him."

Hanley was surprised by this unexpected show of resolve. She stood there now in such stark contrast with the defeated, grief-stricken woman to whom he was accustomed. "But why would he do such a thing?"

"Because he is going to try to take me to his place. Make me his woman. He said he would burn this house down and kill Buck but I am *not going to let him.*"

"I admire your spirit, my dear," said Hanley earnestly, "but I fear it may lead you into harm's way. George Norris is not a man to be trifled with, as you may already know. A house can be rebuilt. As for your dog, well, he is a remarkable creature, but still he is just a dog."

Purdy frowned and Hanley realized he had made a mistake. It was obvious by her expression that she was angry. At times he was just too analytical, too detached. He marked it down to a lifetime committed to logic and reason rather than emotion. He had avoided emotional attachments his entire adult life and in so doing had escaped the turmoil that such attachments often produced. Compassion for people like Jake and Purdy Eddings was as far as he would go in terms of feelings for others. He considered his dispassionate approach a great asset in the practice of the law, but here, now, he could see that it had led him astray.

"He is not *just* a dog," she said sternly. "He is *my* dog. And this is *my* house."

"But dear Purdy, be reasonable. You cannot possibly work this farm alone."

"You're suggesting I let George Norris have his way? Drag me off to be his . . . his slave?"

"No no, not at all!" Hanley exclaimed. "Come with me, right now, to Cameron. Bring your belongings. Bring your dog. Leave the house. You can sell the farm and have a stake for . . . for whatever you wish to do with your life."

Purdy sighed and shrugged off the buffalo coat and stepped forward to hold it out for him to take. "I cannot ever repay you for all the kindness you have shown me, Mr. Hanley. And I can never make up for all the concern I have caused you. I am so sorry you had to go through what you did this morning. I-I was not myself. I was just . . . tired of crying. Tired of hurting inside. The water made me numb. It made me stop thinking. It's easy to do the wrong thing, you know? That's why I have this problem with George Norris. I wanted to hold on to this place, this farm, for my son if for no other reason. That was the right thing to want. But letting Norris help with the fields, realizing what he wanted in return—well, that was the wrong thing to do."

"Don't blame yourself. Sometimes there are no good options."

Purdy shook her head. "That's what Jake thought, you know. Here, Mr. Hanley, take your coat. You really should go, before Norris gets here. You've done so much for me. You've been so good to me, and asked for nothing in return. I just can't bear the thought of you being hurt."

She walked past him to the door and opened it, held it for him to pass through, a grateful smile on her lips. At least, he thought, her anger had passed. He couldn't bear to think of her upset with him.

"But I . . . I can't leave you to face him alone!" said Hanley, distraught. He took the coat and shrugged it on, sighed despondently, and looked out the door at his buggy, then at Purdy. He was afraid for Purdy but also for himself—afraid of what Norris might think to find him here. He abhorred violence. It was so . . . uncivilized. It seemed rather remarkable considering that he had spent the last fifteen years on the frontier, on the raw and bleeding edge of civilization, that he had been spared any form of physical violence directed at him. The thought of confronting a man like Norris made him tremble. He wanted nothing more than to leave at once. But something held him back. Something wouldn't let him go.

He walked to the door, stopped just shy of crossing the threshold, and glanced at Purdy. "I'm not leaving you to face him alone. I can't. I'll put the horse and rig inside the barn if it's all right with you."

She opened her mouth to protest his decision but he didn't wait to hear it and stepped out onto the porch. He saw movement out of the corner of an eye, followed instantly by a searing pain in his head. The world began to spin crazily. The worn planking of the porch came rushing up to strike him. Stunned, he shouted in pure anguish as more breathtaking, blinding agony exploded in his midsection. He didn't realize that Norris had struck him at the base of the skull with a muscle-sheathed forearm hard as hickory, and then launched a vicious kick at his rib cage once he was down. He felt himself being grabbed and rolled over and he was dimly aware of a looming figure as Norris straddled him, but his vision was so blurred that it made him nauseous and he squeezed his eyes shut. Some primal instinct made him throw up his arms to shield his face as Norris, clutching the front of the buffalo coat with his left hand, made a fist of his right and pulled his arm back in preparation for driving that fist as hard as he could into Hanley's face.

"Can't leave her alone, eh?" sneered Norris, furiously. "I'll teach you to move in on my woman, you bastard!"

"Don't hurt him!" shrieked Purdy from the doorway.

Poised bending over the lawyer, ready to strike, Norris looked over his shoulder at her, his face twisted in an ugly rictus of pure rage. "You whore!" he snarled. "Letting this fat pig poke you, aren't you? Spreading your legs for any man who can give you something you need! Well, I know what you need. I'm going to teach you a lesson you won't *ever* forget, you . . ."

Purdy saw his expression instantly transformed from ranging, mindless fury to shock and terror. Then Norris uttered a strangled cry as a hundred pounds of snarling muscle and sinew and fangs exploded through the doorway.

Knocking Purdy off balance, Buck leaped at Norris. The man threw an arm up as he turned, stumbling backward over the prone Temple Hanley. He was off balance when the dog hit him. The collision lifted Norris completely off his feet and hurtled him back off the porch. Before they landed, Buck's powerful jaws clamped down on the farmer's forearm, and Norris snarled in pain as he clawed frantically at the bone-handled knife he wore in a belt sheath. He used the knife for many things—cleaning fish, dressing out game, killing snakes, and whittling as he sat brooding on his own porch in the evening, a habit he had picked up since the death of his wife, which had left him without much to do after supper. Right now he wanted to use it to kill the beast that was chewing on his arm. The searing, breathtaking pain triggered a primal instinct for survival in Norris. It transformed him into a beast, as well.

Locked in a life-or-death struggle, man and dog landed in a spray of snow. Buck was thrown to one side, but his jaws remained locked, his fangs buried in the farmer's flesh—until Norris's blade plunged into his withers. Norris had been aiming for the neck, but the jarring impact with the ground spoiled his aim. Buck yelped and let go of the man's arm. Both scrambled to their feet. The dog began circling, head down, hackles up, his ears back and fangs bared, growling from down deep. Norris kept turning in place, to keep the dog from getting behind him, his wounded arm dangling, ropes of blood dripping from his hand. He held the knife down low, expecting Buck to leap at him, intending to rip the dog open from underneath. "*Come on!*" he roared hoarsely. "Come on, you devil! I come here to kill you anyway!" Buck barked furiously in response, leaving a ring of blood drops on the snow as he circled. Then he gathered himself and made his leap.

Standing in the doorway of the farmhouse, Purdy shouted "NO!" and in the same instant fired both barrels of the 10-gauge shotgun.

The buckshot ripped apart the flesh of Norris's right arm. It shattered ribs and punctured a lung. The impact knocked him sideways, the knife slipping from useless fingers. He lay there stunned, unable to breathe, consumed with agony. The last thing he saw were Buck's fangs as the dog tore his throat out before he could even scream in terror.

The shotgun blast wrenched a startled shout from Hanley, who still lay on the porch, having rolled over on his side to watch the confrontation. He had seen a few shootings in his time in Cameron, but always from a safe distance. He had never seen the damage a shotgun could cause at close range, but as shocking as that was it was nothing compared with watching Norris's throat being ripped open. He stared in horror at an arterial fountain of bright-red blood spurting from the dying man's neck, watched him twitch and flop in the snow as a growling Buck savaged his throat until he lay still. Only then did the dog release his hold, to limp up onto the porch and past Hanley like he didn't even exist and sprawl at Purdy's bare feet. Hanley looked up at her in that moment. She stood in her worn and faded dress with her auburn hair in disarray, a wisp of smoke escaping the barrels of the shotgun she held, looking as adamant and unmovable as a mountain. Then she dropped slowly to her knees and laid the shotgun down so she could cradle Buck's massive head in her arms.

Hanley rolled over on his back and remembered about breathing. The acrid burn of powder smoke lingered in his nostrils. He lay there a moment, his head and shoulders aching brutally, stunned by what he had just witnessed. It had all happened so quickly, much too quickly to allow a man to think. Norris had been on the porch, had struck him from behind when he emerged. That was obvious, and all he could sort through at the moment, because what had transpired after that had shaken him to the core. A man who abhorred violence, who had never lashed out or been struck in anger, he had always held to his conviction that the antidote to violence was reason; that it was better to talk things out than to resort to bloodshed. Now he wondered if he had been fooling himself all along. There had been no time to reason with Norris, no way of stopping Buck from attacking or Norris from trying to defend himself. No logic or rationale could have prevented this, and only violence—that shotgun blast still rang in his ears—could have stopped it from getting even worse.

He got to his feet and saw that Purdy's fingers were smeared with blood. She had been tenderly examining Buck's wound. She wiped those fingers on her dress as though blood on her hands and clothes was an everyday affair not worth thinking about, then looked at him and said, in a calm and matter-of-fact way, "He was going to kill my dog and I wasn't going to let him."

"Perhaps I-I should go fetch Dr. Crighton."

Purdy smiled, the tolerant smile of an adult who hears a child say something silly. "Buck won't let anyone touch him but me. You know that, Mr. Hanley. Don't worry. It's not a mortal wound. Black powder and witch hazel and a lot of rest will do." Hanley was looking at the body in the bloody snow while he listened to her and she added, wryly, "Maybe I'll end up in Huntsville Prison with my husband."

Hanley sighed. As someone who had devoted his entire adult life to the law, he knew he was obligated to go to Tom Rath and tell him about the killing of George Norris. But he had no idea what would happen if he did that. Rath was unpredictable. He might arrest Purdy or he might not. He might see what she had done as murder or as a completely justified act. Or he might just be too put out by the necessity of actually performing his duties as the town sheriff to do anything but complain. It was hard to say, since Rath didn't care about the law except to the extent that it could further his own ends. Hanley wondered if a convincing argument could be made that Purdy had shot Norris in self-defense? There was no question in his mind that Norris had intended to kill Buck, but would he have threatened Purdy's life? *I'm going to teach you a lesson you won't ever forget.* Wasn't that what Norris had told her? Hanley did not doubt that Norris would have been capable of striking Purdy as viciously as he himself had been struck by the man. Even so, he decided it was highly unlikely he could convince a judge and jury that Purdy had been within her rights to take the life of George Norris. Killing a man to save a dog wasn't justified. To save a horse, maybe, in this country. But not a dog.

Getting to her feet, Purdy murmured soothingly to Buck and the big yellow dog rose with another huffing sound, clearly in pain, moving stiffly as he followed her inside. Hanley stepped to the doorway and leaned against it, still feeling dizzy, his neck and shoulders throbbing painfully. He watched Purdy cajole Buck into stretching out by the fire, after which she walked to the door and gently touched the back of Hanley's neck with the hand that had not been covered in blood. "Hot and swollen," she said, solicitously. "You're the one who should see that old sawbones in town." She touched his arm then and smiled warmly. "I wouldn't be alive if it weren't for you, Mr. Hanley. You know that, don't you?"

Hanley nodded, then glanced over his shoulder at the body of George Norris. "I should help you bury him. Or take him off somewhere and bury him."

Purdy shook her head. "No. I'll take care of that. You get back to Cameron and take care of yourself for a change." She touched his arm. Hanley suddenly felt a great deal better. He gazed at her a moment, in wonder, for it was hard to believe that the woman who stood before him now was the one who had tried to drown herself in the Little River the day before. He drew a deep breath, smiled back at her, then turned to leave—only to turn back. "I was about to say I would be back tomorrow to check on you. But my dear Purdy, I don't think you need me to." He sounded a little sad as well as relieved.

She watched him walk to his buggy, climb aboard, and urge the horse into motion; she closed the door. She didn't look at the corpse of George Norris again, and Temple Hanley didn't either.

CHAPTER FIFTEEN

When Mal Litchfield woke, the first thing he did was to check to see if his brother was still in camp. He was relieved to find Lute still sound asleep in the blankets he now shared with the woman named Alise, who was also sleeping. Since childhood Lute had demonstrated a knack for wandering off and getting into trouble. Mal had always managed to bail him out, through either reasoning, bribery, threat of violence, or, occasionally, violence itself. As time went on and the trouble Lute caused became more serious, Mal began to wonder if he was doing his little brother any favor by making things right rather than letting him face the consequences. Now, no matter what he did—even murder—Lute assumed his brother would find a way to protect him from repercussions. The crux of the matter was Mal's promise to their mother that he would look out for her "little darling" no matter what. It was a promise he felt compelled to honor even though she was long dead and gone—and one he suspected would be the end of him someday.

Mal lay there a moment, reluctant to throw aside the blanket that provided his only cover from the bitter morning cold. Brushing the frost off his whiskers, he thought about Dick Turpin. Last night, while they ate a meager supper of beans and shared a single airtight of peaches, Lute had regaled Alise with tales of Turpin while suggesting he was cut of the same cloth as the great British highwayman of lore. Alise had never heard of Turpin, and whether this was because she was unlettered or because Americans were not acquainted with the legend Mal didn't know. But even after Lute was done, she still didn't know the truth. The life of an outlaw was not nearly as glamorous as all the fiction written about Dick Turpin made it out to be. And the subject himself was not nearly as gentlemanly and heroic.

Mal finally summoned the will to get up. By the time he brought the campfire back to life he was shivering violently, the cold a dull ache down deep in his bones. The wood smoke rose up into the low, thick canopy of the thicket in which they had made camp. With the uncertain light of a long daybreak on yet another overcast day, he doubted the smoke would be seen.

Yesterday, after leaving the cabin Alise had called home, they had not crossed a road or seen any other sign of civilization, which Mal found encouraging. He hoped that with just another day or two of travel they would reach the truly wild country he had heard and read about, where those wanted posters—and the lawmen and bounty hunters who might carry them—would be few and far between. Maybe then he could stop looking over his shoulder so much. The life of an outlaw was not nearly as glamorous as all the fiction written about Turpin made it out to be.

A small iron pot was half filled with ice and this Mal moved to the edge of the fire. The night before he had melted snow for drinking water, and what was left froze overnight. Digging around in the sack of foodstuffs, Mal found a bag half full of roasted coffee beans, and he put a couple of handfuls into the pot once the ice melted. He soaked the beans to soften them, so he could use the butt of his pistol to grind them down, as he lacked a mortar and pestle. While he waited he reflected on Lute's pre-occupation with Turpin. He blamed himself. He had been the only one to attend school for any length of time. Like their mother, Lute couldn't read a lick, so Mal had read to him at night, and early on it was evident that his younger brother much preferred being regaled with the outlandish adventures of the Great Highwayman found in the hugely popular *Black Bess; or, The Knight of the Road*, a 254-part penny dreadful, over any other book or pamphlet his brother had produced. Mal had been able to get his hands on a dozen or so issues of the *Black Bess* serial and that was more than enough to keep Lute entertained, even after listening to them many times over.

Dick Turpin was also the subject of William Ains-worth's novel *Rookwood*, a number of well-known bal-lads, and a play. He had even earned a place in Madame Tussaud's wax museum. He was usually portrayed as a dashing gentleman bandit, protector of the weak, a modern-day Robin Hood. The truth about Turpin was quite dif-ferent from the legend. A butcher like his father, he had become involved with a gang of deer poachers who later turned to robbing the homes of gentlemen. Based in London—Turpin had even lived for a while in Whitechapel—the gang was notorious for beating their victims and raping the women, and before long most of Turpin's colleagues in crime were caught, tried, and hanged, their corpses left to rot in gibbets as a warning to the popu-lace. The elusive Turpin managed to remain free for a couple of years more and turned to horse stealing. In that period of time he committed at least one murder. He escaped the authorities after a fight at the Red Lion Inn in Whitechapel in which his friend and accomplice Matthew King was shot—some said by Turpin himself. Shortly after that he was caught, found guilty of stealing three horses, and hanged.

Despite the fact that Turpin had been glamorized in the fiction written about him, there was plenty of evidence to show that he was a violent and unprincipled rogue. But Mal saw no point in bringing this up with Lute. His kid brother wouldn't believe it. His mind was made up. And he really did believe that there was something glamorous about the life of a brigand, despite the hardships that visited a man on the run, and the never-ending anxiety that came from knowing a prison cell, the gallows, or the grave was almost certainly one's destination.

When Mal began smashing the softened coffee beans in the frying pan they had appropriated from the cabin, along with the pot and foodstuffs, he made enough noise to rouse the woman. He noticed her sitting upright, the blanket pulled up over her breasts, watching him with those piercing, emerald-green eyes. When he looked at her she self-consciously pushed her mussed brown hair away from her face and managed a timid smile. Mal glanced at Lute, still sound asleep, and shook his head. "My brother is a real shirkster."

"Brother? I had no idea you two were brothers. You don't look at all alike."

Mal went back to smashing the coffee beans in the rasher wagon. When, a moment later, he glanced at her again, she was looking at the horses, and he said, sternly, "Don't try to run. I've had enough trouble of late."

"I won't," she murmured earnestly. "I don't have anyplace to run to."

Pouring steaming-hot water from the pot into a cup, Mal added some of the coffee grounds. While he waited for these to sink, he glanced again at Alise. "I'm thinking you were a dollymop at one point."

"A what?"

"Prostitute. Baroness or dollymop, I really don't care. It's how easily you have adapted to this situation that made me wonder."

Alise cautiously tried to read his expression before responding. Clearly he wasn't at all concerned about insulting her, and she fleetingly entertained the notion of pretending that she was offended, then decided not to risk it because she didn't know him very well. While he seemed to be in a fairly decent humor, there was a ferocity about him simmering right below the surface. She wasn't ashamed of what she was, but she knew that people responded to women like her in drastically different ways and she had reached the point where she didn't really care what people thought of her.

She nodded. "It's true. I am, or was. Then Isaac came along, throwing a lot of money around. He was a hunter for a railroad, you see. They paid hunters real good 'cause they was obliged to feed all the men on the work crews, you know. I thought he would take care of me. Least he said he would. He liked the idea of having his own personal whore, I guess." She smirked. "And me, I was fine with that. Having just one man on top of you every day is better than ten. Then the troubles began. The railroads started failing, or at least stopped laying new track. Ended up Isaac couldn't do more than keep some food on the table." She twirled hair around her finger as she paused and considered her next words. "Don't get me wrong. He wasn't bad to me or anything. I mean, not real bad. But

I'm kind of glad to be gone from that place." She looked at Mal speculatively. "You and your brother are outlaws, I'm guessing." She looked at him with her eyebrows rising.

Mal had made her a cup of coffee and held it out to her. "A couple of regular Dick Turpins, we are," he said drily.

Alise took the cup gratefully, warming her hands around it. She glanced at Lute, who was beginning to stir but wasn't quite awake. "Well, from what he told me last night, it sounds better than what I've had. More . . . exciting." She glanced sidelong at Mal and smiled a slow, carnal smile. "And being the captive of two dashing bandits, well, there are worse fates. I mean I know I said one man was better but . . ." She shrugged. "So you two are wanted for something? Are you robbers?"

"We've been a lot of things." Mal didn't want to ruin the morning by being specific. That he and Lute were wanted for the murder of the Badham woman in England—and no doubt before long there would be wanted posters out on them for the killing of the two lawmen on the *Mustang*, as well—might prompt Alise into believing she would be better served trying to escape. And if she tried that, Lute would kill her. Even though he considered her an inconvenience, Mal didn't want her dead. It wasn't that one more body left along the trail would make things worse for him and his brother. As far as Mal was concerned, the goal of misleading the law into thinking they had remained east of the Brazos was unreachable now, with the death of Alise's man. Tracks in the snow would tell an experienced lawman or bounty hunter all he needed to know. For once, Mal hoped for fresh snow, since it might serve to cover or at least confuse the trail they had left. Ordinarily he hated snow. He had gotten his fill of it in London. Although he had never seen New York City or Paris or Rome he felt confident that London had the worst climate of any city in the world, and the long winters were a big part of the reason.

Snow had played a big role in his enduring dream of sailing to tropical isles and living in a paradise that was balmy year-round while cavorting with beautiful half-clad native women. What English boy didn't dream of such an adventure following the much-publicized events of HMS *Bounty*? The mutineers who had commandeered the ship, commanded by Captain William Bligh during an expedition to obtain breadfruit trees on the island of Tahiti, had committed the crime not because Blight was a cruel captain—by all accounts he wasn't—but rather because they had been seduced by the opportunity to live the very same dream Mal Litchfield had harbored since childhood. Everyone knew the story, thanks to Bligh, who had written *A Narrative of the Mutiny on Board His Majesty's Ship "Bounty"* following his acquittal at the court-martial that inquired into the loss of the ship to the mutineers.

"So you're on the run, heading west," mused Alise aloud. "Maybe you're going to San Francisco? That's where I hoped to end up when I left home back in Alabama. I hear it's quite a place. A place a person can get plenty rich. Even now, long after the big gold rush."

"You fell short of the mark by a good bit," observed Mal.

"Plenty of marks with pockets full of coin."

"You mean for you or for us?" he asked wryly.

Alise shrugged, smiling coyly. "There's nothing between here and there, from what I've heard. And sure, maybe I could work in one of those fancy houses I hear tell of."

Mal glanced at her, smirking. "So your dream was to be a soiled dove in some fancy bordello, plying your trade in a plush four-poster bed with a feather mattress and silk sheets. Until you found some bloke who seemed to have money and who became infatuated with you and wanted to have you around all the time, to poke for free whenever he had the need."

His words put her on the defensive. "Well, at least I give them something in return for their money. That's more than you can say."

Mal chuckled. She had spirit. Nothing like the fire Sylvie had, though. He sighed as he thought about her—the pretty French prostitute who had been the Litchfield brothers' partner in crime back in London—until Lute had killed her. Or maybe it was the mention of San Francisco. Compared with London, San Francisco was quite a bit closer to that paradise that had fueled his dreams all these years. "As for San Francisco . . ." He shrugged. "Who knows? Won't do to make big plans when you're on the run. It's best just to be happy you get through the day without being shot, or crapped." He noticed the perplexed look on her face. "Hanged," he explained.

Alise touched her neck while keeping her arms pressed against her sides, in this way keeping the blanket up over her breasts. "They . . . wouldn't hang me if they caught us . . . would they?"

"Who can say what men will do when the bloodlust is up?"

Alise fell silent, and Mal gulped down the rest of his coffee, now cold. A moment later, with a cautious glance at Lute to determine that he was still asleep, she murmured, trying to look coy, "Would you want me to come warm you up a little?"

"No. You're Lute's whore, not mine. My brother doesn't like to share. In fact, if history teaches us anything, he will most likely kill you if he catches you with someone else."

"Oh." She looked crestfallen. So much for working in a famous Frisco bordello. Mal felt a little sorry for her.

Lute sat up abruptly and pulled the dead lawman's pistol out from under the blanket, where he had kept it while he slept. He pressed the barrel against Alise's temple. She tensed and cried out and was so startled she let the blanket fall down around her waist. Lute chuckled, took the cup from her shaking hand, and drank the quickly cooling coffee it contained. "Mal's right. You're my whore from now on," he said with melodramatic menace. "So you can forget about your dreams. You had better convince me that you have. Show me why I shouldn't kill you right here and now." Then he laughed at the terrified expression on the young woman's face and pushed her down, rolling on top of her and laying the pistol aside. "Aye, I'm a highwayman and I take what I want! And right now that's you."

Mal got up and saddled his horse while Lute dabbed the whore. He wasn't envious of his brother. Women had their uses, but he had never allowed himself to become attached to one, though that might have happened with Sylvie had she lived a little longer. He certainly didn't obsess over the opposite sex the way his brother did, and he had no intention of laying a hand on Alise—she wasn't worth the trouble it might provoke. He would have preferred she wasn't even with them, but he just had to hope that having her along would keep Lute from wandering off and getting into trouble in the future.

He soon learned how foolish it was to entertain such hopes.

By the time Lute was done Mal had both horses saddled. "What about breakfast?" asked Lute as he started pulling his pants on. "I'm starving."

"We don't have many provisions. One meal a day, for now. No telling when we'll find some more."

"We have guns. We can hunt something."

"We have pistols, and precious little ammunition."

"I'm surprised you don't know how to set a snare for a rabbit," remarked Lute. "You know everything except that, I guess. You set plenty of snares for marks. Maybe we'll stay lucky and find another farm."

Mal glared at him. "No more farms. No more bodies."

A disgruntled Lute muttered about going hungry while he finished dressing, literally yanking the blankets away from Alise and snapping at her to get dressed while he rolled the blankets and tied them behind the saddle on the chestnut. He didn't like being talked to like that in front of Alise. It pricked his pride. But he knew by his brother's tone of voice that he needed to take him seriously. Mounting, he pulled the woman up behind him and they were off, with Mal leading the way. Emerging from the thicket, Mal checked the sky. It wasn't always easy to determine direction when the skies were overcast, but it was early morning and obvious that the cloud cover along the eastern horizon was a bit lighter than the rest.

They negotiated some thinly timbered hills sloping to the south and late in the morning came to thicker timber. Eventually they approached a bluff that steered them south a spell, and then the country began to open up and they spotted a small valley ahead of them. The first thing that caught Mal's attention was a haze of wood smoke; then he saw the sod house. The valley was shaped like a dog's hind leg, with the biggest part, the upper thigh, nearest. It was here that the house had been constructed, along with an outhouse, a smoke-or springhouse, and a large pen made with a palisade of vertical posts. Next to this was a smaller pole corral holding a couple of horses. Mal didn't know much about farming but common sense made him think that the larger pen had been made to hold livestock smaller than a horse or cow. The hills all around were wooded. A creek meandered past the homestead before making its serpentine way down the valley, exiting at the far end. The problem, in Mal's view, was that there was very little cover in the valley, just a batch of brush here and there along the creek, which was sporadically lined with willows and sweet gum. "We'll have to stay up here in the trees and circle around," he told Lute. "Stay out of sight."

A man emerged from the sod house and walked to the stream, getting down on one knee at the water's edge and smashing the coat of ice covering the water with a hatchet. Then he moved to the pen. He opened a gate and entered the enclosure and it was then that Mal saw the sheep the pen contained, which had been huddled together in a bunch up against the northern side of the palisade where they were best protected from the wintry blasts that occasionally swept across the little valley. The man's entrance caused the animals to stir. With their grayish-white fleece they were hard to see against the snow-covered ground until they moved. Seeing the man made Mal eager to move along, so he put his horse into motion. Lute began to follow, then sawed on the reins so abruptly it made the chestnut balk. The horse could sense that Lute was an uncertain rider, and it didn't have the best temperament to start with, so it objected to nearly everything Lute tried to make it do that didn't entail standing still. "Mal! Look!" exclaimed Lute. "Mutton on the hoof!"

"Forget it. Keep moving."

Lute went from excited to petulant in an instant. "The hell you say! Damn your eyes, Mal. I'm bloody hungry! And I haven't enjoyed a good leg of mutton in months.

And you said so yourself—no way of knowing when we'll find more provisions. Well, there are provisions right down there! In the house and on the hoof!" He yanked on the reins to turn the chestnut and then kicked it mercilessly until it broke into a run down the slope. Alise's arms tightened around Lute's midsection as she held on for dear life.

Mal opened his mouth to shout at his brother to to turn back. But Lute had acted quick as thought—or without thinking, mused Mal angrily—and was already so far away that he would have to shout at the top of his lungs for his brother to hear him. Surrounded by bleating sheep, the herder in the pen had not yet heard Lute's horse at the gallop, but he might hear a shout from the top of a hill. Cursing vehemently, Mal flew into a rage. The horse beneath him sensed his strong emotion and danced nervously beneath him. For the second time in Mal's life he had the urge to abandon his younger brother. The first time had been when Lute butchered Sylvie in that Whitechapel back alley. He wanted to now because he *knew* this wasn't about mutton and an empty stomach, at least not entirely. This was about Lute's hunger for killing. The gun to Alise's head this morning should have been a warning that Lute Litchfield was in a sanguinary mood. If Lute killed a person or two every day they would have half of Texas on their heels and would meet their doom sooner rather than later. He had to stop, but Mal didn't know how to stop Lute short of killing him. The words of Coleridge came to him . . . *"God save thee, Ancient Mariner! / From the fiends that plague thee thus . . ."* His own brother was the albatross around his neck, and since he couldn't kill his own brother, if he simply rode away now he would be rid of Lute and have a far better chance of staying alive.

The homesteader was herding the bleating sheep out of the pen to let them drink from the stream. Now Mal understood why he had taken a hatchet to the ice beforehand. The flock numbered about thirty animals, and they compliantly moved in a slowly spreading phalanx to the water's edge. The door of the sod house opened and a black-and-white dog bolted out and began herding the sheep. A raven-haired woman stood in the doorway. It was she who first saw Lute riding in hell-for-leather and called out to the homesteader, a stocky man with a mop of russet hair, who took one look at Lute then turned and shouted something at the woman. Mal kicked his horse into motion, cursing long and fervently under his breath as he rode down the slope and out into the open, following in his brother's wake. The redheaded man snapped a command that galvanized the dog into action. It began barking up a storm, nipping at heels and running back and forth so fast it was a blur, and the sheep began splashing across the shallow stream as the dog herded them away from the house, a few foundering as the thin coating of ice gave way under the herd's combined weight. Meanwhile, the redheaded man loped toward the sod house and was getting close when the woman emerged and handed him a double-barreled shotgun.

When Mal saw the sheepherder arming himself, he pulled the Gasser out of his coat and shouted a warning to Lute, who was thirty yards ahead of him—a warning lost in a sudden flurry of gunshots. Lute was shooting at the sheep and Mal had to wonder if he was even aware that the homesteader was now armed. Several of the animals went down, writhing in agony. Lute was not a good shot, especially from a distance, so he didn't manage to kill a single one right off, even when shooting into the thick of them. He finally looked around at Mal, and then in the direction of the sod house—just as the homesteader brought the shotgun to shoulder. By this time the chestnut, unchecked, had carried him and Alise to within twenty feet of the man.

Yanking instinctively on the reins hard enough to make the chestnut lock its back legs, hooves plowing up a spray of snow and nearly sitting down, Lute had a split second to react. He hurled himself off the horse with such violence that he broke free of Alise's embrace—she had been holding on for dear life as he rode headlong down the hill. Before Lute's body hit the ground the shotgun boomed and the buckshot from both barrels caught Alise squarely in the chest. She was beginning to fall backward over the cantle as the chestnut's croup dropped, easily dislodged now that she no longer had Lute to hold on to. Several buckshot hit the chestnut in the neck up near the crest. Lute landed clumsily, on his right side, and felt a lancing, breathtaking pain shoot through his shoulder. The impact jarred his pistol loose and knocked the wind out of him. He lay there, stunned and hurting, an anguished wheezing issuing from his throat.

As the chestnut kicked and then took off in a gallop, uttering a shrill whinny of pain and indignation, the homesteader saw that Lute wasn't getting up right away. He was also aware of Mal bearing down on him. The woman was standing paralyzed in the doorway and he yelled at her to get inside, then stepped toward Lute, chiding himself for shooting both barrels in his panic-stricken haste. In the ten years he had been trying to make a living and raise a family in this valley he had only shot at someone one time. He had been searching for a ewe that had slipped away unseen by his dog. While scouring the timber up on the hills, he'd heard a single rifle shot, and a short while later came up on a man skinning the dead ewe. You didn't leave the house without a weapon in this country, and he'd had the shotgun with him and cut loose with one barrel, too far away to do much damage, just hoping to run the sheep killer off. He assumed the man was a hungry drifter and didn't really want to kill him anyway.

A little farther west, in cattle-ranching country, cowmen had a low opinion of sheep and the men who raised them, and it wasn't unheard of for cowboys to come swooping down on a flock with guns blazing. But these two men today were no cowboys. He knew that much in a glance. The horses they rode, the rigs they sat on, the clothes they wore—none of it was genuine ranch hand. Even so, he had little doubt they would shoot more than sheep.

He saw Lute's pistol lying in the snow and bent to retrieve it, trying to remember how many shots this sheep killer had fired, deciding he didn't have time to open the cylinder and check. He stared in horror at the body of the woman he had shot and hesitated a fateful second, trying to decide whether he should shoot the man on the ground before he managed to get up, or try to hit the horseman barreling down on him. He wasn't much of a shot, so he opted for the closer, slower-moving target; additionally, for most men shooting accurately from atop a galloping horse was difficult, and he could only hope it would be so for the mounted man bearing down on him. With the empty scattergun gripped in his left hand, he thumbed back the hammer of the Colt revolver, trying to steady his shaking hand and make one shot count—an instant before Mal's bullet struck him in the temple.

Mal made the shot from sixty feet away astride a running horse. Seeing that the sheepherder was about to shoot his brother, he had gone for the head shot as the only sure way to prevent that from happening. As he began to check his horse, he saw the woman burst through the doorway of the sod house and thought for an instant she was going to fly to her man's corpse. Instead, she went for Lute's pistol, now dropped for the second time. Realizing he wasn't going to be able to stop the horse in time, he rode right at her, sawing on the reins at the last instant to turn the horse. The sorrel's barrel collided with the woman just as she straightened with the pistol in hand and sent her sprawling. She lost her grip on the sidegun and as soon as she went down she was crawling, reaching frantically for it. Mal managed to get down off the horse and plant his foot on the weapon at the same time her fingers touched it.

"Don't," he said, calmly. "Just don't do it."

She looked up at him then, a blank expression on her face, but her eyes were the windows through which he saw the flood of overwhelming emotions in that moment— fear, anger, and, most of all, grief. She didn't obey him, instead curling her fingers around the revolver's grip, and he didn't waste time trying to get through to her. He bent over, grabbed the pistol by the barrel, and yanked it out of her grasp before she could slip a finger through the trigger guard. As he turned to see to his brother, the woman rolled over and crawled on hands and knees to the sheepherder's corpse. When she saw that the side of his skull had been cracked open by Mal's bullet, she sat on her heels and her hands flew to her face but she didn't make a sound. Mal glanced at her and felt a sudden, surging rage. He turned on Lute.

"You've done it again now, haven't you! Get up!" He grabbed Lute by the arm and hauled him roughly to his feet. "Get up, goddamn you!"

Lute gasped and winced at the breathtaking pain that

shot through him. Hunched over, he held his right arm tightly against his side. "I—I think I broke my arm," he whined. Mal was looking down at the dead man and the woman kneeling and rocking back and forth, the soundless wail still caught on her tongue, and so Lute looked too. "I don't know what I'm supposed to have done," he said, with the petulant outrage of the falsely accused. "You're the one who shot him, I didn't."

"I shot him," said Mal grimly, "because he was about to kill you. And to think, when you came charging down here I just about rode off and left you."

Lute shook his head. "You would never do that! You made a promise to Mum." Seeing the fury etched on Mal's face, his tone became less stridently defensive and more deferential. "All we have is each other now. Look, I'm sorry. I was . . . I was just bored, okay? It's just . . . when the sheep started running seemed like it would be fun to shoot some of them, that's all."

Trying to tamp down his anger, Mal shook his head in disgust and took a long look around. The sheep were well scattered now and far afield. One had succumbed to its wounds and lay a stone's throw away on the other side of the creek. The dog was nowhere to be seen. He turned his attention to Alise and fresh anger surged through him again. He spun Lute around and pointed at the woman's corpse. "Well, you won't be having any more fun with her now, will you," he snapped crossly, handing Lute his gun back. Lute took it with his left hand. He kept his right arm tight against his side.

Lute had been so focused on saving his own life, and then the lancing pain in his shoulder, that he had completely forgotten about Alise. "Just my bloody luck," he muttered, frowning at her corpse. "I was starting to like her."

Mal huffed incredulously. He glanced at the sod house,

realizing that more than two people might live here. The door was ajar, the interior dark. He turned to the woman kneeling by the dead sheepherder. "Just the two of you live here?" Immersed in inconsolable grief, she didn't seem to hear him. She sobbed quietly, tears streaming down her cheeks. Mal was short on patience. Grabbing her by the arm, he pulled her roughly to her feet, spinning her to face the cabin door and wrapping a burly arm around her waist to hold her in front of him. His right hand, holding the Gasser, was down at his side. Bowing his head down he murmured in her ear, "If there is someone in there you really should call out to them. Tell them to show themselves—and make very sure their hands are empty." His voice was soft, but the menace was like cold, sharp steel.

He felt her body stiffen. Her head came up. "There is no one," she said flatly.

"I'm not sure I believe that." He looked around at Lute. "You think you can keep an eye on her while I look inside?"

Lute was pale. His features were drawn tight with pain. "I think I broke my arm, Mal."

Mal muttered a curse and frog-marched the woman to the door, kicking it wide open before pushing her inside. The interior of the sod house was not markedly different from the cabin where Alise had lived with the hunter. It struck him that these frontier people did not have much more in the way of personal belongings than Whitechapel's poor. What they did have, though, was their own land, and it was the land that could make all the difference. With the land there came hope, and hope was something that was notably lacking in the poorhouses back home. He felt a kind of comradeship with this woman—and her dead husband outside. They were poor people, like his own family. But they had been given an opportunity to make something of themselves and worked hard to do just that. And then he and Lute had come along. As Lute trailed in behind them, Mal looked at his brother with disgust, but managed to hold his tongue. A sweeping glance around the cabin was enough to convince him that the woman had been telling the truth. There was no one else here. He released her. She turned to face them and took a few steps backward until she fetched up against a rough-hewn counter. Grimacing, Lute sat down on a three-legged stool near the fireplace, where the orange glowing embers of a morning fire still provided some warmth. He bent over and groaned.

"He dislocated his shoulder," she said. "It ain't broken or he'd be making a lot more noise. I'll set it. Give you some food. If then you'll just ride away and . . ." She had to stop and fight back the tears. "Ride away and leave me to bury my man."

Mal admired her fortitude. He nodded, lifting his peacoat to shove the Gasser under his belt at the small of the back. "You have my word."

At her direction he helped Lute get to his feet and move to the bed. She had Lute lay so that his right arm and shoulder hung over the edge of the bed. Pulling a chair up, she took hold of Lute's right wrist with both hands, placed a bare foot against his armpit, and slowly, steadily, began pulling the arm away from the body. Lute groaned through clenched teeth, body stiffening, arcing, and Mal had to hold him down until, the muscles stretched, the joint popped back into place. The woman got up and went to a trunk in the corner and, sitting on her heels, opened it, telling Mal she was going to make a sling for Lute's arm.

Lute waited until she was across the room then grabbed the lapel of his brother's peacoat and pulled him closer.

"We need to take her with us."

"No," said Mal, adamantly.

"I need a woman."

"You'll have to go without for a while." He glanced over his shoulder and saw her standing there. She was looking understandably afraid, and her brightly gleaming eyes told him that she wasn't sure he would keep his word. "We had an accord, and I intend to keep my end," he said, hoping to reassure her.

Lute was irate. He was accustomed to getting his way. "No! She's coming with us!"

"You lay a hand on her and I'll break it. Now go and find your horse."

"But you said we wouldn't leave any witnesses behind us," replied Lute, sullenly. He had made Mal angry before, but there was something different about this time. Not one to consider the consequences of his actions, the fact that his older brother had even thought about leaving him to his own devices shocked him. Even so, he felt compelled to complain.

"Aye, I did. But if you will recall, that was to leave no evidence of the direction we were taking after we got off that riverboat." For his part, Mal had in the past tried to explain those decisions of his that ran counter to what Lute wanted, in the hope that Lute would learn something. He realized now that there was no more hope of Lute becoming more circumspect in his actions than there was of his acquiring a conscience. "Killing Alise's husband probably ruined any hope of that. And now . . . this."

"You shot her man," said Lute, gesturing at the woman. "Not me."

"I had to because you were too busy shooting sheep to notice he was aiming a shotgun at you, you bloody glock."

Lute fumed in silence a moment, then shook his head as he turned resentfully toward the door. "I can't believe you'd cut me over that worthless twist there," he groused with a surly look at the woman.

"Hurry the hell up," Mal barked as Lute went outside, then turned back to the woman. "I'm sorry," he said gruffly. "Sorry for killing your man. But . . . I had to. That's my brother and . . . well, he's all the family I have left."

"You have more than I do now," she snapped, and the anger was responsible for the way her nostrils flared as she lifted her chin at a defiant angle.

"Close and bar the door," he said as he turned to go outside. "Don't come out until you're certain we're gone."

Lute was coming around the side of the house when he stepped outside. "Bloody horse ran up into the trees," groused Lute. "I went all the way to the top of the hill but I don't see it."

Mal spotted his horse standing nearby and was relieved when the animal let him walk up and climb into the saddle. Lute got on behind and they rode up the hill, following the errant chestnut's tracks in the snow. Reaching the top of the hill, Mal saw that the timber thickened on the other side. The wounded horse was nowhere to be seen, and Mal wasn't surprised. Ever since the confrontation with the coppers on the *Mustang* they had been dogged by one mishap after another. He had to believe the law was on their trail now, and he was not inclined to linger in the valley looking for a horse that didn't want to be caught up. Without a word he rode into the deeper woods, with only his innate sense of direction to guide him.

Day Seven

CHAPTER SIXTEEN

Sprawled in a rocking chair close by the fireplace, Purdy was adrift in that place between waking and dreaming where the physically exhausted and emotionally distraught often find themselves. She heard a rhythmic tapping sound and found herself at the Cameron undertaker's, watching the man hammer nails into the lid of her son's coffin, sickened by the realization that she had just looked her last upon Joshua Eddings, her flesh, her blood, her joy. She couldn't breathe, and gasped sharply as her eyes flashed wide open, glimmering with tears. The tapping continued and she knew then it was not the undertaker sealing her boy's mortal remains in a pine box but someone knocking on the farmhouse door. Buck was lying at her feet and had raised his head, looking at the door. An irrational fear gripped Purdy. She had this crazy idea it was Norris, standing just outside the door, knock, knock, knocking, his throat still a mass of brutalized flesh, his arm and chest shattered by buckshot. She wondered why Buck wasn't barking up a storm. Perhaps the graveness of his injury had taken too much out of him. Trembling, she moved hesitantly toward the door, then decided to peek out the window first. She was able to breathe again when she saw the corpse still sprawled in the snow. The tapping continued. She opened the door.

A woman stood there in shadows that were gathering under the porch roof in the half-light of those moments when day succumbed to night. She was short and slender and getting on in years, if her long gray hair and creased face were any indication. But her bright, inquisitive eyes and her warm, gentle smile seemed ageless. "Oh good, you're still here!" she exclaimed with girlish delight. She had Purdy's black-and-gray scarf in her hand and now held it out. "This is yours, I believe."

Purdy stared at the scarf a moment and felt remorse as she remembered wrapping it around her naked shoulders right before wading into the Little River to end her existence. Had that happened only yesterday? Time had ceased to matter the way it once had. In fact, she wondered if she had been standing there, staring at the scarf for too long, and looked apologetically at the visitor. "I'm sorry. Yes . . . yes it's mine. But . . . how did you come by it?"

"The river sent it to me. I found it today, caught on some wood along the water's edge right near my raft."

"Your raft?"

"Mhm. I live on a raft a mile or so downriver. Have for many years. It is all I need or want. There is a little shanty on it, you see. The river provides me with plenty of fish and fresh water year-round. I wouldn't want to live in town. Too crowded." She held the scarf up a bit higher than before. "Your scarf, dear?"

Purdy took the scarf, suddenly feeling quite ashamed. She didn't care to explain how her scarf had come to be in the river. "Thank you," she murmured. "I-I was trying to remember where I lost it."

The woman nodded and smiled. "My name is Mary." She glanced over her shoulder at the corpse of George

Norris. "Seems we've lost one of our neighbors," she added, matter-of-factly.

Mary's detachment when it came to a dead body struck Purdy as rather odd. And while it didn't seem as though her visitor was going to ask questions regarding the corpse, the way most people would, she nonetheless felt compelled to explain. "I had to do it. He was going to kill my dog, who was only trying to protect me." She glanced at Buck, who was still beside the fireplace. She noted that he didn't look alarmed at all, which was odd, as Buck never liked strangers. He didn't seem to mind the old woman at all. Or maybe this uncommon complacency was due to his injury. "And Buck, well, he's all I've got left. I thought I'd lost him too, but he came back to me."

Mary nodded. "I confess I never liked Mr. Norris. He was not a good man. No person is born bad but sometimes they go too far down the wrong path to be saved. Maybe next time."

"Next time? What do you mean?"

Mary made a don't-mind-me gesture. "Oh, it's not important right now. Please forgive an old woman for blathering—and for not minding my business—but you probably shouldn't leave him lying out there too long. Will attract the wrong kind of varmints."

Purdy sighed, nodding. "Yes. Like sheriffs." She had tried to put her mind to the problem but just hadn't been able to. She was tired of thinking about death. Trying to dig a grave in the frozen ground was more than she could do. Norris had outweighed her by quite a lot, and she couldn't drag the corpse any great distance. She didn't even feel like making all these points to Mary as justification for leaving the dead man where he lay, so instead she stepped aside and made a gesture for the visitor to enter. "I'm sorry. Where are my manners? Please, come warm yourself by the fire." She glanced again at Buck, whose tail was actually thumping slowly on the floor as the old woman drew closer. "My dog doesn't mind, it seems."

"Thank you, dear. I could stand a bit of warming up. I do believe Norris had a plow mare. I'll go fetch it, and we'll use it to drag the body back to his property. Otherwise you might have coyotes visiting or, worse, a cougar."

"I don't know," said Purdy. "I mean, I'm not sure what to do with the body." A thought occurred to her. "How did you know that was my scarf?"

"You were wearing it at the cemetery the other day. I am so very sorry about your son. I didn't know. Just happened to go to town that day. Noticed people heading to the cemetery and followed out of curiosity, I suppose. Funny how things happen sometimes, isn't it?"

Purdy nodded. "I didn't see you there. I'm surprised I haven't *ever* seen you, since we're neighbors."

Mary chuckled warmly. "I am often overlooked," she said wryly as she built up the fire with fresh wood and then stood right next to Buck and rubbed her hands together in the toasty-warm updraft.

"How long have you lived around here?"

"A long, long time." The old woman nodded and smiled. "I knew your pa, in fact. Even rode on his riverboat once. My, that was a long time ago!" She cupped her chin and looked up at the rafters in a thoughtful pose. "Going on thirty years now."

Purdy sank into the rocking chair, watching the flames cavort under and around the firewood. "You've been alone on a raft all that time?"

Mary turned and looked at her with a soft and sympathetic smile on her lips. "I had a husband, and two strapping sons. My husband was a good man, a farmer. But he had a powerful dislike for Mexicans. I think it was because his father died at the Alamo. I don't think it was so much that he died fighting for Texas. It was how Santa Anna ordered all the bodies of the defenders piled up and burned. Anyway, he wanted to fight in the Mexican War but by the time he got down there, word came that Winfield Scott had captured Mexico City and the volunteer company he had joined turned right around and came home. Then, back in '59, when Juan Cortina quarreled with the town marshal of Brownsville and ended up taking over the whole town, my husband rode south to help take it back. But once again he was too late. He was on his way home and just a few miles shy of it when his horse threw him on account of a rattler. Best we could tell, the fall broke his back and the rattler killed him off."

"My God," said Purdy. "How terrible."

Mary sat on a three-legged stool that stood off to one side of the hearth, and Purdy felt a pang in her heart because the stool had been where Joshua sat on cold winter evenings while she read to him from the Bible. "Both my sons went off to fight in the War Between the States," said the old woman. "One for the North, one for the Confederate states. Lot of people on either side of that war here in Texas. Think we would have all been better off staying out of it. I would have, because neither one of my boys came back. I never knew exactly what happened to them or where, but I'm sure they would have come back to me had they survived."

Purdy was astonished by how dispassionately Mary spoke of these tragedies. "I couldn't hold on to the farm and wasn't sure what would become of me," continued the visitor. "And then one day I was walking along the river looking for a likely place to camp for the night and fish for my supper when I came upon the raft. Found a skeleton in a chair in the cabin. There was a parchment pinned to its jacket. Last will and testament it was. 'I, William Henry Tasker, trader, of sound mind even though my body is ailing, leave all my belongings, which includes my raft, to the first person who discovers my remains, since they are no damned good to me anymore.'" Mary smiled softly. "Just when you think you have no prospects, no hope, no luck . . ."

Purdy was staring at her. Here was a woman who had lost everything, including *two* sons—and she had survived. "You must have been so lonely."

"I was lonely sometimes, yes. But I was never alone. No, never." Mary leaned forward, reaching out to put a hand on top of Purdy's, where it rested on the arm of the rocking chair. "You can't be, as long as the ones you love are in your heart and your thoughts, dear. Do you know why you won't let go of this place?"

"How do you know I won't?"

Mary just smiled. "For one thing, it is your duty to hold on to it. You did, after all, take an oath at your wedding. In sickness or in health. For richer or poorer. In other words, no matter what, you will keep this fire burning. And this is your son's home. He is still here. Surely you feel him. I can. If you left this place he would be lost. So you see, you are doing the right thing. The only thing you *can* do as a loving wife and mother."

Purdy fiercely fought back the tears. She was sick of crying. "My husband is in prison . . . for thirteen more years."

"Thirteen years." Mary squeezed her hand. "That's not too long. I've lived much longer than that without my husband."

"Yes. Yes, you have, haven't you," murmured Purdy,

realizing, for the first time, that thirteen years wasn't forever.

Mary sat back and looked around the house. "Your dog came back to you. So will your husband. And your boy never left. Christmas is only a few days away. I'm sure your son loves Christmastime."

"Oh yes. Every winter Jake would go out and cut a pine sapling and we would decorate it. That was Josh's favorite thing to do. We would dip small pinecones in white or red wax and hang them on the tree. Jake would cut some tin into little stars and we'd paint them yellow and hang them too. And I would make a paper horn of plenty and fill it up with candy from the store in town for him." She paused, lost in a memories of better and brighter days, her eyes unfocused, tilting her head a little with a pensive smile touching the corners of her mouth. She thought she could hear boyish laughter, very faintly. Then the veil of melancholy fell back into place.

"Maybe you should put up a Christmas tree," suggested Mary softly. "He would like that, wouldn't he?"

"Yes. Yes, I suppose he would." Purdy looked at her visitor, eyes quite clear and focused now. "I believe I will."

"That's the spirit!" Mary was delighted. "I would love to stay and help, if you would let me."

Purdy didn't hesitate. Only a day or two ago she would have resented the intrusion, and especially resented the smiles and cheery tone; would have taken exception to anyone being in good spirits in a world where she had lost everything. But she found Mary's presence comforting. Reassuring. This woman had been through what she had been through. There wasn't a doubt in her mind that Mary's concern for her well-being was genuine. And it would be nice to have her around for Christmas.

"Of course. I would very much like for you to stay."

"Thank you, dear. You're so sweet." Mary squeezed her hand again. "Now if you will humor an old woman, I would be so relieved if you would lie down and get some rest. You look very tired. I'll watch over your faithful companion." She turned her smile on Buck, whose tail thumped on the floorboards again. "How long has it been since you've slept in your bed?"

Purdy looked over her shoulder at the bed in question. "I'm sure. It's been a while." That melancholy veil returned as she remembered what George Norris had done to her on that bed just two days ago. She was afraid the smell of him was on the sheet, the quilt. But she couldn't bring herself to say so. "But I don't think . . ."

"Now, now." Mary rose and headed for the bed, pulling off the rumpled quilt and linens. Opening the big trunk at the foot of the bed, she found clean sheets and a Cherokee Indian blanket and made the bed. "There we go! Now come, dear, and lie down. You look exhausted." She bent down and grabbed the quilt and soiled linens and headed for the door. "I'll air these out and then sit by the fire and get acquainted with your dog. What's his name?"

"Buck."

The big yellow dog lifted his head and looked at her, tail thumping yet again.

"The Indians call those ghost eyes," said Mary, studying Buck's eyes as she sat down on the stool again. "They would say that Buck here can see both Heaven and Earth—Earth with the brown eye and Heaven with the blue."

Purdy smiled warmly, rose from the rocking chair, and went to bed. She fell asleep as soon as she lay her head down. When she woke it was still daylight, and she felt rested but groggy and lay there a moment, staring at the ceiling, not thinking about anything, just marveling at how she felt. So relaxed. Then a sound from the main room made her turn her head. Mary was at the fireplace, moving the crane out in order to get to the kettle of steaming hot water that was hanging from it. Buck was standing up, sniffing at a pine sapling about five feet tall, which stood upright in a bucket filled with stones that kept it that way. When Purdy rolled over, the dog looked at her, then walked over. Astonished, she sat up and noticed that a dressing had been applied around his loins.

"Buck is feeling much better, dear," Mary said as she transported the kettle to the kitchen counter. "He's such a strong creature!"

Purdy breathed a sigh of vast relief. Buck *did* look much better, full of his usual vigor. He didn't appear in any sort of pain. She got out of bed and bent down and hugged him. It was then that she noticed her feet were clean. She rose to give the tree a closer inspection. Her nostrils flared as she caught the pine's strong, pleasant aroma, which permeated the house. She ran her fingers lightly over the bristly branches. Mary brought her a hot cup of coffee. As she took the cup, Purdy thanked her, and added, "You washed my feet."

"I took the liberty, yes. I hope you don't mind. They were filthy, dear, and you didn't want to soil those clean linens, now, did you? I hung the sheets and your quilt out on the porch, gave them a beating with the broom. Too cold to wash them right now. They would just freeze right up, stiff as boards."

Purdy became aware of the wind, gusts of wind that made the shutters rattle. She moved to the window and saw wisps of snow blowing across the field between the house and the river, looking like frosty ground fog. It was then that she noticed the body of George Norris was gone. She stared, the cup poised halfway to her lips.

Mary was hanging the kettle of water back on the crane. "I thought it right and proper to take our neighbor back to his home. I fetched his mule and since I couldn't lift him I tied him by the ankles to the mule and the mule dragged him."

Noting that the great splotches of blood marking the site of the battle between Norris and Buck had been covered by the wind-driven snow, Purdy took a deep breath and murmured, "I should go into town and tell Tom Rath what happened."

Mary came to her side and touched her arm. "You feel guilty. You took a life. Well, you and Buck did by the looks of it. And even if it was a bad man's life, it's normal for you to feel bad about it. Buck doesn't feel bad about it, though. He just did what had to be done. Of course, you did too."

"I know you're trying to make me feel better. But you don't know the whole story."

"What makes you think I don't?" Mary smiled gently. "Listen, dear. You did what you thought you had to do, and maybe you made a mistake or two. Making a mistake isn't wrong. Nobody's perfect. It's how close we can get to perfect that counts for anything, and one way we do that is learn from our mistakes."

Purdy stared at her. It sounded very much like Mary knew everything that had transpired between her and Norris. Perhaps she had heard all the rumors and assumed them to be true. But somehow Purdy didn't think Mary was the type to put stock in gossip. "George Norris won't learn from his mistake."

"What he did was wrong. And he knew it. Now, enough about him. He got what was coming to him. Let's talk about how we're going to decorate this beautiful tree!"

Purdy nodded, but instead of joining Mary at the table

she went back to the trunk at the foot of the bed and re-
moved from it a plain wooden box. Taking this back to
the table she unlatched and opened the box to take out a
piece of plank rag pulp paper, along with a small ink
bottle and a metal-nib pen. "I have to write a letter to Jake
first. There is something I forgot to tell him."

Mary's knowing smile gave Purdy the sense that her
visitor knew exactly what she had to write and why.

CHAPTER SEVENTEEN

Sayles and Eddings reached the sheepherder's place early in the morning. The sheepherder's wife had wrapped the corpses of Alise and of her husband in blankets and pulled them up close to the house, as she feared that the carcass of the dead sheep across the stream would attract coyotes and such. She told the Ranger what had transpired with an economy of words that Sayles found admirable, as was her ability to remain composed despite her grief. The sheepdog had returned and lay forlornly beside its dead master all the while.

What she had to say about the two men who had come and gone the day before gave him some insight into his prey. Their accents led her to believe they were British. Maybe Irish. She wasn't sure. The slender one was reckless, unpredictable, and without remorse. He had been the one the dead woman was riding double with, and the one who had wanted to take her with them, a replacement for the one her husband had inadvertently killed. The big one was a crack shot. He had to be that or damned lucky to make the shot the woman described, the one that had dropped her man in his tracks. And the news that one of their horses had run off gave Sayles hope that they were down to one mount, even though it was clear they had ridden off on the trail of the runaway.

The woman asked them to help her bury the dead. It would take her a long time, she explained, if she could even do it, digging two graves with shovel and hatchet in the frozen earth.

"We could," allowed Sayles. "But those men are less than half a day ahead of us. If I push hard, I might catch up to them before sundown, 'specially seeing as how they could be riding double. If we stay and help you, could be I'd still catch 'em, but the odds are longer. Reckon I'll let you decide what you want more."

Jake Eddings didn't fail to notice that the Ranger was talking like he didn't even exist. He sorely wanted to speak out, to tell Sayles that if he was entrusted with a gun he would be willing to help. But he already knew what the answer would be. The man didn't bend. He was a little surprised that Sayles hadn't just answered the woman's request with a flat-out no.

The woman didn't take long making the decision. Her eyes, pools of sorrow, suddenly glittered with a cold, hard anger. "I'll manage," she said firmly. "You go get the bastards who done this."

Sayles nodded, admiring her all the more. "I'll come back this way and let you know." He turned his attention to Eddings. "We're going to push the horses. They both got a lot of bottom."

Eddings grimaced. It sounded to him like a warning, like Sayles wondered if he could stay in the saddle, even with his hands free. "I may just be a farmer but I do know how to ride," he replied, sullenly.

The woman spoke up as Sayles started to turn the coyote dun. "You know who this dead woman was?"

"No idea. But her man is dead, too, killed by the same two men. We tracked them here from her place."

"It's a shame to leave a grave unmarked. But I guess nobody will be looking for her."

"A lot of unmarked graves in these parts," remarked Sayles. He touched the brim of his battered old campaign hat, reined the horse around, and gave it a tap with his spurs. The coyote dun broke into a canter and the bay startled Eddings by galloping right along after the dun without him having to do a thing.

It wasn't long before Sayles knew for a fact that the men he was after were riding the same horse. The runaway had gone over a nearby hill and down into thick woods. The men had followed and then turned to ride along the rim. He wondered if they knew they were heading north now, instead of west, the direction they had kept to since he'd started tracking them. There was little doubt in his mind that these two were the same ones who had killed the lawmen on that Brazos riverboat, or that their intention was to lose themselves in the vast stretch of mesquite plains to the west, a country well known only to Comanches, mustangers, hidehunters, and Texas Rangers.

A few hours later the wind began to blow from the north, escalating Eddings's misery. They had broken camp before dawn and set out without even a cup of coffee to warm their insides. The suit of plain brown wool Temple Hanley had bought for him to wear to his son's funeral didn't do much to cut that wind. He clenched his teeth so tight for so long just to keep them from chattering that his jaw ached. His envy of the Ranger, who seemed just as impervious to the bone-aching cold as he apparently was to all other discomforts, turned into outright resentment. He was like a wolf, relentless in pursuit of his prey.

Now and then Sayles would stop to survey the ground or countryside or both, and once Eddings checked the bay alongside him and in an exasperated tone asked, "You ever get tired?"

"I'm always tired. You get so you don't know how to be anything else. We're getting close. That horse is having a time carrying two men when it gets to deeper snow."

Eddings peered through the scattered trees ahead of them, then glanced at Sayles. He knew the Ranger had that Schofield pistol in his coat pocket. The Winchester was in its saddle boot. And the shotgun he had taken from one of the men he had gunned down on the road from Huntsville was lashed to the saddle under his left leg. "Give me a gun, Ranger. You don't need three."

"I don't need to get shot in the back either."

"I'm not a backshooter," snapped Eddings. "I just don't fancy riding up on men who have killed at least four people that we know of without a way to defend myself."

Sayles impaled him with his piercing steel-gray eyes. "So you're telling me you would pass up the chance to shoot me in the back and run free on account you hanker fer another thirteen years behind bars."

Eddings shook his head. "Well, let's get going then. I want to catch them as bad as you do. I'd rather get shot dead than freeze to death."

When he and Jake emerged from a thick stand of timber into a large clearing and saw the two men they had been tracking just about to ride into the trees on the far side, Sayles wasn't surprised. From what he could tell those two hadn't stopped to rest their mount all day long, and just by its tracks in the snow the Ranger could tell the horse was tuckered out. As he pulled the long gun from its scabbard he told Eddings to get back into the trees a way and wait for him. "You decide to hightail it I'll track you down even if it takes till next Christmas."

"What if . . ."

Sayles kicked the coyote dun into a canter, the butt of the Winchester resting on his thigh. He figured the distance between him and the two men was about 150 yards, and that he had about five seconds before they reached the timber. He could close the distance by thirty yards in that time, and while he was pretty sure he could hit the extra rider right now, even with the wind kicking up strong across the clearing and blowing right at him, closer would make it more of a sure bet. He wasn't too worried about the coyote dun getting hit. He had asked the sheepherder's widow about the guns the killers used, and he thought there was a good chance all they had were pistols. The old Walker Colt of thirty years ago had been advertised as being accurate at two hundred yards, when held with both hands on a solid rest, but not many men could make that shot with the Walker, and fewer still with pistols of more recent vintage. Based on what he knew about the killing of the sheepherder, at least one of those men was a sharpshooter, but if all he had was a pistol Sayles decided it would be more luck than skill if he hit anything farther out than a hundred yards. Then, too, two men on one tired horse were more likely to shoot him off the dun than to shoot the dun out from under him.

He glanced skyward. The day had seemed relatively brighter than previous ones. The overcast was thinning. The clouds were moving fast, something he hadn't seen in a while. Even so, darkness would come quickly when it came, and he figured there was no more than fifteen or twenty minutes of light left, at least light good enough to shoot by. He didn't fancy wandering through woods at night looking for a pair of desperadoes, and he couldn't track at night without moonlight. This coupled with the fact that in a handful of seconds his targets would be obscured gave him cause to hurry.

Pulling the Winchester from its scabbard, he checked the horse sharply and jumped out of the saddle, the reins gripped tightly in his left hand. This swung the horse around and he used the saddle to rest his long gun on while he drew a bead. All this happened in a heartbeat, and the Ranger's heart was beating slow and steady. He had done this many times before. His mind was occupied with range and windage and velocity and distance; he didn't have the time—or the inclination—to think about the fact that he was about to take a man's life. The coyote dun had plenty of experience in this too, and stood steady. Sayles squeezed the trigger, his target the middle of Lute Litchfield's back. Half the men he'd shot had been running away from him. If he called out for these two to surrender they wouldn't. They would either plunge into the woods or start shooting at him.

The Winchester barked and the dun didn't even flinch. The wind whipped the gunsmoke away and Sayles had a clear view of the results of the long shot. The impact of the bullet made Lute's body carom violently off Mal. The forward movement of the horse sent him somersaulting off the back.

Sayles was in the saddle by the time Lute hit the ground. Fighting on horseback seemed the most natural thing to him. Like most Rangers, the vast majority of his fighting had been done against Comanches, who shied away from standing their ground and blasting it out with their enemies. They fought on the move, and the Rangers had adapted. Most had trouble hitting their mark when astride a horse on the move, but Sayles and his kind excelled at it. Reining the dun around and kicking it into motion, once again heading straight for the enemy, he locked his horse-warped legs tight around the dun's barrel while he levered another round into the Winchester's chamber. Less than a hundred yards separated him from his prey now. He set stock to shoulder, took aim at the second man, who was dismounting, and squeezed the trigger.

Mal had checked and turned the horse and was leaping out of the saddle when he heard a loud *crack!* as the Ranger's bullet went right past his head, a sound that triggered a reflex and made him hurl himself down into the snow beside his brother. He pulled the Gasser revolver from his coat and crawled closer to Lute. Reaching out, he clutched his brother's arm, shaking it, calling out his name. Lute was unmoving, though. His body limp. Mal didn't want to believe that Lute was dead. He got up on his knees and grabbed the corpse, shaking it, trying to force some sort of response, hoping against hope and all reason. Then a bullet slammed into him, high on his left side, just missing the collarbone. He heard that *crack!* again when he was thrown violently back into the snow.

Cursing under his breath, Sayles reined in the dun and threw a leg over the pommel to make a running dismount. He had missed his mark not once but twice, and that boiled his water. Both shots had been meant to strike the second man dead center. It was something he could not fathom. Once he had his feet under him he gave the dun a whack on the rump to send it off. If he didn't, the horse would stand its ground, and it was partly for the horse that he was afoot now. He had a pretty good idea that the man who had been his first target was dead or dying. That meant the dun was suddenly expendable. The other reason was it seemed he was not the crack shot from the hurricane deck of a cayuse that he thought he was. Not much more than fifty yards from the two men, both downed now, he began moving forward in a stiff and ungainly lope, hoping he could get close enough for the killing shot.

Mal lay there, trying to breathe, staring up at the sky, catching glimpses of blue between the fast-moving clouds. Then the pain hit him, the most excruciating agony he had ever experienced. His body arched, then writhed in the snow, and he snarled like a wolf caught in a trap. But a sudden burst of rage trumped the breathtaking pain. It was that rage that made it possible, just then, for him to sit up. He couldn't seem to make his left arm work, but the right was just fine; he raised the pistol and with an incoherent roar of wrath emptied it at the man loping toward him.

Seeing Mal sit up didn't surprise Sayles. He knew the second shot had been a little too high. Coming to a stop, he dropped to one knee, Winchester brought to shoulder again.

Mal fired first—and at this range he couldn't miss.

From the other side of the clearing Jake Eddings watched, stunned, as Bill Sayles went down, thrown backward, rifle spinning away as he sprawled in the snow. He fully expected to see Sayles get up and come into view again. But as the seconds passed, the possibility that he was dead was what Eddings had to confront. He rejected that possibility at first, because it seemed impossible that anything but old age could take the Ranger. A cold and painful knot in the pit of his stomach, he tore his gaze away from the downed man and looked at the spot along the far tree line where he had last seen the two men they had been after. He saw a mound of dark clothing, but neither one was standing. Their horse, tossing its head, was loping out into the clearing, away from all the gunfire. The coyote dun was circling around to return to Sayles. Eddings wondered then if all the others were dead. A silence broken only by the whisper of the wind in the treetops reigned for a moment, and in that moment it occurred to him that he could be free. That realization was as phenomenal as seeing Bill Sayles go down and not get up.

Eddings had climbed down off the bay the minute Sayles charged out into the open and now, even while his disheveled mind tried to cope with what had just transpired, he put foot to stirrup and swung back into the saddle. He was free. Free to go anywhere he wanted. Free to get as far away from the prison at Huntsville as it was possible for a man to get. Free from that dank, claustrophobic cell, the thankless labor, the minute-by-minute, soul-killing hopelessness and humiliation of being a convict. He could ride westward and lose himself in the vast, untamed land that stretched for many hundreds of miles between the spot where he now was and the Pacific Ocean. But just as quickly as he became aware of these breathtaking possibilities he realized that he couldn't do it. Because doing it would mean never again seeing the woman he loved. Precisely because he loved her, he couldn't subject her to a life on the run. He would have to leave her behind if he wanted to be a free man today.

His next thought was to fade back into the trees, telling himself he couldn't very well face an armed man without a weapon—especially the man who had gunned down Bill Sayles. He decided not to contemplate whether he would do so even if he did have a gun. But his conscience got the better of him. Had he not prodded the Ranger into coming after these men? Was he not responsible for what had just happened out there in the clearing? The answers were yes—and yes. And he was just going to run away? That answer was no.

"God help me," he whispered and kicked the bay into motion, emerging from the trees and heading straight for Sayles. He didn't cotton to making himself such a big target by breaking cover on the back of a horse so he tried to make himself a smaller one by bending over until the bay's mane was whipping his face. He wasn't sure that either of the men they had been chasing was dead, but that dark spot in the white snow at the edge of the trees yonder didn't move. Still, he kept his eyes glued on it.

As soon as he saw Sayles go down, Mal laid the empty Gasser in the snow and managed to roll Lute over, even though the effort caused him immense pain. He sat there in the blood-speckled snow, cradling his dead brother in his arms. That the man who had killed Lute was himself dead did little to console him. For nearly all his days his purpose had been to look out for Lute. Now he felt empty. Lost. He knew then that he could not have left Lute behind at the sheepherder's. Taking care of his troublesome brother had given purpose to his life. And now that had been taken from him. Rocking slowly, he groaned, and not from the physical pain. "I'm sorry, Mum. I'm sorry." He raised his head to look for the man who had killed his brother, who lay out there sprawled in the snow. That was when he saw another man, riding across the clearing from the far line of trees.

He grabbed up the Gasser, digging into the pocket of his peacoat, seeking the extra rounds he kept there. His fingers brushed the worn leather cover of the dog-eared Edinburgh Edition of the *Reliques of Robert Burns*. "*When from my mother's womb I fell, / Thou might have plunged me deep in hell*," he hissed through teeth clenched in pain. It usually made him feel better to quote from "Holy Willie's Prayer." But not this time. He tried to re-load the revolver. His fingers were numb, whether from the cold—it had never been as cold as it was at that moment—or the breathtaking pain or loss of blood, he wasn't sure. He dropped a couple of rounds in the snow as he fumbled with the Gasser then threw it down in disgust and groped under Lute's jacket until he found the Colt pistol taken from the lawman his brother had killed on the *Mustang*. He couldn't recall how many shots Lute had fired at the sheep, so he checked. One bullet. One was enough. By pure force of will more than anything else he managed to get to his feet.

Eddings saw the black mound move, take shape as a man getting slowly, unsteadily, to his feet—a man with a pistol in his hand, a pistol he was raising. The fear was like an invisible fist squeezing his heart and shoving it into his throat. At the same time, he achieved a sudden clarity that incorporated time and distance in relation to a specific object—the Ranger's Winchester, in the snow about ten feet from where Sayles lay. But Sayles wasn't just lying there anymore. Astonished, Eddings saw that the Ranger, who had been sprawled on his back, was rolling over. The bay was running flat-out, and Eddings had no more time for thinking. He sawed on the reins, checking the horse; the bay locked its forelegs and nearly sat down in a spray of snow. Eddings tried to dismount too quickly and got his boot caught in the stirrup. He sprawled, pushed back up onto his feet, and saw the Winchester within reach. Beyond the rifle was Sayles, pulling the Schofield out of his coat pocket, but doing it slowly, too slowly, like even this was almost too much effort for him. Just staying upright seemed to be all he could manage. And yet he still had fight in him. Eddings felt a surge of admiration for the man. "Stay down!" he shouted, realizing that in that instant the bay was shielding him from Mal, while Sayles was fully exposed.

But Sayles would never stay down—and Jake Eddings knew what he had to do. The bay was standing where he had dropped the reins, which was to be expected since it was one of the Ranger's "god-dogs." Eddings stepped out from behind the horse, which turned its head and looked at him but didn't move. This put him twenty feet to the right of Sayles as he brought the Winchester's stock to shoulder.

Mal was on his feet now, aiming the pistol at Sayles, the man who had killed his brother. He saw Eddings come out from behind the bay, saw him bring the repeater to his shoulder. Meanwhile, Lute's killer couldn't seem to bring his own pistol to bear and was taking it from his right hand with his left. The Gasser, with those extra rounds he had been unable to load, lay in the snow to his left, but might as well have been in China. In the split second he had to make up his mind, Mal decided to use the bullet in the Colt to avenge Lute rather than save himself. He squeezed the trigger, aiming dead center for Sayles. He and Eddings fired in the same instant—and he didn't live long enough to see Sayles fall.

Eddings stood there a moment, breathing high and fast, nostrils flaring as the north wind blew acrid gunsmoke back into his face. To his left, Sayles lay on his back, unmoving. Taking the Ranger for dead, Eddings stumbled forward, levering another round into the Winchester's chamber, keeping the butt tucked into his shoulder as he made his way to Mal Litchfield. Stomach churning, he saw that he had shot the man squarely in the chest. Mal's eyes were wide open, staring blindly up at the sky, and the look of abject horror on his face made Eddings's skin crawl. Made him wonder what this man had seen as he stood for one final heartbeat on the brink of eternity.

Despite the whisper of the wind and the crunch of snow underfoot the clearing seemed eerily quiet after the quick, furious flurry of gunfire. Eddings turned and looked again at the Ranger. The dun had walked over to Sayles and stood there with head lowered. He thought for sure Bill Sayles had to be dead, and he didn't really want to trudge over there and see it up close, but he did, dropping to one knee beside the body. Sayles had been hit in the thigh and chest, high and to the right. There was a lot of blood. The Schofield revolver was gripped in his left hand. The shadows of night were reaching across the clearing. Eddings glanced to his right and saw a bright light beyond the trees. It was the sun, just setting, painting the shredding clouds above the tree line a rosy pink.

The coyote dun whickered softly. Eddings sighed, turned his attention to the horse, and saw the Ranger's left hand, the one clutching the revolver, move just slightly. Then his eyes were opened and he turned his head to look at Eddings. "Is he dead?" His voice was little more than a whispered croak.

Eddings nodded. "He is. I thought you were too."

"I ain't done yet." Sayles groaned through clenched teeth as he lifted his head to look at himself. His pant leg was drenched in blood. "But I'm shot to hell. Reckon you need to tie off that leg or I'll bleed out."

The rope that had tied him to the bay for days was now coiled and lashed to the saddle on the dun. Eddings borrowed the bowie knife stuck in the Ranger's boot and cut off a length of it, which he used as a tourniquet on Sayles's leg. He didn't think it would do much good. Even if he stanched the bleeding it seemed unlikely the Ranger would survive for long.

"Go check the bodies," said Sayles. His voice was hoarse, weak.

"I'm not much for looting the dead, unlike some people."

"Hurry up."

Eddings grimaced, but he wasn't going to argue with a dying man. He walked to where the Litchfield brothers lay and came back a moment later with the Gasser and the Colt stuck in his belt and two wanted posters clenched in a hand covered with Mal's blood. He slid the bowie knife back into the Ranger's boot. "Five hundred pounds apiece. How much is that?"

"Damned if I know. Hold on to them." Sayles tried to sit up. It took everything he had to accomplish that feat. He looked up at the saddle on the dun, then at Eddings. "Help me get on my horse."

Eddings could only imagine how much it pained Bill Sayles to ask for assistance. Since there was nothing to be gained by arguing, he helped the Ranger to his feet. "How far do you think you can get?"

"Far as I need to. But you better tie me to the horse. Likely I'll pass out soon."

"Where do I take you?"

Sayles didn't answer. Once he had the Ranger in the saddle, Eddings took the rest of the rope and secured him atop the coyote dun in the same manner he had been bound on the bay for most of the past week. By the time he was done he had made up his mind. "The sheepherder's place. I'll leave you there and ride back to Cameron to fetch Doc Crighton." He looked up at Sayles. The Ranger's head was down. He had passed out. Or he was dead. Eddings sighed and looked around. The sun had set. He could see stars and he figured the moon would be on the rise soon. He got on board the bay, gathered up the dun's reins, and put the north wind to his back as he kicked the bay into a walk.

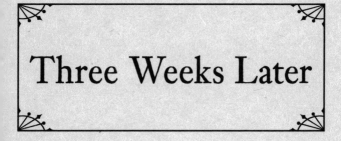

Three Weeks Later

CHAPTER EIGHTEEN

"Mr. Eddings, I suspect you're nervous, sitting here today, with your life, at least the next thirteen years of it, hanging in the balance. I urge you to relax. Remember, this is a hearing, not a trial. Just tell your side of the story, beginning with your departure from the prison in Huntsville in the custody of the Texas Ranger Bill Sayles."

Eddings kept his eyes glued to the smiling face of Temple Hanley, who was standing directly in front of him as he sat in the witness chair, hands in his lap, wrists shackled together courtesy of Sheriff Tom Rath. The chair was beside a battered kneehole desk behind which sat Circuit Judge Jacob Greve—the same judge who had presided over his trial two years earlier. He didn't look at the crowd of about forty people packed into the small Cameron courtroom, or at the judge either. From what he understood, it was Hanley who had convinced the judge to allow the public into the courtroom for this occasion. In fact, it was Hanley who was responsible for the hearing in the first place, as he had been the one whose telegram to the governor had initiated the process that resulted in him spending three weeks in the city jail instead of being returned immediately to Huntsville. He resented the casual, almost bantering way Hanley addressed him, as though this was all a relatively minor matter. Aside from that, he had no idea what to say. Hanley came to his rescue.

"You were allowed, by order of the governor, to attend the funeral of your son here in Cameron and arrived here without mishap, isn't that correct?"

"Well, yes. Unless you call seeing the Texas Ranger who brought me gun down three men a mishap."

"Those three men were bandits, were they not? I would call it a mishap if they had succeeded in holding you up." Hanley's glib response elicited some laughter from the onlookers. "Then after the burial of your son, Ranger Sayles set out to deliver you back to prison, and it was then that you crossed the path of the Litchfield brothers."

Eddings nodded. "We found a dead man inside a cabin. It was clear he had been killed. Tracks in the snow showed that two men had come to the cabin and left with a woman who lived there."

"For the record, the woman has been identified as one Alise Graham, a soiled dove who had plied her trade up and down the Brazos River for a few years before she began living with the dead man, an Isaac Smith, hunter by trade. You already knew that two lawmen had been killed on a riverboat a few days before because you overhead a ferryman tell that to Ranger Sayles. So what happened next?"

"Sayles decided to go after the two men—the Litchfields."

"And why did he do that? To try to rescue Miss Graham, who had clearly been kidnapped by the Litchfield brothers?"

"I don't know for sure." Eddings shrugged. "It's just . . . what he does."

"The next morning you came upon the scene of another crime, did you not?"

"Yeah. They'd killed a sheepherder. But not his wife. We found the Graham woman dead too. The woman told us that the smaller of the two men had been hurt, and that he'd wanted to take her along but the bigger one wouldn't allow it. They'd lost one of their mounts, so they weren't traveling very fast, and we caught up with them that same day."

Hanley had been pacing slowly back and forth with his pudgy fingers laced behind his back. Now he stopped and seemed to tilt forward. "Were you armed, Mr. Eddings?"

"No. Sayles wouldn't give me a gun. He had untied me, though, so that I could ride and he didn't have to pull my horse along by a lead rope."

"I see. And did the thought of trying to make a run for it, as they say, ever cross your mind?"

"Sure it did."

"But you didn't make a run for it. Why not?"

Eddings thought a moment. "One reason is, had I made it to China, Sayles would have tracked me down." He paused, having a difficult time putting finding the right words to express himself.

"And what was another reason?"

"Because I didn't want to be a fugitive. I'd already made enough mistakes." He glanced briefly at the crowd, as what he perceived to be some skeptical murmurs arose. "I know. I know what you're thinking. What man would choose thirteen more years in a prison cell to being free? But the outlaw trail—that's not freedom. The only way I could be really free was to serve out my sentence. Besides . . ." He looked down at his hands, clenched together in his lap. "I've done enough that my wife—and my son—would be ashamed of."

Hanley's smile faltered. More than a few times he had heard witnesses wax sentimental in the hope of gaining favor with a judge or jury. But there wasn't a doubt in his mind that Jake Eddings meant every word. He glanced over his shoulder at the onlookers. No one was snickering.

"Let's move this dogie on down the trail," said Judge Greve sternly, being no fan of sentimentality, and looked at Eddings. "So what happened next?"

"We came to a big meadow. The Litchfields were about to ride into the timber on the far side. Sayles told me to stay put and rode after them. About halfway across he shot one off the horse. Then he dismounted and traded fire with the other, who had dismounted as well. He hit the second one but that one got up and fired back and he went down. I went out and reached the rifle he had dropped and shot the one called Mal Litchfield. Killed him." Eddings drew a long breath. "I had never killed a man before. Sayles was in a bad way. He had two slugs in him. I tied him to his horse." His mouth curled in a wry smile. "He told me to, said he was going to pass out. Thanks to him, I knew just how to tie a man to a saddle so that he wouldn't fall off." There was a hint of irony in his tone. "We rode back to the sheepherder's place. I never thought he'd make it, but he did. Bill Sayles is a hard man to kill. I left him there in the care of the widow and rode straight here to get the doctor." He glanced at Tom Rath, who was sitting in the front row. "The sheriff arrested me. Doc Crighton said he knew where the sheepherder's place was so I wasn't needed to show him the way. From what I'm told he got the bullet out of the Ranger's leg but he couldn't get at all the pieces of the one that hit him the shoulder."

"If I'm not mistaken, you must have passed close to

your farm on the way into Cameron. You didn't stop there?"

"I saw it. From across the river, through the trees. No, I didn't stop. God knows I wanted to. But I was . . . afraid."

"Afraid of what?"

"Of making another big mistake."

Hanley stepped closer and put a hand on Eddings's shoulder. "And where is your wife today?"

Eddings drew a long slow breath, making sure he had his emotions held in check before replying. "She's at home. She wanted to be here but I asked her not to be. It was . . . very hard on her, that day I was sentenced, here in this very room."

Hanley nodded. "One final question, Mr. Eddings. Why did you ride out into that meadow? Was it an attempt to save the life of a Texas Ranger? Was it to stop Mal Litchfield? What was it that compelled you to risk your life, exposing yourself to a man who was, by all accounts, an expert shot with a pistol? In my opinion that was a pretty heroic thing to do."

Eddings shook his head. "Nothing heroic about it. I had no choice," he said.

"That's all, Judge." Hanley smiled reassuringly at Eddings then retired to his front-row chair.

Greve nodded. "Mr. Eddings, you can take your seat," he said as he turned his attention to the small, wiry old man with an arm in a sling and a crutch between his knees. The man's head was down, face hidden from the judge's view by the battered brim of his campaign hat, but even so, Greve was fairly certain Bill Sayles was asleep. "Mr. Sayles? Mr. Sayles!" The head came up sharply. "I am sorry to wake you, sir, but you said you wanted to speak your piece here today?"

Sayles mumbled something, pushing the hat back on his head. He fished the Elgin out from under his coat, then began the process of getting to his feet, relying on the crutch, since he could not depend on his right leg.

"No need for you to sit in the witness chair, Mr. Sayles." Eddings had relocated to a chair between Hanley and Tom Rath. "You can stay where you are."

Sayles acted like he didn't hear. As he made his way slowly but resolutely to the witness chair, Temple Hanley smiled. He had already discovered that the Ranger was a man with an indomitable will and fierce pride, and now the judge and the rest of Cameron knew it too—unless they thought him just a doddering old fool who hadn't heard or understood Greve's offer.

Once in the chair Sayles sighed with relief and only then acknowledged the judge's presence. "Yer Honor, I only got a few words to say."

"By all means, Mr. Sayles."

Sayles looked at the faces of the spectators and cleared his throat, seeming a bit nervous. "I don't put much stock in words. But I have to say that I would have been shot dead by that son of a bitch Mal Litchfield but for the bravery of that man over yonder." He pointed at Eddings with a crooked trigger finger. "He could have run. Any other man would have. Now, I ain't never been one to give a bad man any rope. But Jake Eddings isn't a bad man, and he deserves a second chance." He paused, rubbing his chin, as though trying to decide if he had anything else that needed saying. Then he glanced at the judge. "I reckon that's all." He began the slow, laborious process of getting up.

"Thank you, Mr. Sayles, and thank you for your service to the people of the great state of Texas." Judge Greve fastened his gaze on Eddings. "I believe that the sentence

I gave you two years ago was a fair one, Mr. Eddings, considering that you were involved in a robbery during which a law-abiding man was gunned down. You may not have pulled the trigger on that day, but you were just as culpable as the man who did. You could have been hanged. While I believe that a person who does wrong should be punished, I also believe he who does a good deed should be rewarded. The law cannot serve the people if it has no compassion. The prophet Micah said, 'He has told you what is good and what the Lord desires of you, that you love mercy and do justice and walk humbly with your God.' Have mercy *and* do justice. Because of your selfless act of heroism, Mr. Eddings, I set aside your sentence and declare you, as of this date, a free man. Sheriff, remove those shackles."

A collective gasp rose from the spectators, as though all of them had forgotten to breathe while the judge spoke, and then everyone seemed to be talking at once. Eddings hardly noticed the commotion. He was aware of Rath, as he leaned over to unlock the shackles, saying, "You're still a no-good longrider in my book, and you always will be." And Temple Hanley, who sat to his right, leaning over to murmur, "And I must say, Sheriff, I've always thought of you as the southern end of a northbound horse, and I believe I always shall."

Rath glowered at the lawyer as he got up and joined the other people filing out of the courtroom. Eddings realized he could do the same. He could get up and walk outside a free man. He could go anywhere he wanted. But there was just one place he wanted to go.

"I need to get home," he told Hanley. "I need to tell Purdy. I hate to do this, but could I borrow your buggy?"

Hanley was beaming. "Follow me, Jake."

The lawyer led him down a short hallway past the

small room where records were kept, and where the judge could deliberate in private. A back door opened into an alley, and in the alley stood the bay mare, ground-hitched. Once he was certain no one was around, Hanley reached under his buffalo coat and brandished a large pouch, which he handed to Eddings.

"There was a reward for the Litchfield brothers, you know. Seems they murdered the daughter of a very powerful and influential man back in London. A rich man, as well. He offered a bounty of five hundred pounds sterling for each of the brothers. Comes out to be about five thousand dollars, American. I hope you don't mind but I took the liberty of using a portion of it to pay off the lien on your farm. That left more than four thousand dollars, and it's all yours."

Eddings stared at the bag. "Four thousand," he murmured, in disbelief. That was more money than he could even get his head around. "But . . . I don't deserve this, Mr. Hanley."

"Well, I think you do. And the only other man who would have a claim on that reward thinks so, too. He said he had no need of it. He also said he didn't have a need for this fine steed, since he wasn't going to be transporting prisoners anymore."

Eddings looked at the bay. "No, I don't suppose he will. He doesn't take any prisoners. I should thank him. But I need to see Purdy. Would you do me one more favor, Mr. Hanley? Tell the Ranger I'll be back to see him."

"I think he's already gone, Jake."

"Gone?"

"He told me he was riding out as soon as he gave his testimony."

"But how could . . ." Eddings couldn't fathom how a man in Sayles's condition could walk, much less ride. But then Sayles was no ordinary man. "That sounds about right."

Hanley chuckled. "Now you better get home and let Purdy know that you're a free man."

Eddings nodded, but he stood there a moment, struggling to find the right words. "This wouldn't be happening if it weren't for you, Mr. Hanley. I owe you my life. Purdy's too. She told me what happened at the river. I won't ever be able to repay you."

Hanley shook his head. "I have been repaid a thousand times over. Now go home, Jake."

Jake Eddings had imagined a happy homecoming countless times in the early months of his incarceration at Huntsville. Toward the end of that ordeal those dreams had become nightmares, of coming home to an empty house, Purdy having moved on. When he rode up to the house on the long-legged bay it still seemed like a dream to him as he tried to come to terms with the fact that he was a free man. Not only free, but, by frontier standards, a rich man too. He was glad he no longer owed the bank anything, but the money didn't matter to him nearly as much as did the woman who came out onto the porch. He checked the bay and dismounted, transferring the gold-laden saddlebags to a shoulder.

Purdy stood there, with Buck by her side. Her heart galloped in her chest as she held up a lantern so that she could study her husband's face while he climbed the porch steps. His grin told her all she needed to know. With a sob of pure joy she put the lantern down and threw her arms around his neck and just held him, leaning her trembling body against him, up on tiptoe as she nuzzled into the angle of his neck and shoulder. He felt the wetness of her joyful tears on his skin, even as he tried to fight back his own tears. In that moment it struck home. He was free. The long ordeal was truly over. His heart filled with such love and joy that it was hard not to break down.

He held her as long as he could. When she let loose of him, she glanced at the ground-hitched bay. "I'll take care of the horse. You must be frozen clear through. Go warm yourself by the fire."

Eddings glanced at the bay. "The horse can wait a bit. He's not going anywhere, believe me." He turned to Buck, who had been waiting with tail wagging, and knelt to give the massive dog a hug. "Thank you, Buck," he said, from the bottom of his heart. "Thank you for saving my girl." Buck lapped at his face, a sloppy wet lick that made Purdy laugh. Eddings had forgotten what a wonderful sound his wife's laughter was.

Purdy had visited him daily in the Cameron jail while they waited for the circuit judge, and she had told him everything—about Joshua's illness, about George Norris, about Mary, and the attempted suicide in the Little River, and of course her rescue thanks to the heroic effort of their dog. Much of it had felt like a knife twisting in his gut, but through it all his love, respect, and *need* for this woman became stronger than ever.

She had also given him a letter, a letter she had intended to post to the prison at Huntsville, but which she passed through the bars of the cell on her very first visit to the jail. She had written just four words, but they were four words that turned his world right-side up again.

I will wait forever.

He picked up the lantern, took her by the hand, and led her inside, with Buck following. Dropping the saddlebags on the table, he looked around. "Where's your friend. Where's Mary?"

"She left. Yesterday. She was absolutely sure you would

be home today." Mystified, Purdy smiled pensively and shook her head. "She seems to know . . . everything."

Eddings gestured at the saddlebags. "The reward money for the Litchfield brothers. That Ranger didn't want any part of it. There's a whole lot of money there, Purdy. The bank has been paid off. We'll get us some pigs, a milk cow, a plow mare. Oh, and we need to get some mules."

"Mules?"

"Yes, absolutely. We need a couple of mules. You won't want for anything ever again, Purdy."

She wrapped her arms around him again, resting her head on his shoulder this time. "I have what I need most," she whispered.

He gazed at the Christmas tree in the corner, the pine sapling in its bucket of river stones, gaily decorated with pinecones dipped in white and red wax. Seeing the tree produced a stab of grief that felt like a knife in his heart because it reminded him of how excited Joshua had been at Christmastime. The house had rung with his laughter. It hadn't seemed to matter that they were too poor for Eddings to afford store-bought gifts. Joshua had been overjoyed with the handmade one—a new shirt Purdy had sewn, the bow and arrows Eddings had carved by hand.

"Joshua would have loved the tree, darling," he said, his voice husky with emotions that nearly unmanned him.

Purdy looked up at him and touched his cheek, a gentle smile on her soft lips. "He does love the tree, Jake. He *does.*"

Eddings sighed. "I want to bring him home, Purdy. He belongs here."

She wrapped her arms around his waist and leaned her slender body into him, resting her head on his chest. "I would like that," she murmured, wondering if she should tell him that, according to Mary, their son was here and always would be, as long as they were.

Buck was sprawled in front of the fireplace. His massive head came up and he barked. Purdy leaned a bit to one side and peered past her husband at the big yellow dog, expecting him to be on his feet and looking at the door. But Buck was still lying down, his long tail thumping the floorboards, and he was looking toward the Christmas tree, ears alert.

Purdy could almost hear Joshua's infectious laughter. Smiling softly, she lay her head on her husband's chest again, and held him tighter still.

EPILOGUE

When he set out to find Bill Sayles, The Captain looked
high and low all over Waco. His first stop was the White
Elephant Saloon, which he knew to be Sayles's favorite
watering hole. Then he went by the boardinghouse where
Sayles had been a lodger for many years. No luck. Next
were several other saloons in town, just in case Sayles had
grown fond of another place that served the Old Overholt
he favored. When that didn't pan out he visited the livery
where he knew Sayles kept his horses. The grizzled old
freedman who took care of all the animals, and who lived
in a corner of the tack room, was cleaning out a stall. He
knew more about all the comings and goings than the
owner of the place, who spent an inordinate amount of
time at one of the town's bordellos. The hired hand confirmed that Sayles had ridden out early in the morning on
his coyote dun—"smartest gol-durned horse I ever done
seen"—but of course, being Bill Sayles, had not seen fit
to inform the man of his intended destination.

Growing increasingly exasperated, The Captain went
outside and stood in the sun and watched the business of
the street awhile. He expected winter would go on for a
time, but the past couple of weeks had been a pleasant

respite of sunny days above the freezing. It was a pure blessing to feel the warmth of the sun on one's face. He considered giving the job intended for Sayles to another Ranger, one who was easier to find. But that he would have to explain to Governor Coke, who had requested that the task at hand be given to the man who had taken down the Litchfield brothers—"the two most dangerous and despicable villains who have come over from England since Bloody Ban Tarleton," Coke had said of them, referring to the British cavalry officer responsible for the massacre of Continentals who had surrendered after the Battle of the Waxhaws.

Being a man who had political aspirations of his own, The Captain decided not to give up just yet, wanting to avoid the task of informing the governor that his wish would not be fulfilled. Unable to think of any person in Waco who could be categorized as a friend to Sayles, he bent his steps back to the boardinghouse and shared his predicament with Mrs. Doubrett.

"Bill has lived here with you for many a year, ma'am," The Captain said. "You probably know him better than anyone else in town."

"He is a hard man to know. Would you like some coffee, Captain?"

The Captain didn't want any coffee but he said yes anyway, because Mrs. Doubrett was very proud of her reputation as a good hostess, and he didn't want to get on her bad side by declining. It wasn't until he was seated at the kitchen table with a mug of steaming-hot java that she gave him the information he needed.

"Were you aware that Bill has property outside of town, Captain?"

The Captain confessed that he had not been aware.

"Yes. Over near Haddock's Hill. He's had it for a long

time, I think. And ever since he came back from that business with the Litchfields he struck me as . . . different. I don't think it has anything to do with him being shot to pieces. Or maybe it does. I would find him in the parlor, sitting by the fireplace, lost in thought. I would ask if he was all right and the only thing he ever told me was that he was thinking about old times. Something about the way he said it, the way he looked, made me think of his wife and daughter. You do know he lost them both many years ago? To Comanches, I believe. He told me once, long ago, when he was in his cups." She smiled pensively. "I don't think he remembered telling me. I never brought it up."

"Oh yes," said The Captain, sipping the coffee. "Now that you mention it, I do recall hearing that, from the man I replaced."

"So it may be that he rode out that way, because he has been acting much like he did years ago when he first told me of the tragedy. Or maybe not." She shrugged. "Who can ever say about Bill? He is a hard man to get a handle on."

The Captain hurried to finish off the coffee—he didn't want Mrs. Doubrett thinking he didn't like it—and was about to leave when she caught him by the sleeve of his shirt.

"While Bill is a hard one to read, I can tell you this, Captain. He needs something to do. For a man like that, sitting around idle is downright unhealthy."

The Captain smiled. It was obvious that Mrs. Doubrett cared very much about her lodger's well-being. "Don't you worry, ma'am. I'll keep him busy."

It took The Captain an hour to find his man. The Sayles place was nestled in a horseshoe-shaped hill covered with scrub brush and a handful of live oaks. There looked to be a small spring at the base of the hill. The ruins of what had once been a house lay in the shade of two big pecan trees, and The Captain wondered if Sayles had planted those when he built the place. At the foot of one of those trees were a pair of graves marked by headstones. Sayles was sitting with his back to the tree's trunk, and the coyote dun was ground-hitched close by. A warm southerly wind cavorted through the branches and made them dance. Checking his horse some distance away, The Captain was struck by the scene. There was something poignant about it and for a moment he was hesitant, not wishing to intrude. But then Sayles got slowly to his feet and walked in his stiff, horse-warped gait out into the sun. His left arm, bent at the elbow, was pressed tight against his side. The Captain rode on in.

"Afternoon, Bill. Sorry to intrude, but I need to talk to you."

"Where's your manners, Captain? Climb down and we'll jaw some."

The Captain chided himself for forgetting that Sayles was a stickler for frontier etiquette. He climbed down and followed Sayles, who was making for the nearby spring, and he got the distinct impression he was being steered away from the graves. When he pulled up alongside Sayles he noticed the grimace on the old Ranger's creased, weathered face. "That bullet what's still in you giving you some trouble?"

"Nothin' to speak of. Feel it when I walk."

"How about when you ride?"

Sayles fished a half-smoked cheroot out of the pocket of his shirt and scraped a thumbnail across the sulfur tip of a strike-anywhere to light up. He inhaled deeply, then let the smoke trickle out of his nostrils before speaking. "You got a job for me." He wasn't asking.

"That's right. Governor Coke wants you to handle something."

"You're not sending me back to Huntsville." Again, it wasn't a question.

"No. We want you to bring in a killer so we can put him in the Huntsville prison. A real hardcase."

"Who might that be?"

"John Wesley Hardin. We think he's in Florida. Have a Ranger working undercover over there and he intercepted a letter addressed to Hardin's father-in-law that said John Wesley is hiding out near the Alabama border and using the name James Swain. Reckon Hardin's killed so many men here in Texas he finally had to go somewhere else and crawl under a rock. You're to go track him down and catch him. Or kill him." The Captain paused to study Sayles's profile, trying to read the old Ranger's expression. But he couldn't. "Listen, Bill. Hardin is the most dangerous man alive. I know that doesn't spook you, but you've just been shot all to hell and if you don't feel up to making the trip, then that's fine. I'll send someone else."

Sayles watched the water trickling over the rocks into a small pool as he reviewed what he knew about Hardin. The Captain hadn't been exaggerating when he called Hardin the most dangerous man alive. Born in Texas to a Methodist circuit preacher, Hardin was in his early or mid-twenties and bragged about killing around forty men. Sayles figured the true number was closer to half that. Hardin demonstrated his violent nature at an early age. As a schoolboy he stabbed a fellow student, nearly killing him. He was fifteen when he killed his first man, claiming his victim had waylaid him, seeking retribution for Hardin beating him in a boxing match. As the dead man was a former slave, and Texas was under Reconstruction law, three Union soldiers were dispatched to bring Hardin in. He killed all three. At seventeen he was arrested in Marshall, Texas, for killing the Waco sheriff, a man Sayles knew personally. While being transported to Waco to stand trial, Hardin killed one of the two lawmen escorting him, and escaped.

Even while pushing a herd of cattle to Abilene, Hardin continued to take lives, tangling with Mexican vaqueros and castle rustlers. Arriving in Abilene, he quarreled with a man who thought poorly of Texans and shot him in the mouth. A few months later, while staying in an Abilene hotel, he shot through a wall into an adjacent room because a man's snoring was keeping him awake, and killed the snorer. Hunted by town marshal Wild Bill Hickok, he hid himself in a haystack until morning, then stole a horse and made his getaway. The next year he became embroiled in the Sutton–Taylor feud over in Trinity, and was credited with killing two local lawmen known to be allies of the Sutton family. While celebrating his twenty-first birthday with some friends in a Comanche, Texas, saloon, Hardin shot a deputy sheriff. After that he disappeared. Sayles calculated that had been about a year and a half ago.

Being busy fighting to end the Comanche threat during Hardin's brief but bloody career, Sayles hadn't paid much attention to the man's exploits. He remembered hearing that Hardin carried a brace of pistols in holsters sewn to the inside of his jacket, using the cross-draw technique to brandish them. Clearly, having killed so many men, he was quite a pistoleer. And one couldn't elude justice as long as he had without being pretty smart. None of that worried Sayles too much. One well-made shot could end even the most dangerous man's career. You just had to make sure you didn't miss your mark.

"There's a reward," said The Captain. "Four thousand dollars. That's a lot of money. You could fix this place up with money like that."

Sayles looked around. What was left of his house was overgrown with brush. The Comanches had burned it down and he had never even considered rebuilding or replacing it, the site of the greatest tragedy in his life, and the biggest mistake he had ever made. Now, though, it was something to consider.

The Captain didn't expect the bounty offer to influence Sayles, who had never been a man who seemed concerned about money as long as he had enough to buy ammunition and an occasional bottle of whiskey. So he was surprised when Sayles nodded and said, "That's a purty fair number. Reckon I'll go." Noting the look of surprise on The Captain's face, he added, "After this I think I might just settle down here. It's where I should've been all along."

Deciding it was best to steer clear of that remark, The Captain glanced past Sayles at the grave markers and then turned to his horse. Once mounted he said, "Does that mean this will be your last job, Bill?"

Sayles shook his head. "Just sayin' I've been away from home for going on thirty years."

The Captain nodded. There was something right and comforting in the knowledge that Bill Sayles would do what he was made to do, that when he died it would be violently, not falling to sleep for the last time sitting in a rocking chair.

"When you get to Florida, find a man named Jack Duncan in Gainesville. He's one of us. I'll take care of your horses while you're gone."

"No need. Only got that one over yonder now, and I'm taking him with me. He and I been through too much together for me to leave him behind."

The Captain smiled faintly. He suspected that was Sayles's way of saying the coyote dun meant too much to him to leave behind. It meant extra cost to haul the horse across the country by train and The Captain was a notoriously parsimonious man, but he decided to take care of the cost. After all, it would be a feather in his cap if a member of his company was the one to bring in the notorious and elusive Hardin. "Come by the office and I'll give you enough to get you there and back. You can catch the Great Northern at Hearne and connect with the Texas and Pacific at Longview and then . . ."

"I know which way Florida is."

Sayles gave a wave of the hand as he turned to walk back into the shade of the pecan trees, with the smoke from the cheroot between his lips trailing over a shoulder. The Captain turned his horse and urged it into motion. To those who didn't know any better, Bill Sayles would seem like nothing more than a broken-down old man. But The Captain knew better, and he felt sorry for John Wesley Hardin.

Standing in the shade at the foot of the two graves, Sayles finished off the cheroot and ground the butt under a heel. He had spent the morning walking around the place, or sitting under one of the pecans, setting free all the memories he had locked away, memories of the good times he had shared here with his wife and daughter. Those times hadn't lasted long but now he was glad to have had them. This hadn't always been true. More than once, when those good memories had become too painful to bear, he would conclude that he'd have been better off never to have made them. Today, though, he had let them out and was glad of it. Now this place felt like home again. He could feel the presence of his loved ones. He could see his wife's warm smile again. Could hear his young girl's laughter. He still had his family. Even tomorrow, when he started after Hardin, he would have them with him.

Sayles sat down between the crosses, wincing as his old bones complained. One of the crosses was tilted a little, and he straightened it, firmed up the dirt around its base. He wiped at his squinty, steel-cast eyes and softly murmured, "Well, gals, have I got some tales to tell you . . ."